IN BLACK AND WHITE

WEATHERHEAD BOOKS ON ASIA

WEATHERHEAD BOOKS ON ASIA

WEATHERHEAD EAST ASIAN INSTITUTE, COLUMBIA UNIVERSITY

IN
BLACK
AND
WHITE

A NOVEL

TANIZAKI JUN'ICHIRŌ

TRANSLATED BY PHYLLIS I. LYONS

Columbia University Press
New York

Columbia University Press
Publishers Since 1893
New York   Chichester, West Sussex
cup.columbia.edu

This publication has been supported by the Richard W. Weatherhead
Publication Fund of the Weatherhead East Asian Institute,
Columbia University.

Columbia University Press wishes to express its appreciation for
assistance given by the Pushkin Fund in the publication of this book.

Library of Congress Cataloging-in-Publication Data
Names: Tanizaki, Jun'ichirō, 1886–1965, author. |
Lyons, Phyllis I., 1942– translator.
Title: In black and white : a novel / Tanizaki Jun'ichirō ;
translated by Phyllis I. Lyons.
Other titles: Kokubyaku. English
Description: New York : Columbia University Press, 2017. |
Series: Weatherhead books on Asia | Includes
bibliographical references.
Identifiers: LCCN 2017022741 | ISBN 9780231185189
(cloth : alk. paper) | ISBN 9780231185196 (pbk. : alk. paper) |
ISBN 9780231546256 (e-book)
Subjects: LCSH: Authors—Fiction. | GSAFD: Autobiographical
fiction. | Psychological fiction.
Classification: LCC PL839.A7 K6513 2017 | DDC 895.63/44—dc23
LC record available at https://lccn.loc.gov/2017022741

Cover design: Jordan Wannemacher
Cover image: © Keystone Pictures USA / Alamy Stock Photo

For MVC and JMC

CONTENTS

TRANSLATOR'S PREFACE

I t is astonishing that there could be a major Tanizaki novel that no one has ever heard of, but that is the situation with *In Black and White*. Hidden in plain sight for more than eighty years, it has been almost invisible in both Japanese and Western scholarship, is unknown to most Japanese readers, and naturally has not been available to readers outside Japan. This translation redresses a puzzling blank in the Tanizaki record, with a novel that shows Tanizaki's writing on the cusp of turning from interesting to masterful.

In Black and White is a murder mystery that folds Escher-like in on itself: a writer kills another writer with his writing—only he did not kill him. We follow the ludicrous and increasingly terrified measures of the writer as he struggles to extricate himself from an inexplicable dilemma with potentially fatal implications. The translator's afterword addresses features of the story that show it to be far more than a crime thriller or a witty, ironic view of the Japanese social and literary scene in the late 1920s. It is in addition a sharply observant critique of literary culture and the theory of fiction itself, and it hints at complications in the author's life that go beyond simple equations of autobiographical fiction. And while it is not a polemic against police power and the use of torture in interrogation, it reveals acquiescent attitudes that contributed to the transformation of civil Japan into a military-police state in the 1930s. It does all this even as it details the tribulations of a would-be man-about-town falling into the hands of a sophisticated Ginza streetwalker in his attempts to create an alibi he imagines he might need—for a crime someone else will commit.

AUTHOR'S WORDS IN PLACE
OF A PREFACE

P eople often ask, "When you publish a newspaper novel, have you completely worked out the whole story beforehand?" Of course, when you publish anything (and not just in newspapers), you ought to have it all completed before you present it to the world. But to tell the truth, few writers work that way. That's especially true in this case, where I've had a publisher's request and have had to start it quickly. It will be no easy thing for a slow writer like me to have to keep turning out four pages or so a day for at least the next three or four months. On the average, it's all I can do to write four pages a day. And so while this newspaper thing is running, I'll have to spend every day locked up in my study without a break for even a little trip, even though the good weather season is coming upon us.

What's worse, newspapers are different from magazines. With a newspaper, once you start writing, you are stuck with having to keep it going, no matter how it turns out in the end. It's like sending a rock rolling down from the top of a hill—once it gets going, you can't stop it. Let me tell you: it can be terrifying because even if you think it's not working out, you can't just start over again partway through, so you're stuck not knowing what the outcome will be and just stringing it on one day after another. On the other hand, there's no pleasure greater than when you really get going smoothly. It goes on day after day, propelled as if by natural energy, and you open the newspaper every morning to see it happening just as you want it to—well, if you're not a writer, you just don't know what a great feeling that is. Because I'm such a slow writer, my work wouldn't really make much progress if in fact I didn't throw myself into such a precarious situation.

It's not that I don't have any plan at all, but we won't know how the game turns out until we play it. Please, readers, join with your writer in praying to the God of Art, that we are favored with good fortune.

IN BLACK AND WHITE

1

Mizuno always hated getting up in the morning. That day, he opened his eyes around ten, lit a cigarette and lay on his back, staring at the ceiling. Suddenly a thought floated into his head.

"Oh, wait . . . that's right . . . did I actually use his real name?"

For a moment he didn't even realize he'd spoken out loud. Then, even though there was no one to hear, he glanced around uneasily—not because he'd blurted out something that shouldn't be heard but rather because he was worried that his recent habit of talking to himself out loud might be taken as a sign that he was going crazy. To be sure, it was nothing new; he'd been doing it since his twenties. But recently it had gotten quite a bit worse. His head was always fuzzy, and any kind of concentrated thinking exhausted him. One thought would lead to another, and then he would be off on all kinds of tangents, and strange, disconnected fantasies, and thoughts of an instant would suddenly appear, like the shadow of a bird falling on the screen—and before he realized it, words would pop out of his mouth. Sometimes he even cried out as if scolding himself for talking to himself.

"I've got to stop doing this!"—Time and again he'd tried to pull himself up short, but his control didn't last even five minutes.

Before long he'd already have forgotten, and his mind would once again be drawing up another picture on its own, and he'd erase that one and bring up another image and then extinguish it, too. It was as if his mind had a mind of its own, his heart was not his own heart. Perched on top of his shoulders was not his head, but a tank, and some horribly stinky, filthy sludge precipitated in it, and there was liquid on the surface that dripped out, drop by drop, and those were the words he spoke to himself. . . . That's how he thought of it.

He couldn't control his own mind—his brain seemed to have become a self-propelled movie projector, arbitrarily streaming out whatever goblins and evil spirits it wanted while he simply stood there with his arms folded, watching as if his own life had no connection to himself. Was this then a sign that he was crazy? No, but he was more than halfway there. He realized that he talked to himself because he was usually all alone. He had no real friends and he lived by himself, so he often went all day without talking to a single person. With no chance to talk to anyone, he felt a deep isolation within himself, although he didn't want to think of himself as lonely. For that matter, two or three years ago, when he was still married, he wasn't always talking to himself like this. His wife would say something, and all he had to do was grunt in response. He could hardly even remember what she looked like—she was that kind of wife. But still, they did exchange words at least a couple of times a day. She'd been the talker, even if he had no interest in chatting. But now there never was a human voice in his room, not his or anyone else's. That's why he talked to himself: he wanted to hear a human voice. The proof was that he spoke out loud like that—sometimes running on, sometimes just growling out sounds—only when there was no one else present.

"What difference should it make, his real name . . . ?" he muttered to himself once again. The long, thin tower of ash poised at the end of his cigarette collapsed and fluttered down onto his lips. With a bitter grimace he crushed out the butt in the teacup beside his futon even though it was only half gone. As if ashamed to be seen, he flipped the bedclothes up over his head. And then for a long time he just lay there blinking his eyes, staring out into the darkness, not thinking of anything at all.

This "real name" he was talking about to himself was in a manuscript he'd finished writing a couple of days earlier. The story, which he'd been working on for almost three weeks, was supposed to be in the April issue of *The People*, and just the day before, he'd squeaked in under the deadline and handed it over to a runner from the press. The storyline was something he was particularly good at, and he'd been looking forward with quite a sense of anticipation for the magazine to come out. Although he'd been writing for fifteen or sixteen years already, he did still get excited sometimes. He'd been enjoying playing over this part or that in his mind when suddenly it hit him: in two or three places, he was sure, by mistake he'd put the real name of the man he'd used as the model for a character in the story.

"Codama, Cojima, Codama, Cojima . . ."—the third time, he blurted it out loud as he lay in his futon staring into the darkness. He'd done this before: once, he'd used his first girlfriend as the model for a character in a story, and he'd written her real name by mistake. Luckily that time he'd noticed it while it was still in draft and managed to take care of it before it was printed. He had imagined the mess such a slip might cause, and since then he'd been very careful about what he did with names.

The problem was one of verisimilitude. Say in this case with "Cojima" he'd changed it to something that sounded or looked completely different—he'd lose the sense of realism that had been precisely the reason he'd modeled it on a real person in the first place. And the more important the character was, the worse mixing up the names would be—it would cause the model even more trouble. That's why he tried to figure out a name that was close enough to make the model vivid, so that it would produce a similar effect for readers. But if he made it not different enough from the real name, that might make the model recognizable. So he really worked very hard at it. If the name were too close to the real one, then he'd change the age or the appearance, anything to give him some space. This time, however, he'd not had time to go over it. It wasn't that it hadn't occurred to him that "Codama" would make for an easy mistake, but he was hard pressed, and as he gathered speed in the last day or two before the deadline, he'd been up practically all day and night, his pen flying. And so "Codama," "Codama," at some point became "Cojima," "Cojima."

That need not have been much of a problem, of course, but this story was one of those "diabolistic" plots he specialized in: a man gets fascinated by whether he can kill another man—any man, a stranger—without leaving a trace, and he does successfully manage to kill the man in such a way that no one will ever know he did it. The model for the killer would be the author, Mizuno himself; the man he chose as the model for the man to be killed was this Cojima.

The protagonist of the story was, like Mizuno, a literary man. . . . He loved no human being but himself. He saw everything in the world as random and accidental. This was the fundamental view of human life that permeated his works, but before long he felt his artistic genius begin to weaken, and eventually he got to the point where he had to try acting out his aesthetic position in real life.

There were several considerations in his decision. First of all: given that he was that kind of person, of course he didn't have any close friends and he lived a calculating, solitary life. So if no desire to write came bubbling up naturally, his isolation left him with no way to replenish his stock of creativity. Second: whether or not he felt such a thing as the prick of conscience (even to think this way he'd have to be crazy already, but he didn't realize it), he thought of it as a kind of nervous prostration: human nerves were quite fragile, and if one overused one's head and was stimulated even a little bit beyond the ordinary, one would immediately become sick and exhausted, and not just from doing something immoral. And so it seemed to him that if he wanted to do something evil without feeling the promptings of conscience, either he had to find a way to trick his nerves or he could try to numb his nerves by accustoming them to evil bit by bit. And since "tricking his nerves" was in fact "to lead them rationally," it was not something to fear at all. Rather, it meant that he should train himself to be heroically faithful to his own beliefs. In this way, while attending to the state of his nerves, and by working at it bit by bit, eventually he would be capable of performing some great act of evil with perfect ease.

Accordingly, he worked out his plan and secretly set about carrying it out. First he worked at ensnaring someone—in such a way that the man would think him a noble and kindhearted man, and even thank him. Just as he had expected, his nerves gradually became numb, and he came not to feel any of those pricks of conscience. "Look at that!" he said in his heart. . . .

Soon he became the embodiment of evil. How far can I go before I feel a pang of conscience? Is it here? . . . Here? . . . Gradually he was so drawn into it that he felt he had to enact the height of evil: he would have to cause harm to another human being. He thought to himself, "If I don't try this at least once there will be something missing in my commitment to resolving the riddle of 'conscience.'" Slowly he looked around and sought out a suitable victim.

His crime would be evil for the sake of evil. That was the only reason for it. . . . Why it should be that way is that otherwise there would be room for some moral "justification." For that reason it would be better if the intended victim were someone he didn't have much of a connection to. That way there would be less danger of getting caught. After all, if he managed to snare the man but were caught by the law, then there would be no point to it. . . .

As he looked around him to see who might fit his conditions, into his field of vision wandered—the very man. Why this man Codama caught his (the story's protagonist's) attention is that, just as stipulated, they had almost no connection. This fundamentally cautious criminal knew that no matter how careful he was to erase all evidence, all the same something might remain somewhere to be sniffed out, and that last trace would remain, at least in his own conscience. Even if he could erase the external footprint, he could not easily wipe away the mark left in his heart. Of course he had no worries on this point, for his conscience was already numbed. But as long as he paid scrupulous attention, inside and outside, spiritually and materially, he would be able to erase the trace completely. For the rest of it, given that he wasn't very competent at planning things, even if there wasn't any actual evidence there might be some vague rumor going around. If all eyes turned toward him and all fingers pointed at him and people became suspicious of him, there would be the possibility for disaster to grow from that.

Now, this man Codama had once been a reporter for some women's magazine and had visited him two or three times, but other than that the only connection they'd had was to pass each other on the street occasionally, or see each other at the motion picture theater. All the writer knew was what he'd picked up here and there: that after quitting the magazine, the man had withdrawn to somewhere in the outskirts of Omiya off in Saitama prefecture and now was involved in compiling the collected works of some writer; that he went into Tokyo twice a week for that, Mondays and Fridays, and while he was in Tokyo, generally he had dinner and then returned by train around eight or nine. The writer just happened to hear bits and pieces of the man's life: his house was some three-quarters of a mile or so from Omiya station, outside the town, and he had to pass along an isolated section where at night there were hardly any passers-by. He'd learned these things when occasionally he had run into the man on the Ginza or at a movie theater. It was always when he had come into Tokyo for work, and he would say something like, "Yeah, I come in on Mondays and Fridays," and then, "Oh, sorry I have to rush off before you—I've got a long way to go, and if I don't make this train . . ." And even if they were in the middle of a movie, he'd always get up and leave around 8:00 P.M. They'd had five or six accidental encounters of this sort, but once he'd been talking to a friend of the man, a journalist at some magazine, and the topic of living away from the city had come up. The journalist said, "You know, living off in the country is all right, but it's pretty inconvenient," and went on to talk about Codama's house as an illustration of how isolated and dangerous it was to live in the hinterlands. He continued in considerable detail about what the road was like and concluded, "Well, I suppose since it's only once or twice a week, it could be okay, but there's no way I could live in such a place if I had to commute every day."

This was all he knew about Codama, and none of it was the result of any special research. Given that their relationship was so tenuous, there was virtually no way that he could know anything other than this about the man's activities and living situation. When he thought it over, he realized that he was probably the only one to know this much about Codama. For the unsuspecting

Codama, it was just his bad luck that the writer chanced to be in that position. . . .

No one can know when disaster will befall him. He could be walking along below a cliff somewhere and a rock could fall and crush him. His foot could just happen to slip on some clay, and by just the difference of an inch or two, he could plunge into a gully. He could suddenly have a heart attack right there on the street. In other words, Codama's death should be a death of that sort. The only difference was that it was another human being who did it, rather than a rock or clay. Like a rock or clay, however, this other person was a man without conscience. And Codama, until the moment he was killed—no, even his ghost after he was dead—wouldn't have the slightest notion of why he had died.

Before setting things into action, he definitely had to make sure that Codama really did go into the city on Monday and Friday, or if he really was still living in the outskirts of Omiya, and he had to do it in such a way that no one would notice him checking. But that didn't mean that there was some deadline by which time the plan had to be carried out, so he didn't have to rush with his investigations. He would do it in a perfectly natural way, taking whatever opportunities came up. He would gather information here and there, in passing, from people connected to Codama's editing work or journalist friends of his, so that no one would be suspicious. Furthermore, he would secretly go to Omiya himself to check the layout of the neighborhood where Codama lived and actually walk the route from there to the station to calculate the distance and the time it took.

What he paid closest attention to was the method for murdering him. As he thought it out, he decided it would be best to use a weapon that came to hand by accident. On the intended day, he should pick up something just lying by the roadside, do the deed with it, and then drop it back on the side of the road. That would be the most ideal. It certainly wouldn't be good to steal some kind of knife or gun—that would leave quite a trail of evidence. Rather, the weapon he was looking for was something completely ordinary—say, a towel, a rope, or an empty bottle, a stick, or something like that. And as long as he was putting his order in, it should be something that would do it without leaving blood traces, that would knock him out at the first blow, and further, something that he could use to achieve his purpose with precision from a distance of ten or twenty feet away. There must be something he could find accidentally lying at the determined spot on the lonely road from the station. On the day he went out for his survey, these were his thoughts as he walked along the road. He found at least four kinds of weapons easily obtainable on the road. One was in a vacant lot at a construction site on the town's outskirts, an iron bar used in the concrete. Another was firewood piled at the side of the road. The other two were a hoe and a hatchet leaning against the wall of a farmer's barn. Surely he'd be able to get at least one of these on the appointed night. If it happened that he couldn't find anything that night, well, there was no hurry, he would just quit then and wait patiently, however many nights it took, until chance let him get what he needed.

A "rational man"—from when he found Codama until he was able to carry out the project, this was how much deep thought he put into it. He ended up having to wait about half a year before the most propitious conditions presented themselves. Finally, one moonless Friday night following one of those short days at the end of November, he leisurely left his rooming house in Kagurazaka, wearing his usual strolling outfit of kimono with a cape. He took the train before Codama's. While he was hardly likely to meet anyone he knew on the train line from Ueno to Omiya, he could imagine such an encounter and so tried to be as inconspicuous as possible.

"So, finally Codama gets killed. But I wonder what a reader would feel if he read it as 'Cojima'?"—Mizuno traced along the plot of the story to that point, but now he cocked his head doubtfully.

Would Cojima notice that he had been used as the model for the Codama of the story? Or—would Cojima even read it? Mizuno at first lightly assumed somehow or other that maybe he wouldn't read it, but now that he thought about it that was pretty wishful thinking. While Cojima was fairly distanced from the literary world these days and all he was doing was editing some encyclopedia, originally he had been a staff writer for an entertainment magazine called *Humoresque*, so undoubtedly he was a man with literary tastes. Accordingly, he was not likely to miss checking out the new fiction columns of the magazines every month—especially that of a first-rank journal like *The People*. To be sure, a man who was knowledgeable about magazines or happenings in the literary world would probably be cynical about current fiction, and he'd likely just flip through the pages and not read very carefully. After all, that's what Mizuno did: he looked through all the magazines that were sent to him each month, but what he mostly read were the easy-reading essays and feature articles. As far as serious fiction was concerned, unless it was by a writer he especially liked, or by someone he knew well personally, or he had some behind-the-scene information about the content, or it was reported to be extremely good, or something like that, he rarely read the rest of it. Maybe Cojima was the same. Mizuno was not a writer Cojima "knew well personally," and he probably wasn't "a writer he especially liked." It's just that, if it became an issue in the literary world, he might read it. Another thing he could imagine: what if some third party read it and got him interested by saying something like, "Hey, you're the model, you know—he's even used your real name"? Of course, that wasn't likely to happen. A third party wasn't going to notice a connection with a model. Whether or not "Codama" turned into "Cojima," "Cojima" was a very common name. There's nothing strange about mixing up the two.—No, no, wait: "*Ko*jima" is pretty common, but not the way he spelled it, "Cojima." So if it's *Cojima* in the story, surely that would make them connect the two, wouldn't it? But that he had used Cojima as the model: who, other than the man himself, would think of that? Be that as it may, it was too early to decide that Cojima would not read it. There was at least the possibility that he would. Mizuno had a strong feeling that he couldn't *not* read it. Rather than assuming he wouldn't read it, he'd better think that he *would* read it. . . .

So he was back at the beginning: supposing Cojima did read it, would he notice? If he were reading casually he probably could be expected not to notice. But if he got toward the end and the word "Cojima" instead of "Codama" caught his eye—wouldn't he sit up and take notice? And then wouldn't he go back and read it again and start to feel, "Hey, this is peculiar . . ." And once he began to *suspect*, there would be any number of things that would make him feel uneasy. For example, Codama had been a writer for a women's magazine, but now he was on the editorial board of a certain writer's collected works. For his part Cojima had been a writer for the entertainment magazine *Humoresque*, but now he was on the editorial board of a certain encyclopedia. Codama's house was in Omiya, while Cojima's house was in Urawa, the station just before it on the same line. And they both went into Tokyo on business twice a week. Even worse, the degree of acquaintance between Cojima and Mizuno was almost the same as that between the story's protagonist and Codama: from time to time they ran into each other in passing, they both were friends of the same magazine writer, and Mizuno had learned about Cojima's daily life from that magazine writer, Suzuki.

When he discovered so many similarities, Cojima probably wouldn't think of them as accidental. He'd be sure to think, "Huh, so he used me as the model." Now if this was the full extent of the correspondences, he probably wouldn't feel too unsettled, but the author in the story had gone to excessive lengths in describing Codama's personality and looks, his build and even his voice. Not only were these, too, just like Cojima's, but also Codama was described as if he were not a pleasant person at all. Of course, the protagonist of the story had not the slightest bit of personal feeling in choosing Codama as the victim; but Mizuno couldn't say that he hadn't felt a tinge of malice in choosing Cojima as the model, as if he were implying, "That guy is a disgusting piece of work." There's probably no such thing as a man whose face says, "Kill me," but if there were such a person, Cojima was it. . . .

Something like that had been in Mizuno's mind for some time. You can't weigh the relative seriousness of the crime of murder on the personality of the victim, but illogically he had a feeling that some men were more killable than others. You might not feel so bad killing some people. For example, there's that scene in kabuki called "Mitsugi's bloodbath," where this guy goes toddling out in his summer *yukata* and suddenly, as he passes, for no reason, just on some whim, he is set upon by a swordsman and cut down. He's generally played as thin, with bad color; his face and build are weak, and although it's mean to say so, he is so insubstantial that he looks as if he'd fly away if you blew at him. Mizuno himself wasn't very substantial; he was thin and unsteady on his feet, and at the time he was staying over at the Kakuebi teahouse fairly often, he'd be sitting in the main room at the hibachi in his yukata, nursing a fading hangover, and find himself thinking, "What if some other guest runs amok and I get slaughtered like Mitsugi, even though I'm an innocent bystander?" Cojima, in a word, was just that type. From the first time they'd met, when he'd gone

visiting with Suzuki and they chatted about this and that, his immediate impression was, "What a stupid face this guy has."

A stupid face: you could spend an hour or two sitting right
across from him, looking directly at him, and five minutes after
he leaves, you forget him. But it was precisely because Cojima's
face was so stupid that he remembered it. He didn't know where
he came from, but clearly it wasn't Tokyo. No man from Tokyo
had such a slick, hairless face. His coloring: you could call it tan,
or brown, or even black, but it gave the impression of worn-out
shoe leather. His nose was flat, and his eyes were dull; as for his
mouth and chin, they had no special features but were just dry
and blunt. His face was as flat as his cheeks, and at the same time,
his facial features were small and pinched. And so you could say
that it was not just his coloring: his whole face was just like a shoe.
Further, his voice was what you'd expect to issue from such a face:
it was dry, toneless, and rough; the enunciation was unclear, and
he rolled his tongue around in his mouth so you couldn't understand his mumbling. A voice issued from him, but when you looked
at his face, it was just like a shoe was talking to you.

In addition, he didn't know how to deal with other people. It
seemed to be beyond his talents to be lively or joke or be witty. He
seemed to have a kind of reserve, as if he were weighed down by
his own miserable appearance. And yet what really got on one's
nerves was that, at the same time, there was something strangely
thick-skinned and pushy about him. The first time Mizuno met
him it wasn't so apparent, but when they happened to be riding
the same train some time later, Mizuno opened his newspaper
and pretended not to see him. But Cojima deliberately stood up
and familiarly called over to him, "Well, hi . . ." This greeting was
delivered in his characteristic mumble, with nothing friendly or
comfortable about it. And what was all that familiarity about?
Did he not mean to be familiar, but just thought that he had to

make some kind of acknowledgment? Mizuno couldn't read his attitude at all.

Once when he'd been at a motion picture house in Asakusa, Mizuno had felt someone silently tap him on the shoulder from behind, and when he'd turned around and looked, it was Cojima. He said, "Haven't seen you for a while . . ." Because he seemed hesitant, Mizuno, too, responded noncommittally. But there was nothing particular to talk about, so he turned back to the screen. Yet Cojima didn't leave, and from time to time he continued to ask questions as if something had just come to mind: Are you busy these days? What are you writing? Do you often come to the movies? . . . And although Mizuno didn't respond much, he persisted. Of course, Mizuno, too, was that kind of man himself, with something indecisive and persistent about him. So while he found Cojima irritating, he didn't cut him off, but continued to make neutral appropriate responses. As for the irritation he felt: Mizuno had a feeling that somehow or other, if he were never to see Cojima's face again, there would be something missing in his life. And so he did continue to engage with him occasionally. While he did find Cojima worthless and irritating, he couldn't say that somewhere there wasn't a certain entertainment value in the contempt he felt for him. Accordingly, for all that Cojima was of no consequence, for Mizuno he had a singular existence, always squatting like a jailer in a corner of his head—so that even when they ran into each other on the street, he'd stand there and join in several minutes of conversation with him.

Mizuno had not been aware of it until then, but it was just this quality of Cojima himself—or at least the picture of Cojima he had in his head—that had given him the idea of the story in the first place; this picture had unconsciously given him the *hint* and led him on. If he hadn't seen the image of Cojima passing back and forth in his mind's eye, he might never have come up with

IN BLACK AND WHITE ᴄ℞ 15

that plot. He couldn't even say that there hadn't been a degree of lighthearted maliciousness to it, as if he'd said to himself, "Okay, okay, let's use that guy—he's so thick-skinned he'll never know!" And so his contempt had been helped along by a kind of desire to make fun of him. That's why in the story, while there was not the slightest personal antipathy between Codama and the protagonist, and there was the man's unfortunate appearance, the author took advantage of his third-person position to maliciously dot in here and there traces of his own ill will, as his pen slipped along, finding it entertaining to describe Codama with such phrases as "What a dismal face . . ." or "Just looking at him you could tell what a pinched, miserable existence he led."

To be sure, no matter how bad Cojima's circulation was, he could hardly feel good about seeing a phrase like "a complexion like calfskin shoe leather." But there he was: as a writer, he wouldn't be able to write anything if he worried about whether readers would arbitrarily connect a character in a story with an actually existing person and comment on the connection. A story is a story and reality is reality, and if they won't distinguish between them, that was a problem. He could be evasive by acknowledging that to have a model means that there is some sort of relationship between story and reality, but he could also assert that a writer writes purely from his conscience as an artist, so considerations like "good faith" or "ill will" are irrelevant, because an artist does not insert his own personal motives into the story. But all the same, he should have made more of a difference between "Cojima" and "Codama." If Cojima lived in Urawa, he shouldn't have had Codama live nearby in Omiya but put him in Yokohama or Chiba instead. To have one editing an encyclopedia and the other editing a story collection—he could have made him a professor or a businessman, at least. And to have them both be former magazine writers— that was entirely too similar, and changing it wouldn't have made any difference in the plot. To have Codama killed in Tsurumi instead of Omiya wouldn't have weakened the story's effect. Mizuno hadn't really paid much attention from the start because he was writing as fast as he could to make the deadline. But he was in fact making fun of Cojima. And so he had no defense against a charge that he was intentionally pointing at him.

But wait a minute—what was he thinking? Would the man even suspect? Would he get angry? Right—wasn't his opponent only Cojima, after all? What was he going to do, even if he *was* mad? "That's mean, to say 'calfskin shoe leather' . . ." The only thing that would happen is that I would grin at him, right? My nerves must be getting bad these days, to have me worry about something like this.—Mizuno, still in his futon, rapidly blinked his eyes and tried to persuade himself that he was being stupid. But oddly enough, his mind immediately circled back and once again he found himself caught in the same thoughts.

He'd already written quite a number of murder stories, and the murderers were more or less modeled on himself. How many people had he killed in his stories? Not just that—even if it hadn't been as blatant as it was this time, usually there had been a model for the victim, and people who knew his personal life could generally guess who it was. In fact, the reason his wife had left him was that he'd written three or four wife-murder stories in a row, and at the time, letters flooded in to her from sympathetic readers, saying things like, "Dear lady, your husband is horrible. What must you have felt as you read it?" Rumors kept spreading in the literary world that he had killed his wife. There were more of those rumors than critiques of the stories themselves. His wife did eventually flee the house in terror, with no notice. While he hadn't actually borne her any ill will, and his primary purpose had not been to drive her away, it is true that he'd felt the inclination to use the stories to do just that. He had snickered to himself: "Well, that certainly went well, and now I'm finally free." And without question he was delighted that his plot had worked so well.

When he thought about it, there had been so many episodes of this sort that by this time there could very well be quite a bit of rancor toward him out there. So with this "model problem," the possibility of disaster was not out of the question.—Of course, it was only because he was so obsessed with it that he could even imagine such a thing. But then, even if by some remote chance Cojima bore him a grudge, what could he do about it anyway? What means of retaliation could he have by himself? And given that Cojima was so removed from the literary world these days, he probably wouldn't even have the wherewithal to gather support to drive Mizuno out of it. So would he resort to legal appeal? But Cojima hadn't suffered any actual injury. He couldn't say that this story had made him lose his social position or had lost him a job. The fact is, other models had suffered even greater losses than someone like Cojima. All that would have happened to him was that he had been made fun of in a story; if he claimed that he'd been insulted, wasn't being compared to shoe leather just some stupid little thing? And besides, if the author firmly continued to deny that he had used Cojima, and the author had gained nothing by frightening him—unlike the situation with his wife—how could he find any grounds for claiming that he was actually the model? Not only would Cojima fail to achieve anything; he'd have to testify in court that his face had been compared to shoe leather. Not likely! So what could Cojima do? Would he try to kill Mizuno himself to get even?

Mizuno snickered out loud. And then it occurred to him that such a man *could* go against expectation and actually kill him. It was not inconceivable that hidden within his tricky, ambiguous attitude was a criminal nature. If he worked out a plan just as Mizuno described it in his story, there couldn't be any more intensely satisfying a form of retaliation. Even if he didn't have the guts to actually do it, at least the idea might float around in his head. And if Cojima became obsessed with the idea and thought about it day and night, he could become seduced by his own fantasy. That could happen, with such a morose, closed-off guy like him. Or since he was such a cold fish, he wouldn't even have to go through such a complicated process—right from the start, he'd head straight to the "okay, I'll just kill him" step.

"Nervous breakdown, nervous breakdown . . ." The fourth time, Mizuno said it out loud.

Then it came to him. The tangled threads of his thoughts had been twisting around in crazy directions, and he suddenly realized that it was more complicated than the base problem of Cojima's hurt feelings. What if—what if—Cojima were to be killed in a fashion identical to the murder of Codama in the story. Wouldn't *he*—Mizuno—be suspected? Of course that would never happen, and if it did, it would be very, very bad luck. But to say that it *couldn't*—well, say some third person had a grudge against him and killed Cojima precisely to entrap Mizuno. Oh yes, suppose there was this person who had been lurking in the shadows, waiting patiently for some opportunity. This would be the perfect chance. To be able to arrange the perfect moment to kill a man and shift the blame to someone else—such chances don't come along very often. And yet here it was, as if Mizuno had created the opening for someone else and had himself taken on the role of being blamed for it.

He had meant to put a clever murder in his story, but instead he had planted a seed that would grow to kill him. He'd dug a trap to catch another man, but before he knew it, he'd fallen into it himself. Most cleverly, unbeknown to anyone else in the world, he'd come up with the means to do away with a man. The crux was not what was in the story but the relationship between four elements:

the story; the writer, Mizuno, who wrote it; Cojima, the model; and one more—the man lurking in the shadows. In the instant of putting them together, the chosen victim became not Cojima but Mizuno. Cojima would undoubtedly be killed in the course of working it out, but he was only the means to an end: the ultimate goal of the man in the shadows. *His* aim, his fascination, was to have the crime successfully laid on Mizuno and to have Mizuno killed at the hands of the law. This plan, once the story was published, was quite possible. It was far more possible than what the protagonist of the story had planned for Codama. A man who noticed this possibility might come to want to make it happen simply for the fun of it, even if he had nothing against Mizuno.

In short, there was a sequel to his story. He should have conceived of Codama's murder as a story-within-a-story, with what he'd written already as the first part. That is, the larger plot should be that on the basis of a story dealing with a murder, an actual murder takes place. Then the author of the story is suspected and executed.—The whole thing should have been a single story. It would have been so much better than what he'd written instead. Not just that—if he'd done all that in the story, he could have prevented the ominous second part from actually happening. If the second part had been already written, the Shadow Man might not have been particularly interested in imitating it in real life, and it would have made much more doubtful the possibility of pinning the crime on the author. Rather, the Shadow Man would have feared inviting suspicion to fall on himself.

"Damn. If they'd give me just another month, I could rewrite the whole thing. But I don't suppose they're likely to give me the manuscript back." Mizuno's disquiet doubled. He'd taken great pains to write this story with its ingenious conception. Instead, he realized that in fact it was half-baked, and he'd lost the chance to devise something more complex and natural. Even worse, because he'd missed that chance, now he was exposed to real danger. Clearly, even if he tried to get the manuscript back, it was already far too late to do anything about it. *The People* deadline was around the tenth of the month at the latest, and it generally appeared on the stands before the twentieth. But he'd been handing over five or ten pages to the company messenger every two or three days, and when it got to the office they sent it on immediately to the printing plant. And he'd given over the last section on the morning of the thirteenth. Three days had passed since then, so they were probably finished with the proofreading and were already typesetting it. Even if they hadn't actually started, they weren't likely to just instantly pass back to him something that was already planned to be in the next month's issue. There'd have to be some exceptionally important reason, and while Mizuno felt his whole fate lay in the balance, even if he raced over to the printing plant at this moment and pleaded with the editor, would he be likely to agree?

"Hey, listen—if you publish the story as is, I'm sunk. If it appears like that, the real man that Codama is modeled on will be killed. Believe me, that will really happen. And then the police'll arrest me. Two lives are in the balance!"

But would the editor hear his anxiety as real? "You're joking! What a crazy thing to say. . . . What's up with you?" The more serious Mizuno was, the more he was likely to ridicule him.

Mizuno himself thought it was ridiculous, but just as a cluster of clouds gradually spreads to cover the whole sky, so did his fear gradually spread over him as he lay rigidly burrowed into his futon. Big disasters sometimes come from little things. From the start, he'd had a premonition that something *would* happen. The more he tried to push it away, tried to think of it as a silly little misstep, the more he heard a menacing voice threatening him: "No, it's not a little error. Retribution for your long-standing evil is drawing near." It was better that he realize sooner rather than later that bad luck was still ahead of him; at least he could be prepared. But supposing he couldn't get the manuscript back—what should he do?

Wait a minute—maybe he could have them change the "Cojima" to "Codama" for him. There was still time for something like that. The mistakes were in just the last ten pages. He had handed them in on the morning of the thirteenth, so no matter how fast they went, they might still not have printed it yet. Maybe the proofreader was smart enough to have seen it, and he'd corrected it himself? If so, he was in luck. But he'd been three days past the deadline, so probably there was no chance it was noticed. And as far as *The People* went, the owner was impatient, the employees were all careless, and the work was always done in a rush. So the magazine was always full of typos, and it was not likely to have been fixed. Wait—yes, I'll negotiate by phone, and the sooner the better!

At that thought, he threw off the covers and stood up. But then he began immediately to worry about where to telephone from. There was no telephone booth in the boardinghouse—the phone was right in the vestibule. He didn't really care if he was overheard, but what if he got carried away and started shouting? Wouldn't it be a bit strange to hear him going on about "Codama" or "Cojima"? Wouldn't they wonder why he was so exercised over such a trivial misprint? It would be depressing to imagine them thinking of him in such a context. Well then, should he use a public phone? But the boardinghouse had a phone—wouldn't it be strange for him to go outside just to phone?

As he battered his nerves this way, he became totally confused about what to do, and although it didn't really matter where he telephoned from, for a while Mizuno wavered in utter confusion, leaving the room and coming back in. In the end he finally decided to use a public phone after all, but it took him another thirty minutes to get himself to do it.

He got to the nearest public phone, but then for some reason or other he went past it and trotted on to the one at the next corner. Then after suspiciously checking out the neighborhood and the passers-by, he furtively entered the booth.

"Ah, yes, you are . . . oh, Mr. Mizuno, is it?"

He had called the printing plant, and by good chance *The People*'s chief editor, Harada, was there.

"Oh, Harada . . . listen, in that manuscript I recently sent you, there's a big mistake, and I'd really like you to fix it, but . . . well, it's in the last ten pages, right at the very end, but . . . have I made it in time?"

"Yeah, well, it is too late. I got right on it the day it came in and stuck with it through the night until the editing was done. The next day it went into printing, so there's nothing we can do now, you know." Harada's Kyushu drawl made him sound like a cop in some melodrama. The oddly expansive tone of his response was provokingly cool.

2

"But there's a mistake, something that's really going to cause quite a problem, you know . . ."

"What's the mistake?"

"The story has . . . there's a . . . ," he was about to say, "model in it," then he hurriedly corrected himself. "The name 'Codama' appears in it, right?"

"Yeah, yeah, the guy who gets killed, right?"

"Yes, right, but I got mixed up at the end part and wrote 'Cojima' instead. Can't you do something about it?"

"How many places are you talking about?"

"Well, five or six for sure . . . no, well, there could be more. But maybe I'm in luck and the copyeditor fixed it for me. Did you notice it?"

"Hold on a minute. You say it's in the last ten pages or so? . . . Let me go and ask him."

He left the phone and came back two or three minutes later.

"Yeah, well, I just checked the proofs and sure enough, it wasn't fixed." Harada's naturally deep voice got even louder as he growled over the noise of the press, as if he were calling from a long distance.

"But if we leave it as is, it'll embarrass not just me but the magazine, too, don't you think?"

"Nah, something like that's no problem. The readers can pretty well figure it out, you know. Actually, I didn't even notice it when I read it through."

"No, but listen—suppose there's some guy named Cojima. Mightn't he think he was the model for the character? Then I'd really be in trouble."

Mizuno had been mulling over whether or not to say this. Harada was far from sharp and observant, so it was probably unlikely that his attention would be drawn in dangerous directions. But all the same, Mizuno broached the topic as cautiously as he could. Sure enough Harada didn't answer, but his cheerful laugh echoed from the phone for some time.

"No, really, it's no laughing matter. . . ."

"Mr. Mizuno, do you know how many people there are in Japan named 'Kojima'?"

"Well, yes, that's right, but my 'Kojima' isn't spelled with the usual 'K'—it's 'Cojima,' you know."

"So what's the problem?"

"The problem is, it's . . . it's not the ordinary, everyday 'Kojima.'"

"So—are you saying you modeled your character on an actual man named 'Cojima'?"

Harada was probably just teasing and meant nothing by it. But to hear these words fly out of his mouth meant that he'd have to be ever more careful. "No, it's nothing like that at all."

"Well, then, there's nothing to worry about."

"Right—but I do actually know someone named 'Cojima,' and that's what I'm worried about."

It was hopeless. No matter how much he went back and forth with Harada, the man just continued to chortle and refused to engage with him. Even after he hung up, he could still hear the man's laughter ringing in his ear.

Now there was nothing he could do. There was no way to correct it. A less first-tier magazine than *The People* would have listened to what the author wanted, and the editor-in-chief would not, like Harada, have been so high-handed with him. With other magazines the work would not have been so rushed and there would still have been plenty of time to change it. But when your luck is bad, this is how it works out. There was nothing he could do—within the next four or five days, it would be out on the stands for the whole world to see. And then, maybe at the same time of year as the murder in the story—around the end of November, when the days are short—at some point, Cojima will be killed. And I will be thrown into prison. . . .

Mizuno returned to his room on the second floor of the boardinghouse and sat brooding at his desk, his chin propped in his hand. The funny thing was that even as he worked himself up with these ridiculous and embarrassing fantasies, somewhere in a corner of his heart he felt a kind of pride: "I am a hero, an artist willing to brave danger, staking my very life on my creative work." Isn't that remarkable? No matter what they say, I am no ordinary writer. My work is always born out of this kind of suffering. Suppose by some remote chance I am suspected of murder because of this story: then even if I were to be executed, my death would be for the sake of my art! At that final moment, I would cry out at the top of my voice from the scaffold: "My fellows, hear my last words—see how a true artist offers up his life for his art. From the start I knew that if I wrote this story, disaster could come upon me. But there was no way my artistic passion would let me avoid this. Not in the least do I resent the laws or the courts of our nation. Hear my prophecy: after my death, the real criminal is sure to be discovered, and that fact will eternally validate my writings, the work I have dedicated myself to in this world!" . . . Under ordinary circumstances I'm a coward. But in the face of that challenge, I could unexpectedly become heroic and meet it with splendid resolve. By contrast, Cojima would be the pathetic loser. After all, he probably doesn't even realize the danger my story poses to him. "To use a real person as the model—even if it's just a story, to model the murder victim on an actual man—that's really disgusting!" . . . That's probably as far as he can understand. He doesn't even realize that it's not a matter of "just a story"—in fact, it's his personal fate to be used as someone to be actually killed. That's the consequence radiating from him as a man in a story. If he understood that, he'd probably be ten or twenty times more panicky than I am. It's a blessing that he's so insensitive. There is after all nothing he can do about being killed. . . . A malicious half grin rose to Mizuno's lips.

From that point on, the first thing he did every morning, even before he got out of his futon, was to open the newspaper that had been left beside his pillow. With terrified expectation, he pored over the advertisements announcing the contents of the next month's magazines. It was not until the morning of the twentieth that the bold, showy lettering of *The People* assaulted his eyes. His story had been relegated to the last item in the fiction column. Below the title, "To the Point of Murder," the editor had appended his usual provocative comments: "This diabolist has finally accomplished his true art. This is the ultimate summation of his view of human existence. What are the torments of conscience to such a man—a philosophical murderer who has no conscience? The latest masterpiece of this writer, relentlessly pushing to the farthest extreme of the individual's state of isolation, the farthest limits of violence, complexity, intensity, truly ranking with De Quincey."

Reading it, he again felt ominous premonitions spreading to every corner of his heart.

The announcement was clearly Nakazawa's work, produced at Harada's behest. It was just his style to refer to De Quincey. The worst part of it was that you couldn't tell if he was outlining the plot of the story or referring to the actual author himself. From "This diabolist . . ." to ". . . has no conscience" was a synopsis of the plot, and from "The latest masterpiece" on was boosting either the author or the work, but which one was not immediately clear. "This diabolist has finally accomplished his true art." The "diabolist": even though that meant the man in the story, it rather gave the impression that it referred to the author. If even he felt momentarily startled as he now read it, how much more would the general reader be likely to misconstrue it? Of course that was the purpose of the advertisement: to arouse a confusion in the "he"— the protagonist in the story, the writer Mizuno—to make the reader think, "The writer has murdered someone." The magazine would consider it all to the good if it aroused curiosity. If so, then these lines would be even more dangerous than his story itself. Why? Because even if they didn't read the story, people who read the advertisement would be sure to pick up a preconceived notion that Mizuno was "a loathsome man who wouldn't stop at murder." If at that point Cojima were killed, the conclusion would be obvious. Everyone would think that Mizuno, "this diabolist," had "accomplished his art." In fact, the advertisement itself was supremely dangerous. Now that it had appeared, his position was immensely more precarious. The person who would be most aroused by this ad is surely the Shadow Man. When he reads this, the Shadow Man will see that things are now turning out quite as he hoped, and he will be even more encouraged.

That afternoon, the accursed magazine was delivered to him. For a while all he did was open the envelope and set it on his desk. He gazed reproachfully from a distance at the words *The People*, on the cover. And then with dread, sighing all the while, he took the magazine onto his lap and flipped through it quickly until he found the story. Haphazardly, as if choosing a fortune slip at the shrine, he glanced at one part and then another, from the beginning, from the end, out of order, starting and stopping, until finally he read every word of it. Then he slowly read through it again, from the beginning. Next, he counted how many times the name "Cojima" appeared. He had thought it was five or six times, but to his surprise there were only three places. However, even once or twice was too much—that it was only a few times did nothing to assuage his worry. And besides, as he continued to check through it he realized he had chosen the worst possible places to make his mistakes. One was, "Cojima grunted and fell face up. And that was all there was to it." Another was, "It was dark, and so he couldn't recognize his face, but he felt nothing at all toward the corpse. It was as if he were throwing away a piece of trash. . . . Cojima's existence had been contingent while he was alive, and now that he was just a dead body, it was still contingent." And the third was the part where the protagonist reads the article in the paper reporting the murder:

> It was just two or three lines with the headline, "Suspicious Death," in an inconspicuous corner of the page. "The body of Naojiro Cojima (age 35), formerly a writer for XX women's magazine, was found dead early yesterday morning around 6:00 A.M. by passers-by at a spot several hundred yards away from his residence near Omiya in Saitama Prefecture. Investigation is currently underway to determine if this was a homicide."
>
> —That's all there was, along with articles about a drowning and a man who had dropped dead on the street. It was treated in the paper as if it were just an accidental death.

Of all the slips, this is what worried him most about the newspaper excerpt in the story: "Naojiro Cojima (age 35)." That's because Cojima's real name was Nakajiro, so three of the four syllables—

actually, five of the seven syllables—were the same. It was strange that he should have been so careless. But then maybe it was natural after all that when a writer is thinking of names to give to characters in his stories, the names of actual people would come floating into his mind, so it would make sense that he would tend to make them close approximations. Mizuno had not really been conscious of whose name it was; all he had remembered was the euphony in "Nakajiro Somebody-or-other." So when he changed "Cojima" to "Codama," the sound of "Something-o Codama" or "Something-uemon Codama" didn't work, and "Something-jiro" came out naturally. And so without much thought he made it "Naojiro." But he could see now that it obviously had come from Cojima's "Nakajiro." Then there was the problem of the age. He had chosen thirty-five at random, but in a curious turn of fate, some malicious devil had created a coincidence with real life. Even if he'd picked something other than thirty-five, it would have been only a year or two different anyway.

Until now, Mizuno had been wrestling with seemingly groundless fears in his own private imagination. But now they had taken shape, and there they were, standing right before his very eyes in clear print. For a moment he could imagine Cojima's protest. No matter how thick-skinned the man was, when he read this he was bound to be horrified.

With luck he wouldn't see it, but in time what might the critics say about it? How might the literary world view it? Terror that Cojima would hear about it made him want to bury himself in his futon covers and hide until things quieted down. In times of stress like this, his habit of talking to himself got even more intense, and now, like a man with an earthquake phobia who causes his own body to shake during an earthquake, he started to rattle on to himself as if to block the comments of bystanders:

"You jerk—what are you doing?"

"Yeah, well, there's no way for me to escape my fate."

"Hey, this isn't a joke!"

"Codama, Cojima, Codama, Cojima . . ."

"Um, hello, hello? Is this Mr. Mizuno?—"

There were all kinds of ways he talked to himself, but whenever he started calling himself by his own name as he just did, it could turn into a long dialogue:

"Um, hello, hello? Is this Mr. Mizuno?—Yes, this is Mizuno.—You wrote a story like that, and now it's most unpleasant that you're playing the innocent.—What, me? I'm not playing the innocent, you know.—Ooh, you're awful, when you've gone and committed murder.—It was just a story.—No, it was real. I *know* you did it.—"

It went on and on, even longer than when he was simply uneasy. One party spoke in Mizuno's natural voice; the other was coquettish, like a young woman speaking on the telephone.

From this point on he kept track of the monthly literary reviews as they came out in the newspapers. He got a sense that the literary establishment had grown tired of his diabolism. He had put so much into this serious piece of work, and now it was being dismissed. The attitude seemed to be, "What, this again?" The monthly reviews generally brushed it off with contempt.

One of them put it sarcastically: "Mr. Mizuno's 'To the Point of Murder' seems at first to be conceptually different, but in fact it is just like all the others. He seems to be stuck: it would appear that he can't be diabolistic if it isn't a murder story."

Another was quite harsh: "His seriousness is forced; trying to make the conception significant, he only plays around with the structure and does not give it true profundity. This writer's work is always like this. There is no one who is totally without a conscience, like the protagonist. If there were, he would be a madman. Even in 'diabolism' there is genuine human suffering in feeling the pain of conscience, and complex problems come from that. This writer does not understand human beings." And one was lightly dismissive: "As a psychological story, it is shallow; as a crime story, it is simplistic."

He'd been a writer for a long time and was used to negative reviews of this sort. In fact at one level he was rather pleased that this time he wasn't being flattered but instead was being put down with some subtlety. And more important: fortunately, from what he'd read so far, no one had touched on the matter of the model. Whether they hadn't even noticed, or if they did notice, it was beyond the scope of the critique, or a measure of courtesy toward Cojima, at any rate even though there had been a great public hue and cry over the incident with his wife, this time there was an almost eerie silence. He wondered if it might have been mentioned in the gossip columns, but no rumors appeared in either the newspapers or the weekly magazines. As the month progressed he got gradually bolder and, as he took his walks, he would be quite comfortable as he looked through the various magazines set out in front of the bookstores. But surely at least one person ought to have noticed, yet there was nothing. That it hadn't been noticed, and the silence over it, he found vaguely unnerving.

If he'd had some sort of close friend, he could have tried exploring the situation indirectly. But unfortunately he hardly ever had a visitor, so he was stuck, completely on his own. One day Nakazawa came from *The People* to commission him to do another story for them. Usually after their business was finished Mizuno would abruptly get rid of him, but this day he continued to talk, and gradually he turned the conversation to his topic of concern. Even as he probed delicately, it became clear that the matter wasn't on Nakazawa's mind at all.

"Well, then, how about it—this time we'd like to get the manuscript just a *lee-tle* bit earlier, you know? Couldn't you do it by the fifth of next month, at the latest?"

"The fifth . . . nah, the fifth is too soon . . . couldn't you wait until the tenth?"

"Well, now . . . no . . . that would be a problem for us. The last issue came out late, and our owner was quite vocal about it. Starting this month we've made the deadline earlier."

"You guys work fast, so you'd still be able to get it out if you had at least a week after the deadline . . ."

"Yeah, but look what you did the last time . . . if you said the tenth, and it got to be the thirteenth, we'd be up against it, you know, and then we'd get grief from the printers."

"And so there'd be lots of typos."

"Yeah, inevitably that's what would happen." He suddenly grinned as if remembering something.

"Hey, that's right. This last time, you really shook Harada up, you know."

"Oh—why?"

"Didn't you phone him all upset?"

"Oh, yeah, there was something like that. Did he say what it was about?"

"Something about how you'd made some mistake in writing the names, and you wanted him to fix it for you because if he didn't there'd be some kind of mess. He said it was some piddling thing, but you were hysterical."

"Yes, yes, yes—but that was because I thought that if I didn't put it in extreme terms, Harada wouldn't even listen to me, you know."

"But Harada says you were practically crying on the phone, and then you got all serious and said Cojima would hate you—"

Mizuno suddenly looked as if he'd gotten a body blow, and the startled Nakazawa swallowed his words.

"Co . . . ji . . . ma . . . ?—Who do you mean by this Cojima, eh?"

This is bad, I mustn't lose my head. . . . Even as he thought this, Mizuno couldn't keep his voice from rising.

"A while ago, there was that staff writer for *Humoresque*—Nakajiro Cojima? Aren't they saying you used him as the model?"

"Who said so?"

"Hey—he said you said it yourself on the phone."

"N-n-no joking!" Mizuno finally managed to say with a laugh. "I didn't say that. Cojima is a very common name, and what I said was that there must be hundreds of thousands of them in Japan, maybe even millions, and I could imagine that among them there would be someone who accidentally resembled the character, and I was afraid that that person would think he'd been used as the model—" At some point, even though he hadn't planned to *lie*, in a self-serving rationalization he began to think of Harada's words as his own. "—and if by some remote chance—well, it's a bit silly to think such a thing could actually happen, but if, by a one-in-a-million chance, this Cojima happened to get killed under the same conditions as described in the story, well, they'd suspect me, you know."

Nakazawa burst out laughing.

"No, really, it could be.—I didn't go into this much detail with Harada, but the fact is, when I'm pulling a story together, my fantasies come bubbling up, and my nerves get strangely overexcited, and I lose the distinction between the story and reality. I imagine lots of stuff, you know, and if that doesn't happen, I couldn't write anything good."

"Yeah, I suppose that's right." Even though his job was only to pick up manuscripts, Nakazawa spoke as if he seemed to have an immediate appreciation for the mind of the writer. "—And yeah, they say that Balzac always talked aloud to the characters in his works as if they were actually there."

"Right—I do that myself. If someone who didn't know me heard me, he'd think I was talking to myself, you know?"

"'Poison would be the way to kill the servant girl'—isn't there some story about that nineteenth-century writer Takizawa Bakin doing that?"

"Yes—there, you see? Every writer has experiences like that."

Chattering on, Mizuno began to feel himself calm down. And as he gradually warmed to the topic, he began to feel that he, too, was a great writer like Balzac.

"Well, it's not that we don't understand that. In fact, that's just what Harada said at the time, you know: he did think it was strange, but he also said that you were always writing murder stories, so you must sometimes find yourself terrified at the things you write. In other words, he realizes just how serious you are."

"Yeah, yeah, well, it's something like that. On top of that, you know, I'm generally working in the middle of the night, two or three o'clock, right? I'm glued to my desk, and it's real quiet and very late, and I'm writing a story like that, and you can bet it doesn't make me feel good."

"How *is* it—do you get terrified yourself, do you ever hesitate to continue?" Apparently believing that flattery would be the most effective way to encourage Mizuno, Nakazawa cynically asked this with a straight face, as if he were a young aspiring writer himself.

"Well, yes, it is terrifying, but no matter how frightened I am, I can't stop—that's just how it is, you know. To stop is just as terrifying, so I hold my breath and continue writing in a trance. It's like a frightened horse that can't stop running once he starts."

"Mr. Mizuno, they call you a diabolist, but you're actually probably a very good person, and that's why such a thing would worry you—that's what everyone on the editorial staff said, you know."

"A *fake* diabolist, they say, and my reputation's shot everywhere, it would seem. . . ."

"No, that's not what I mean. '*Fake* diabolist' and 'good person' are not the same thing. . . ."

"I don't mean you. The others—they've been criticizing that story pretty much everywhere."

"Really? No, surely that's not so, is it?" That Nakazawa's ignorance was feigned was transparent. "—Were some people really running it down?"

"'Some people'? You must know that all it's gotten is criticism? Not one critic has had anything good to say."

"Gee, that couldn't be . . . No, that's not true. I'm sure I saw something positive about it somewhere. In the first place, it's extremely interesting. That part where you say that guy Cojima was like shoe leather—the feeling comes out really well there. No one else could write that but you!"

"Hey—hey—it's C*o*dama, not C*o*jima!" As he spoke, Mizuno's face began to cloud over again.

"Ah, really?—But I'd been completely convinced from the first that it was our Cojima, you know—"

"You—but do you know that Cojima?"

"Well, in fact just a month ago I was helping out at *Humoresque*. You must know Cojima, too, surely."

"Let's see—yes, maybe I met him two or three times? Not so much that I could say I know him. Anyway, do be careful that you don't get me caught up in some sort of mess about fictional characters and real-life models."

Not long after, Mizuno saw him off at the entrance. As Nakazawa tied his shoelaces, Mizuno stood behind him fidgeting. Furtively stealing a look at his profile, he asked, "Say, that thing about models I mentioned a while ago—you're not the only one, does everyone think that?"

"No, probably no. It's just that I know Cojima, and he suddenly popped into my head."

"But what about the insiders at the magazine? Have the editors heard any rumors about it?"

"Well, if they did, they've forgotten all about it. It isn't something that would stick in your memory, is it?"

Mizuno felt that there was still something or other that he wanted to ask him about, but Nakazawa finished tying his shoes and quickly slipped out, leaving behind him an ambiguous "Well . . ."

"The hell with you," Mizuno spat out abusively at his retreating figure. His thoughts whirled about in disorder: he had been comfortable, but then specifically asked about something he needn't have; then again, maybe it was a good thing he had asked. The biggest surprise was that Nakazawa's relationship with Cojima was close enough for him to know him by sight. Cojima was such an amorphous person that Mizuno had arbitrarily decided that he would not attract public attention and his circle of acquaintances must be small. So for Nakazawa, who knew him, to suddenly appear from the inner circle of *The People*, as if there was something going on, was a bolt out of the blue. When he thought of it that way, rather than feeling bitter at his own carelessness, he felt rage that Nakazawa, the creep, knowing what was what, hadn't told him early on, but, as it were, intentionally hid it from him.

He realized now that to have telephoned so heedlessly was the biggest mistake he could have made. If he hadn't called, Harada wouldn't have laughed at him, and probably there would have been no rumors spreading throughout the editorial staff. To know that Nakazawa made an association like that meant that it was not unlikely that sometime, somewhere, he'd make another slip of the tongue. What was it he'd said?—"That part where you say Cojima was like shoe leather—the feeling comes out really well there." If that's what he really felt, then without a doubt there are other guys who know Cojima, and they'll all feel it. No matter how much I deny it they'll probably all be thinking, "Yeah, for sure he's writing about Cojima." And they'll maliciously spread the word, just for the fun of it. Come to think of it, he must have been the jerk who wrote that advertisement that caused such a fuss. God, how I hate the guy . . .

He'd had a hidden agenda in their conversation just now: if Cojima were in fact murdered, and if he were arrested as a suspect, Nakazawa would be certain to be called as a witness, and he'd have to make a detailed statement about the particulars of this conversation. It was actually a clever ploy when he had said, "Of course it's pretty ridiculous to think that such a thing could actually occur," and that's why he had prefaced his comments by seeming to reveal such a trivial concern.

He began to imagine the exchange between the judge and Nakazawa at the preliminary hearing:

JUDGE: . . . So then what did the accused say to you?

NAKAZAWA: Mr. Mizuno said that he was just joking to think of such a thing, but that he was worried anyway, because if by some one-in-a-million chance a murder took place just as it was depicted in the story, he would be suspected.

JUDGE: And when you heard that, how did you feel?

NAKAZAWA: It was such an off-the-wall fantasy that I laughed it off.

JUDGE: Then what did the accused say?

NAKAZAWA: Well, then he told me various things about the creative artist's psychological state of mind when he was engaged in the process of creating.

JUDGE: Would you please give us some details about what exactly his explanation was?

NAKAZAWA: He said that when he's creating, his imagination bubbles up wildly and he's under nervous stress, and he becomes unable to distinguish between the story and reality. And then he thinks all these crazy things and he's is horrified to find himself writing them—that sort of thing. And I said that I had heard the same of Balzac and Bakin, so that made sense.

JUDGE: When you cite Balzac and Bakin, you mean—?

—Of course, if the questioning went on like this, the conversation wouldn't be so bad for him. That Nakazawa had spontaneously thought up the examples of Balzac and Bakin was probably the most effective way to get the judge to understand his psychology. At least the judge wouldn't be able to determine on his own whether, just because Mizuno wrote the story, he did the deed.

But come to think of it: if in fact they thought he had the desire to do it, couldn't they think he'd revealed all of this on purpose? In the process of writing the story, he became carried away by the desire to translate art into action. Mightn't he be suspected of layer after layer of nefarious scheming, of doing things in order to fool the world: to deliberately make such a phone call, to let slip that "stupid concern" to Nakazawa and then manipulate Nakazawa by leading him to remember the examples of Balzac and Bakin? "If there were someone named Cojima who got killed in the same way as the story says, I would be suspected"—he hadn't done that quite right. If he was going to mention it, it would have been better for him to have been clearer, to have confided it in full detail. Instead of trying to hide Codama's resemblance to Nakajiro Cojima, he should have asserted that he had used him as a model before he was even aware of it. He should have made Nakazawa fully realize that Mizuno knew that a number of people bore him grudges, and that if one of them were looking for a chance to get even with him this would be absolutely the best time to do it. He should have made these things clear, and others: the danger that Nakajiro Cojima would really be killed, his fear that he would be ensnared by the Shadow Man—all these reasons that this was not such an off-the-wall fantasy. And not just Nakazawa— he should have made the world in general understand his anxiety, and imagine the existence of the Shadow Man.

But maybe there was still some way for him to remedy it. He could actually make what he'd already written a Part One and do the manuscript they'd just commissioned as Part Two. Since he hadn't started "To the Point of Murder" with such a plan in mind, the transition would possibly be awkward, but this was not the time to bother about that. Given the pressing need to avoid being sucked into a whirlpool, and not that he had a perfect harmonious whole, he would abandon any artistic pretensions. All the same, the problem remained that it would still be a month and a half before Part Two would come out. Would the Shadow Man hold off setting things into action? He might think that no matter how bizarre Mizuno's tastes were, he was not likely to actually kill a man within a month of writing a murder story. He would proba- bly think that the time was too close between the story and reality and thus wouldn't work to transfer suspicion onto him. Accord- ingly, for the time being it probably made sense to assume that nothing would happen. And then when the Part Two came out the Shadow Man would be forestalled and wouldn't be able to do anything stupid after all. Of course, Mizuno couldn't say positively that he was completely out of danger, that if by some remote chance Cojima was killed, he wouldn't be the one to be suspected . . .

3

The very next day he sat down at his desk to work. His first perplexity was the title. Should it be

To the Point of Murder: Part Two

or

Part Two: To the Point of Murder

He tried the two on standard manuscript paper, but neither caught his fancy. To put his thoughts in order, he wrote down the following:

1. We have here a writer with diabolistic tendencies. He publishes a story called "To the Point of Murder." Originally, the whole of it was to be Part One. In other words, the story "To the Point of Murder" makes up only a part of Part One. However, out of necessity this current "To the Point of Murder" was separated off as a solo piece and it stands as what now makes up Part One.

2. Part Two opens with a man who wrote a diabolistic story just like the Part One. After he writes the above story, by chance

he discovers that there is an actual man named Koyama who in a number of ways resembles "Codama," the man who gets killed in the story, and he becomes terrified that if this Koyama is killed in the same circumstances as those in the story, he might be suspected. He tries to act as if he is tough and evil, but actually he's just faking, and is in fact quite a decent person and a coward to boot. And then just as he'd feared, an incident occurs, and Koyama is killed. The man is eventually picked up by the police and an investigation takes place. He pleads tearfully, "I'm absolutely telling the truth, I did not kill him, there must be someone who has it in for me, and this is his work, to entrap me." But the detective doesn't believe him. "That's crazy, isn't it a part of your diabolism to lie like this and pin the crime on someone else?" The detective mocks him. And then they torture him horribly. Finally, unable to bear the pain, he says, "Yes, I killed him." The case is moved from hearing to trial and he recants his confession, but the prosecutor delivers a scathing summation and the judge finds him guilty. During the trial, his ex-wife appears in court as a witness and gives damning testimony. Among other things, she says, "This man can't keep himself from acting out his art. I myself was afraid he would kill me, and that's why I left him. There is no doubt: this man killed Mr. Kojima." And then he gets a death sentence, and before long the sentence is carried out. However, after his death the real criminal appears. He brags, "I destroyed that diabolist for the sake of public order. It's better that someone like that is dead." He goes on, "It's too bad I had to kill Kojima, but it couldn't be helped, and between the two of us (Kojima and I) we got rid of that devil," and with a smile he pleads guilty. The world shudders at the criminal's horrific vendetta, but no one has any sympathy for the writer who died for a crime he did not commit. Rather, they hate him even more and feel he has gotten his just desserts. . . .

He vigorously underlined the words "by chance" in item 2 of his memo so that he'd be sure not to forget it. But near the end, where he should have written "Koyama," once again he began to write "Kojima."

When he stopped writing and looked it over, he realized that because "To the Point of Murder" was the title of an independent story, it didn't work to cover the whole thing. "Two" was the continuation of "One," but it was not Part Two of "To the Point of Murder." To be precise, it should be, "To the Point of the Murder of the Man Who Wrote 'To the Point of Murder.'" That was just too long for a story title, but he wanted this work to be read by as many people as possible, so maybe it would be good to have a striking, unconventional title that would draw attention. Not only that—just the title itself would telegraph quite a bit of the content of Part Two. Come to think of it, up to now he had killed off quite a number of people in his stories, but this time he was writing a story where he himself was to be killed. Wouldn't this in some way be making amends for his own sins?

And so he started again and wrote on the first page of his manuscript paper, in two lines, the title:

To the Point of the Murder of the Man Who Wrote

"To the Point of Murder"

"Now, this is great, what a relief! I'll write it as fast as possible and foil the Shadow Man!"—

Day after day, he went on writing. But as usual, he had trouble getting past the first ten or twenty pages. He knew that once he made it over the hump he'd pick up speed, but he always found it terribly hard to begin writing, and it always took quite a while before he picked up the pace. To start with, he didn't get up until around eleven in the morning each day, and by the time he'd lain in bed awhile smoking, let his mind wander in fantasies, read the newspaper, washed his face, and eaten his breakfast-cum-lunch, it was generally already around two in the afternoon. At that point, he would sit down at his desk, but he hardly ever got more than one page a day written. He thought, I'll be tough with myself and write at least one line, but already extraneous fragments of thoughts that had nothing to do with the story roiled up, gathering like clouds in his head. Until he could tame them somehow or other, there was nothing he could do about it, so he'd helplessly lean his cheek on his hand and stare out the window or lie on his back with his legs outstretched, glaring at the ceiling. Then, spying a clearing in the clouds, he'd take up his pen again and write another line or two. But as he wrote, the hazy clouds would come welling up again. It was like trying to make his way by paddling between waves that came pressing in one after another. But when the commotion of the clouds wouldn't stop, he'd angrily throw his pen down and abruptly go out for a walk, wandering around the neighborhood until nine or ten o'clock at night. Whenever he started writing something fairly long, this was invariably how the first week or two would go.

It happened one day during this initial period. That day, too, he was making no progress at all, so he gave up on getting any work done during the day. Hoping to soothe his edginess, he headed for the Ginza. Around five in the evening, having eaten at a stand-up sushi bar for the first time in a while, he went into the Royal Cinema to see *Chang*, the movie that was playing. When he got to his seat in the special balcony, the scene on the screen was the part near the end where the herd of elephants comes out of the forest and tramples down the natives' huts while the white monkey flees, swinging from tree to tree. Just as Mizuno was thinking how beautiful it was, someone silently tapped him on the shoulder.

"Um, yaa . . ."

Even without turning around, he realized that there was no question: it was Cojima . . .

"Yaa . . . well . . ." In the same ambiguous tone of voice he, too, gave a light greeting in the direction of the shadowy figure bowing in the semidarkness, and then immediately turned back to the screen. He was bound to run into Cojima sometime, wasn't he? . . . It's not that he hadn't imagined it from time to time, but, well, it was fortunate that it happened in a place like this while he was right in the middle of watching a movie, instead of bumping into him unexpectedly on the street in broad daylight. And so even though Cojima made the first approach, the picture was ending in twenty or thirty minutes, and he could fake it until then and then get away. Well, no, to sneak away like that would be rather strange—but as he was covertly working out a plan, Cojima came around from the row behind him and dropped onto the seat just at his right. The springs in his seat back continued to squeak for some time, as Cojima slowly took off his hat and set it on his lap. Just as Mizuno was wondering how long he was going to watch the picture, Cojima stirred and brought his shoulder a bit closer to Mizuno.

"Are you . . . alone?"

"Um . . . ," Mizuno muttered with his mouth closed so that he could hardly be heard and deliberately resisted turning toward him. But as he continued to face forward, he could see out of the corner of his eye that the other man seemed again to be engrossed in the picture. Cojima smoothed the knees of his trousers and placed his shabby, folded coat on them. Silvery light reflected back on them whenever the beautiful white monkey appeared on the screen, and Mizuno could see Cojima's face illuminated from his forehead to the bridge of his nose. Why has he deliberately come to sit next to me—does he have something to say? Why is he sneaking around—does he think I'm trying to avoid him? Is that why he's trying to hunt me up? The tip of Cojima's shoe began tapping nervously as Mizuno pondered the situation. Tap, tap, tap, tap . . . it went on for two or three minutes and then suddenly stopped. Then it started up again: tap, tap . . . Hell, if he's so nervous and keeps jiggling like that, isn't that a sign that he's crazy? If he were actually keeping tabs on me, or if he were obsessed with some secret plan, surely he wouldn't be twitching like that. Maybe he's just being sneaky, and this is a trick to disarm me. Jiggling is contagious, so what if I start twitching too to get at his plot? Or maybe he's not being sneaky at all—maybe he's just got to piss.

"Heh, heh, heh . . ." The nervous jiggling stopped, and Mizuno could hear him laughing, as if something funny was happening. Wrinkles gathered around Cojima's nostrils, and his mouth twisted with the laugh. And then suddenly he turned toward Mizuno.

"Interesting, isn't it . . ."

"Ha, ha." Mizuno laughed as if it were being pushed out of him, but in fact it wasn't a laugh—all he did was say "ha" twice.

"Say, have you been here from the beginning?"

"Uh . . . nah . . . and you?"

"Just got here . . . now."

With that, the two again subsided into silence. Cojima always talked in broken phrases, so this would not seem to be anything out of the ordinary, but all the same, Mizuno was worried to some degree at his silence. Anyway, the film would be over in another five or ten minutes and then the lights would come up in the theater. Should he wait until then to leave? Or should he leave before? At any rate, Cojima had just come, so he would stay behind, but which would be the more natural for Mizuno to do? He'd run into Cojima before at places like this. How had he handled it at such times? He should do it the same way now. But as Mizuno thought about it, he realized that he had never once been the first to leave. Just as Codama in the story says, "My house is far away, and so . . . ," so Cojima had always used those words to leave before Mizuno. On top of that, when he asked Mizuno if he'd seen the movie from the beginning, Mizuno's "Uh . . . nah . . ." was an evasive mutter, but it was also definitely a negative answer. If he hadn't seen it from the beginning, then it would be strange not to wait to see it through again. . . . But why am I so afraid of Cojima? Mightn't I learn something from meeting and talking with him a bit? It wouldn't be so bad. I could ask him some stuff: has he even read the story? How does he feel about me? Does he still live in Urawa? If, for example, he had recently picked up and left the Urawa area and moved to live in the middle of Tokyo, then that one element alone would make me quite a bit less anxious. . . . Oh wait, a guy who's jiggling again like that—would even he make such a big deal about a "model"? Hey, Cojima, "Mr. Shoe-Leather" . . . Yeah, that was great, that "shoe leather" was the perfect way to put it . . . when you look at it that way, this man is just asking to be killed. Hey, you—Right? Stop it—stop that jiggling! Before long, you're going to be killed, you know. . . . With a start, Mizuno grabbed onto the arms of the seat. He had almost spoken those last words out loud, but he stopped himself and said it only in his head. Fluid was starting to leak out of the tank at the top of his neck. At the same time, Cojima stopped his nervous jiggling. And then the lights suddenly came on.

At that point, Shoe-Leather looked at him, and with a grin made his customary opening: "How about it . . . these days . . . are you writing something?"

"Uh . . . yeah . . ."

"Is it long?"

"Um . . . a bit . . ."

"So you're busy?"

"Uh, no, not—" he started to say but then realized that saying he was busy would be convenient for getting away, so he continued, "—very, but I am writing on a strict schedule every day, so . . ."

"You write at night? Usually?"

"Uh, yeah, generally from about now . . ."

Cojima made a series of long, drawn-out nasal responses: "A-ah" or "Really?" or an uncomprehending "Oh?" And after some time, he asked, "So it's something like the one before, what you're writing?"

Although Mizuno hadn't been conscious of it, in the conversation so far he had been talking as much as possible without turning his head toward Cojima's face, driven by a fear of looking at him. The crowd in the unreserved seats on the floor below and the pattern of the sparkly curtain that hung down over the stage reflected meaninglessly and hazily in his eyes, and Cojima's indistinct outline appeared in a shadowy corner of his eyes' blurry focus. His eyes, too, treated this man, who lived so ambiguously in the world, quite ambiguously. So when he heard Cojima's words now, Mizuno continued to face forward, as if paralyzed, with a snake creeping up on him. The crowd in the cheap seats and the pattern of the glittery curtain were even more wildly jumbled up in his eyes at that moment.

"By 'something like the one before,' you mean—?" he was about to say, but in the act of coming to his lips, it came out something completely different.

"Uh . . . well, I don't know how it'll come out . . ."

"Where will you send it? *The People*, as usual?"

"Ah, yeah, maybe . . ."

"Next month's issue?"

"Ah, yeah—"

Then it felt to Mizuno that another two or three minutes of silence followed.

"That one was interesting, wasn't it, the one before—"

"Ah, that one?"—he wanted to say quickly, nodding with his chin, but instead he jerked two or three times and his whole body twitched as if he had been tickled in the armpit.

But even though Cojima had persisted in his empty questions, now he seemed to have nothing more to say and again subsided into that vague nervous jiggling. Mizuno had never found this man's inscrutability as irritating and infuriating as it was today. The things he was letting slip bit by bit could be taken as frightening, but whether this was intentional or nothing at all, Mizuno couldn't tell with this man, and in the end he was left in total disarray. "That one was interesting, wasn't it?"—there, too, if any other man had said it, it could clearly be taken as irony, but what it was to this man, Mizuno couldn't say. It could have been just to have something to say. And had the man heard what he'd been muttering to himself before? You might think that it definitely had entered his ears because he suddenly stopped jiggling, but if he had actually heard it clearly, then really there should have been more of a reaction . . .

At that point, Mizuno realized that without his noticing it the theater had gone dark and the next movie showing had started. But what picture he was watching, what was fantasy in his head and what was the illusion manifested in the film, he could not distinguish. What he was experiencing was a comic short feature before *Chang* came on. In one scene, a white flour slurry was being poured over the head of a fat man, but Mizuno found the flour paste dripping in globs over the man's face like lava strangely horrifying rather than comic, and he thought of it as a cruel trick. Even the sudden uproarious laughter of the audience was frightening.

"To have this kind of comedy in the middle of a movie is most dangerous," he thought.

Had the two of them been sitting beside each other like this for two hours? Mizuno had come in here around five o'clock, and the grandfather clock at the end of the hall said it was exactly seven o'clock. Given that he had kept him company this long already, it probably wouldn't seem as if he were fleeing even if he left first, would it? But the fact was that now that they'd reached this point he was curious to sound him out by trying to bring up other topics of conversation. "That one was interesting, wasn't it, the one before?"—No matter how many ways he mulled over those words, sure enough, they worried him. This man would never get to the point, regardless of how much time they spent together. And not just that: the longer they were together, the eerier it seemed to Mizuno. If his nerves were so on edge here, he'd get into a state where he'd not be able to work again for the next four or five days. He'd be better off leaving quickly and burying himself in his manuscript.

"Say . . . well, I'm sorry but . . ." Aiming at a time when his companion was intently watching the picture, he said this suddenly and stood up from his seat.

"You're leaving?"

"Yeah . . . well, I've got to get back to work and so . . . You should come visit me some day."

This "Come see me one of these days" was to create the opening he'd been looking for so he could ask the following question: "These days, you're still in the same place? In the Urawa direction?"

"Eeyaa." (*Author's Note*: There's no other way to write Cojima's answer, which lay somewhere between "Aah" and "Yeah" but was neither. At any rate, it was a sound that didn't exist in Japanese. Probably its truest representation was with the International Phonetic symbol *æ*.)

"Ah, yeah, well, 'bye."

Mizuno bowed his head lightly and started to go. But Cojima showed no sign of returning his bow and instead slowly got up. As his seat creaked, he took his hat out from where he'd been sitting on it.

"Well, then, me, too . . ."

Mizuno, forgetting that he was obstructing the view of other viewers, couldn't keep himself from stopping right where he stood.

"You're leaving, too?"

"Eeyaa."

"But . . . you're not going to see the beginning part of *Chang*?"

"Eeyaa . . . I have to return on the eight o'clock train, so . . ."

By the time Mizuno had pushed his way through the packed audience and reached the stairs at the end of the hall, Cojima had overtaken him and they were completely shoulder-to-shoulder. They went down the staircase together, and Mizuno, who was wearing Japanese clothing, got his shoes back from where he had checked them and stepped ahead of him out into the street, stopping in front of the box office.

"Which way, for you?" At this point again it seemed strange to immediately get on the streetcar. "Well, shall we walk a bit?"

"Yes."

This time his "Yes" was unpleasantly clear, as if that was just what he was waiting for. . . .

It was that middle of the month—"November when the days are short." Night had fallen completely over the Ginza streets already, and a biting wind was blowing, making one think of the end of the year. The two of them walked without speaking at a leisurely pace toward Kyobashi past the rows of night stalls, even though one was supposed to be getting back to his work and the other said he had to make the eight o'clock train. Mizuno walked along with his head facing down, feeling it hard to breathe; he felt as if Cojima's face was looking up at him from the ground. It might have been his imagination, but somehow it seemed to him that Cojima was walking with great, deliberate slowness, as if to bring his broken-down shoes even more to Mizuno's attention.

"It's cold, isn't it . . ."

After some time, the shoes finally said something.

"Yeah, it is cold, tonight."

That alone was enough to make Mizuno parrot back a response. Attempting to joke, he added, "So, you know, it must be because I'm getting old, but year by year I've come to feel the cold more. At this rate, you can imagine how the winter will be, right?"

He intended to laugh at that point, but he couldn't get his voice out right, and it was Cojima who laughed.

"How old are you, Mr. Mizuno?"

"Next year will be one of the big ones."

Suddenly he realized it was necessary to get Cojima's age clear.

"How old are you, anyway?"

"Thirty-five."

"Oh yeah, you're still young, aren't you . . ."

In his ears, it was as though he could hear a devil sneering at his words.

"But there are times I can seem old, into my forties . . ."

"Why? Surely not?"

"Yeah, well, it's because I'm thin and dark." Cojima spoke and laughed again.

How long was this man planning to walk, for God's sake? Is he going to keep pulling me along with him, and stabbing me with the things he says?—Even as he thought, "What a pain this guy is," he felt himself being crushed, and there was nothing he could do about it. Not only that—before long a new worry began bubbling up in his head. What would he do if some third party—say, someone like Nakazawa—saw them walking along like this together? What would he do, if sometime later this man was killed? . . . At that point Cojima was walking along the Ginza with the writer of that story, just a little while before he was killed. And so it was indisputable that the writer and Cojima had considerable contact.—That's probably the conclusion they'd come to.

"Well, Mr. Defendant, you say you didn't know Cojima enough to use him as a model, but isn't it a fact that on November 15, 19—, between 7:00 and 8:00 P.M. you and the victim were walking together from the Royal Cinema toward Kyobashi?" That's how the judge would cross-examine him, isn't it? If this whole thing was the devil's doing, then without a doubt someone would be sure to notice them. Yet if that person called out to them, that would be all right. But what if they didn't notice him, and he just observed them—that would make it quite a bit worse. It would still have been all right if they were in the movie theater, but to have specifically chosen to walk along the Ginza in the company of this man, on a street so crowded with passers-by, and just where the night stalls were set up—how careless that had been.

"I wonder what time it is," he said, ostentatiously taking out his pocket watch from his waistband. "Let's see—seven thirty-two . . . are you still all right for your train?"

"Eeyaa, it's still okay."

"Didn't you say it was at eight?"

"I can do the next one . . . might have dinner somewhere . . . how about you?"

"I'm done—had sushi at a stand-bar earlier."

This was unbearable—to have to go beyond this and keep him company at supper. It would be the wisest course of action to part here, but if he got on a streetcar, mightn't the guy follow him on? And the problem was that his boardinghouse was in Yushima, in the same direction as Ueno Station, where Cojima was going.

"Well, then, we can go as far as Ueno Hirokoji together. You can get supper around there."—It looked as though that was what was going to happen, when a taxi came from the other direction. He raised his hand to hail it and got in quickly, saying, "Oh, here's where I have to leave you," closing the door before Cojima had time to pull himself together.—At least, that was how it was supposed to work. But unfortunately the cab made a wide U-turn, and by the time it was finally facing in the right direction and had stopped in front of him, there was enough time for Cojima to take his cigarettes out of his pocket, strike a match, composedly light up, and come behind as if to get in with him.

"Are you . . . what are you going to do?" Mizuno, his hand on the door and one foot on the running board, had no option but to say this after all.

"Is it all right with you, if part of the way . . . ?"

"It's fine with me, but . . . your supper?"

"If I could have you drop me off at Hirokoji, I could eat around there"—the exact words he had been hoping to hear.

Never in his wildest dreams had he imagined that he would be riding in a car with this man, but now here they were sitting side by side locked in a cramped box, being shaken up together as they ran along the street through Nihonbashi. However, there was probably less danger of attracting peoples' eyes this way than on the Ginza sidewalks or a streetcar. It worried him that the interior lights were on in the cab, but the passers-by on the busy Nihonbashi streets were not likely to notice what was going on inside a vehicle. Oh well, never mind, at any rate it's only another ten or fifteen minutes, and even if he seems not ready to get out at the Boulevard, it's only a bit more until we deliver him to Ueno Station.

"You appear to like the movies . . . haven't we run into each other there on occasion?" This time Mizuno spoke.

"Eeyaa . . . and I can never see it to the end . . ." Then, after a pause, he continued, ". . . If I'm late, my wife worries, it's such an unsettled area . . ."

"Oh, yeah, you're pretty far from the station, aren't you?"

"Over half a mile . . . part of the road runs through rice paddy fields, and on moonless nights it's totally pitch black."

Mizuno suddenly raised his head to find Cojima's face right in front of him, as it reflected in a little mirror affixed to the ceiling of the box. Seeming not to have noticed, Cojima continued to turn his expressionless eyes here and there as he spoke. Mizuno looked fixedly at it. This was the first chance he'd had tonight to see the man's face from this perspective, and he couldn't help thinking that the shadow of death was upon it. He didn't know what a "shadow of death" looked like, but somehow it was different from Cojima's usual face. Shoe-Leather was Shoe-Leather, but his face was branded with the mark of the God of Fate. He was hit with the feeling that this was the very shadow of death, that this was without a doubt what a person looks like before he dies; this is how it shows even on a person who doesn't know it's coming.

"Ah, stop here . . ." At Cojima's voice, the car stopped. They'd come to the Boulevard. "Well, then, I'll take my leave here, sorry I've been so . . ."

"Nah."

"Um, I'm looking forward to your next story."

"Nah," said Mizuno, nodding again. At the same moment, Cojima laughed.

His figure, tottering off toward Ueno, disappeared into the night crowd. The cab immediately turned left and went up the hill street cutting through the heights. But now Mizuno wondered if he oughtn't rather to return for the time being to the Ginza. It was clear that if he went home now and sat himself at his desk, he wasn't going to be able to settle down to his work. He had carelessly gone out for a walk, and look at the mess he'd gotten into. And he'd been completely disrupted. It wouldn't be so bad if it affected only today, but for the time being—or even the next four or five days—he wouldn't be able to do anything. . . .

He had been laughing at his worries, sure they were trivial and needless; but his misgivings were actually becoming fact, one by one. Cojima was now living in Urawa, he said. He was thirty-five years old, he said. These details were already a horrible enough coincidence, but then his house was some distance from Urawa station on a lonely road through paddy fields, over half a mile—even the numbers matched Codama. One thing he could imagine: mightn't Cojima have actually made these details similar to the story's in order to frighten Mizuno? The man's appearance today was certainly quite enough to bring the matter of the "model" to attention. This business of his family being frightened if he came home late—maybe his wife or children had started worrying about his situation since the story appeared, and he wanted to get even. Even Cojima must have his boiling point—how angry might he be? If so, could he be angry enough to do this maliciously by way of revenge, when he lacked the strength of character to confront Mizuno directly? The man didn't seem to have that kind of shrewdness, but to think of it this way somehow made the most sense. If not, it was too strange for so much to be just coincidence.

"So—was that it?" He felt a bit relieved at the thought, but immediately the death face he saw earlier reflected in the mirror floated before his eyes.

Actually, the original problem of whether or not Cojima bore him a grudge was secondary; rather, whether or not Cojima would be killed was the crucial issue. But the man himself seemed not to have noticed that at all. Professor Shoe-Leather, you should be frightened yourself rather than frightening someone else.

Should you quickly pack up and move back into the city; should you not wander around the Ginza at night and instead return home right away? He should be cautious; his carelessness would seem to indicate that he just didn't see how dangerous it was. The Shadow Man now effortlessly seizes his opportunity. Accordingly, the thing Mizuno had to worry about again was that the "end of November when the days were short" was pressing on. Until today he had completely overlooked that the time would come within the next ten days or so. He ought to have realized that those critical days were sandwiched between the publication of his Part One and Part Two. Mizuno's nerves were always unpleasantly oversensitive, but still he kept leaving things half done because he was somehow missing some essential quality of attention.

Before long he returned to the boardinghouse, and when he came up into the entry hall, he spoke into the screens closing off the office. "Say, Missus, might you have an almanac for this year? If so, let me borrow it for a bit." It had occurred to him to see if there was a "Friday night without a moon" at the "end of November when the days were short."

"Would this be what you want?"

Snatching it up, he put the booklet she handed him into the breast of his kimono and climbed up the stairs as if he couldn't wait. As soon as he entered his room, without even taking off his cloak, he turned on the light. He continued standing just as he was right under the light, and opened it to the late November section.

There—there it was, November 25 is the day, the Friday that was the last day of the month by the lunar calendar. It was right there, just as he'd written it in the plan for his story. "How about it—this is the way it is," the almanac was saying to him. Mizuno stood stock still, like a log, gazing at the words for some moments, illuminated with a halo from the bright lamp above. I shouldn't be especially surprised; I've pretty well known that this is how it would work out. And he wasn't just making a virtue of necessity, he felt. Then he sat down at his desk and sat for a long time staring at the almanac, still forgetting to take off his cloak and hat.

How long had he sat there? When he came to, the sound of the streetcars had stopped completely. It was around two thirty in the middle of the night. He was startled and looked around at the room like a man who had just awakened. The single room that had been the stronghold of his unmarried life for the past couple of years was deeply silent. Brightly, quietly, the things arranged within it glowed like the objects in a still-life painting. The futon bedding was spread near the display alcove. While he'd been out earlier, the maid had prepared it for him. The white of the freshly washed sheets sank painfully into his eyes, bright enough to make them hurt. He got a clear impression of each of the books lined up in order on the bookcase, the gold lettering on the spines telling what book this was, what was the next. . . . How in this situation can my head be so clear and calm? What I had feared was, unexpectedly, not frightening. If this state continues, I'll be able to stay composed even if the twenty-fifth comes at last and Cojima is killed. And if I'm arrested by the police and thrown into prison, even if at the end the death penalty is handed down, I could be able to face the moment with equanimity: "So it's finally come." Of course, that I can be so composed may actually be because my nerves are paralyzed. Such quiet may be a sign of the final upsurge of an enormous terror from the very center of my heart.

On the desk the almanac was still spread open, and beside it was piled all of the manuscript that had already been written, only about ten pages. He gazed at them disinterestedly, as if he were looking at a still-life painting. He could not think of them as something he had written. Or if he had written them, between the time he had written them and now was a long separation of ten or twenty years . . .

Here I am, in the middle of the night, looking at this almanac, and maybe the Shadow Man is also holed up secretly in his one room, sitting at his desk in the same way and looking at his almanac.—That Mizuno guy, could be he's writing his Part Two. If so that means I'll have to act before it is published. Fortunately, here we have that day, the twenty-fifth. There might not be another suitable "moonless Friday" at the end of November next year, so it would be a waste to wait. Okay, it's a bit rushed, but let's do it this twenty-fifth.—The Shadow Man takes up his pencil and draws a black horizontal line under the twenty-fifth in the almanac . . . I can see him drawing it . . .

Mizuno, too, took up his pencil and was about to write beside the twenty-fifth in his almanac: This day is Great Danger, the day that will determine my fortune, if I don't pass through this day without incident, I will not be safe. But then he stopped. The maid could open it and see this when she comes to do the housekeeping. It's enough for me to write it in the almanac of my heart and keep it there.

Well then, there are some ten days between now and that day, so how'll I spend them? There's no point in writing the Part Two until my fortune is set for the day, and I've lost interest in everything else. From the start I've thought of this work as a means of self-defense. Now it doesn't seem likely to achieve its aim as a protection.

Mightn't there some other means of defense? There would seem to be no way to prevent Cojima's murder, so it would be best to see it as a fact: it will happen on that day. Then in that case, the thing to do was to make sure suspicion would not fall on him.

Oh wait: he should arrange to avoid being by himself as much as possible for the next ten days. Especially that day—from 8:00 P.M. on the twenty-fifth until morning the next day, he should figure out where he'd be and who he'd be with—that's the best way. During the day, he could be sure not to stir a step outside his room on the second floor, and if he called the maid in from time to time and had her do things for him, that would generally be proof enough. But the problem was the period from night until morning. At a time like this it would be good if his wife could come over; but she wasn't even a friend anymore, so that wouldn't work. Instead, could he go on a trip to somewhere far? That was a real plan, but he didn't have any travel money at the moment, so there was the problem of the time between walking around getting the money together and the several hours on the train. What's worse, all his life he had hated traveling. Regardless of the destination, there was no inn he knew well or anyone who would know his face, so it was not impossible that he'd find himself thrown out all on his own for a long period.

Yes, after all it would be safer to stay here in the boardinghouse. So where he should be was clearly decided at this point. It's just that he couldn't ask someone else to stay here with him. At any rate, it was impossible to cover all the time, but as much as possible, he should cut down the time that he was all alone. At least he should be sure not to have more than an hour go by without meeting with someone. This much he had to put into effect from dawn today until the twenty-fifth. And so for the nights, if he couldn't find some appropriate person to keep him company, well, he'd go in the evening to a pleasure house and spend the whole night . . . He didn't have to do anything; it would be enough for him to have a place to sleep. After all, it's not that he didn't have some favorite houses or women who knew him . . .

From that morning on, the comedy began. He crawled into his futon some time after five in the morning, but from the time he began hearing doors to rooms opening here and there and the sound of footsteps plodding down the hall, he would open his eyes and do things like cough or get up and go to the bathroom down the hall.

"Mr. Mizuno, you're up quite early today, aren't you?" It was around eight when the maid came to the door to the bathroom.

"No, I'm still planning to go back to sleep—I don't know why, but since last night, I've had to piss an awful lot—"

"Are you sick?" The maid chuckled as if poking fun at him.

"Don't be stupid."

"But there must be some reason, mustn't there?"

"Yeah, well, maybe I brought home a souvenir from some-where—that's what happens when you're a single man, I guess."

Mizuno thought: *This is great—for the time being I'll have the clap and spend my time commuting to the bathroom.*

4

B etween then and around ten he went to the bathroom twice. But it wasn't easy to pretend he had gonorrhea. Furthermore, he hadn't had any real sleep since the previous night; drowsiness was gradually spreading in him, and if he wasn't careful, there was the danger that he would oversleep the next hour. After ten, he had hoped to doze off in a light sleep, but before he knew it, he had fallen into a deep slumber. When his eyes popped open, he was surprised to find it was already eleven thirty.

"Ow—this is bad, it's been an hour and a half already."

He hastily went off to the toilet and managed to be seen by two or three people. Of course, a plan that had him going to the bathroom every hour seemed crazy even to him. If Urawa was to be the place for the crime, the round trip from the boardinghouse to Urawa took two hours, no matter how fast you went. So up to two hours was okay. If he couldn't get solid sleep for two straight hours at a time from now through the next ten days, he'd be totally exhausted, and then he'd be lost if he got to the crucial twenty-fifth and overslept because he was so tired. Rethinking his scheme, he decided to stretch the one hour to two. And so, after the eleven-thirty visit, he let himself sleep exactly the two hours, until one thirty.

He usually had his lunch meal around two, and the maid he'd talked to earlier brought it in to him on a tray.

"How's your illness doing, Mr. Mizuno?"

"Hey—what do you mean, 'illness'?"

"But didn't you say so yourself, sir? Where did you catch it?"

"How should I know, I have it pretty much all the time. It's chronic, and I'm often hit with it at the change of season. This recent shift from fall to winter has been particularly bad. Don't be so mean to me—I need a little sympathy."

She chortled. "How should I be sympathetic?"

"Well, never mind. Despite your kind offer, I have other people who will sympathize."

"Well, I'm amazed—even though you've been sick, you still haven't learned from experience? Really, should I go buy some medicine for you?"

"Oh yeah, you certainly are kind to me. You could go get it for me, but I have trouble remembering its name."

"What's it called?"

"Sandalwood oil smells and it's bad for the stomach, so that's no good. Let's see—is it Santolmonal, or Methylene Blue, or could it be Aleol? That might be it, maybe . . ."

He kept the maid for as long as he could, idly chatting, and then he suddenly thought of another plan: he could take a diuretic. That would in fact make him have to pee often, so even if he were asleep, he would wake up naturally. And besides, while it was vulgar to say so, if he took the medicine with the Blue in it, his urine would be dyed blue, and that alone would catch people's attention and advertise that he was ill.

When he finished eating, he set out for a pharmacy in the neighborhood of the rear gate to the university. There he bought a bottle each of Santolmonal and Methylene Blue and ostentatiously placed them on his desk. It had taken him thirty minutes to do all this.

But anyway, in the evening he had to go find some place to be with a woman. Unfortunately his wallet, which had held only a single ten-yen note, now had only five or six yen remaining because of the medicines he had bought. It was hopeless to think of going out to seek entertainment every night for the next ten days without two or three hundred yen in his breast pocket. Furthermore, he was blocked in every direction because he owed quite a bit to a number of the houses he frequented. It was even awkward to go to the pawnshops because he was behind in paying the interest to them; besides, as he looked out over his possessions, he saw nothing at all left of any significance to pawn. Well, his pocket watch was the only thing he could possibly take to them, but at this point his watch was more essential than anything else.—Oh wait, that's right, he mustn't forget to wind the watch! He'd be in real trouble if he got careless and made a mistake in the time.— So there was nothing to do but go whine to *The People* and get them to give him an advance on the manuscript fee. But here, too, in addition to piling debt upon debt, there was the question of whether this time he could even write the manuscript.

It was well over ten years since he had appeared in the literary world as a creative writer, and now he was approaching the age of forty. He should be more trustworthy, but when it came to money matters, his reputation was bad everywhere. That was because from his youth he had believed that to be a genius one had to lead a self-indulgent life, and that narcissism was still indelibly impressed on his mind. His "diabolism" was essentially a means to evade payment to teahouses, houses of pleasure, the magazine companies, and friends.

And then, too, he took pride that he lived alone, feeling it demonstrated his qualification as a brilliant writer and diabolist, but that was probably no more than a self-defensive rationalization, basically a result of having lost friends and being ostracized because of his real-life money problems. Another thing he took as a point of pride was that he never wrote too much at any time, but this, too, was not really a matter of his deep artistic conscience but was simply because he was a loafer. Actually, all he wanted to do for the next ten or twenty days until his money gradually ran out was just lie around.

The debt he had long put off paying back to *The People* must probably have reached around a thousand yen at this point. He didn't even remember the exact amount. Over the past two or three years he had borrowed a hundred or two hundred yen at a time, always with the same promise: "I'll return it for sure with the next one." But it kept piling up and must have reached that much. The company had finally resigned itself to cut its losses and leave what he'd already borrowed unredeemed and instead decided to absolutely refuse to make him any new loans. Indeed, the company owner, being a sharp man, and knowing that Mizuno was the kind of man who wouldn't really work unless he was shown the money, came up with the bright idea that they wouldn't pay except in exchange for the exact number of pages actually written, whether it was ten pages or even five. Even so, these terms were quite a bit more generous than other magazines, and for the present he put up with the humiliating conditions and made *The People* his favored client. So while he was writing "To the Point of Murder," whether he wrote five or ten pages, he'd hand them over and get paid for just that much.—"'Well, give me this much or that much, and I'll take off my petticoat. And, um, for the next one, give me this much and I'll take off my stockings . . .' Mizuno's way of getting paid for his manuscripts made him just like a Western prostitute. The owner of *The People* has really worked it out." That's how the gossip of the day cynically had it.

But because he had no other recourse, when he went to the bathroom around 4:00 P.M. he tried making a phone call to Nakazawa.

The man was flustered, but he openly pressed Mizuno: "Oh, hey, I was just thinking I'd stop by to see you one of these days soon. How about it—how's the manuscript coming along? Have you gotten a good bit of it done?"

"Oh, yeah, well, it's coming along bit by bit, but not as fast as I'd hoped . . ."

"About how many pages are done?"

"Well, let's see, there's finally at least—" Hell, he couldn't say only seven pages, and so he went on, "seven—teen, eighteen, maybe around twenty?"

"Is that enough, just that much?"

"It's fine, you know, I've almost gotten up to speed, and I'm planning to really push up my output from here on." He left it at that, and then immediately shifting into a plaintive tone of voice, continued,

"Actually, um, the reason I called you was that this would be the chance to ask something of you. . . . How about, well, I haven't asked for an advance in quite a while, and I just wondered if I couldn't get a loan of, say, three hundred yen or so?" There was no response from the phone; he could almost see Nakazawa's conflicted face shrunk into silence.

"Ah, hello, hello . . . ?"

"Yeah."

"Well, how about it? . . ."

"Um, that's a real problem . . ."

"But anyway, do talk to the owner for me, won't you? If I don't get that money, the fact is, well, I'm . . ." Until then he hadn't thought of an excuse, but he was accustomed to such things, and so instantly the words slipped smoothly from his mouth:

"It's about that high-interest loan I must have told you a bit about at some point. The guy's been making a big stink, threatening to sue. . . . It's not that I'm afraid of being sued, but he comes around threatening just about every day, and as a result I can't get down to work, and I'm just wiped out with the commotion." He emphasized the phrase, "as a result I can't get down to work."

"I don't think it'll work, but . . . ," Nakazawa said, leaving the phone and going off to be Mizuno's intermediary with the company owner. He returned directly within two or three minutes. "Um, this is what the owner says, that just as he'd stated before, he can't very well pay without receiving the manuscript in exchange. But how would it be if I came over to pick up what you've done so far? If you have twenty pages, that would amount to 160 yen we could pay out . . ."

"If that's the best you can do, well, that'll have to be it, I guess."

"But, you know, these cutthroat lenders, even if they talk about suing, they don't do it, you know. If it's three hundred yen, and you offer them half, that'll hold them for a while. As for the rest, you can only pay if you can write, so they really can't complain."

When it was clearly laid out that way, Mizuno had no comeback.

"Ah, hello? Hello? How about it? If that's all right, I'll come right away to pick it up . . ."

"Ah-h-h, so you'd come over?"

"I'm actually busy today, so I'll just ask one of the office boys to do it."

"You'd have him bring the money with him, the 160 yen?"

"Yes, of course. In exchange, there's no mistake, is there? We'll get the twenty manuscript pages from you?"

If it's only a clerk, I've got it made, I'll get the money from him, and I can give him an envelope with just ten pages in it.— He decided this was his last resort.

"Mr. Mizuno, a clerk is here from *The People*." It was past five fifteen when the maid conveyed this information to him.

"What kind of person?"

"An office boy, sir, around sixteen or seventeen. He says he'd like to see you, and you have something to give him."

"Ah, that's right, I'm coming right down, so tell him to wait." He quickly took a piece of manuscript paper and scribbled on it in pencil:

Apologies for my recent phone call. This is inexcusable, but even though I've done twenty pages, when I just re-read it, there were a number of things I didn't like, and I think I'd like to do some more work on them. But anyway, for the time being, here are at least the first ten pages, and after revising the rest post haste I'll deliver them to you. I've truly never put so much effort into a work . . .

Maybe this was too much of a lie, doesn't writing this way seem rather sleazy, he wondered. Well, it is shameless, and if that makes Nakazawa too angry, he may come right away to negotiate with me. . . . He ripped it up and tried re-writing the main paragraph:

Nakazawa, I am truly, truly sorry, I've deceived you, I didn't mean to, but the result is that I have come to deceive you . . .

But this too was unseemly: this made it seem that he was groveling. Maybe it was after all better to simply, frankly apologize, as if it were no big deal . . .

The clerk had come an hour ago, and it would have been better if Mizuno had used the time to think and write. But he was the type to want to put off something unpleasant even a bit longer, so he would have had trouble writing such a letter if he had not been pressed by this very present crisis. If he could, he would have, like with those automatic writing game boards, let his hand move by itself and write out random phrases while he kept his eyes closed. He always felt that way, and he wanted to write so quickly that he wouldn't even remember what he had written. But the faster he wrote, the more he got caught up with trivialities of phrasing, and only after writing and ripping up two or three pages would he get to the point of being able to write something smoothly in one move. In the end, that day, too, he wasted five or six pages and finally returned to the first opening line, "Apologies for my recent phone call," and from there went on like this:

> . . . I've truly never put so much effort into a work, and I have not in any way been slacking off [the "in any way" sounded to him a bit brazen, so he immediately crossed it out heavily and made it "intended to be"]. The fact is, these ten pages are not as fully realized as I had hoped, but it would be unforgivable for me to take the money without giving you a single page, and so I entrust this to you on the assumption that whenever it comes time to print, I will be allowed to go over them again. I should properly take payment for just the ten pages, but as I have told you, because that bloodsucker would not let me off without getting at least half the amount, I have had to take advantage of the exigent circumstances. Under these serious conditions, I beg your understanding.

Even as he imagined how furious it would make them, he folded the letter in fourths and slipped it into the envelope; and then he opened it again two or three times and rewrote the address. But having now put so much care into the letter, he pulled the pages in question out from the drawer where he'd stuffed them and, as if handling some cursed object, put them in the envelope without re-reading them, and sealed it.

Manuscript Fee: One Hundred Sixty Yen

After removing the bills and putting them away at the bottom of the drawer, for a while he sat gazing at the square Western-style envelope on which this was written. So I did a good job of squeezing this out of them; this is the money I got by cheating— even as he thought this, the thick black well-formed letters came to look blurry.

"So—what'll I do now? Maybe I should go out somewhere."

As he continued staring fixedly at that "One Hundred Sixty Yen," after a while it seemed to him that the letters began taking various foul shapes. The inside of his head became a kaleidoscope, and various faint white curved lines, like the branches of a tree, waved back and forth here and there. Were these women he knew, or movie stars he'd seen on film? Whichever, these objects, which had at various in the past stimulated his senses, became resurrected as fantasies, all of them vivid and even more beautiful. At the same time, angel-like wings sprouted from his body, and he began to float from branch to branch between the lewd trees. . . .

It was only 160 yen, but as he looked down at the money, he realized that it meant that anytime he wanted he could go right out and have a good time, restless as he was. And his first objective completely flew out the window. Strangely enough, from the instant that square Western envelope came fluttering into his heart, what he had been fearing until now, what he was worried about, what on earth his motive had been for contriving to get this money—all of it completely evaporated, and all that remained behind was the single passionate desire: "Woman." . . . No matter how bad a person was or what kind of bad things he did, surely he must feel some kind of remorse. But Mizuno, even after taking money under false pretenses, still didn't feel as dirty as he had from similar experiences up to now. Instead, rather to the contrary, he thought, "I did well; cheating or not, I did right to take it." Not only that: did this money just buy him pleasure? No, it swept away the shadow of the fear that had been menacing him like a bad dream these past several months. In that sense, it was a double god of salvation.

"Hmm . . . well, what do you know, it was worth resorting to these extreme measures like that." As usual, he couldn't help but rationalize his actions.

Oh, yeah, this is so right I don't know why I didn't get the money earlier. Just 160 yen—and when I see how effective it is, the menacing worries I've had all this time seem pretty trivial. If I just had money, my nervous attacks would stop. Not having been with a woman for so long is what messed up my head . . .

"Oh—are you going out, Mr. Mizuno?"

Ignoring the smirking maid, sometime after sunset he walked out onto the slope that cut through the hills in the direction of the Boulevard, cheerfully twirling his walking stick.

"Ah-ha—the means has become the end!" He spoke out loudly to himself, and there was excited happiness in his voice. In this state, the threads of his associations were being paid out even more violently, and like the motion of microbes under a microscope, they variously bonded and separated. So for some reason at that point he found himself thinking of that Kabuki hero Oishi Kuranosuke. Yes, that's right, even while he was plotting, Oishi Kuranosuke went out to enjoy himself . . . just as I'm doing now, he must have been restless and sallied forth from Yamashina. "Oishi, Oishi," he blurted out as he walked on.

It was strange that even though he was near forty, his heart still leapt like this when it came to going out to play. Now that he thought about it, he felt the same as he had when he first got a taste of dissipation, when he was around twenty. It might seem that it was because he was single now, but even before, when he was married, it was even more pleasurable to sneak out precisely because he had a wife. So it could very well be just the same when I'm fifty or sixty, maybe. Because the anticipation was so intense, whenever at last he arrived at his intended destination and found one of those women right before his eyes, he hardly ever experienced as much pleasure as he had been expecting. Was this really the woman he'd been so much longing for, he asked himself, and mostly he'd be disappointed and leave with a sense of disgust. But still he never seemed to learn from experience and would set right out again, and his heart would be pounding just as much as before. And so times like this, when he had money stuffed in his wallet and walked along with wild imagination for what lay ahead of him in the next hour or two, that's when he was most happy. "Don't rush, you mustn't rush," he firmly admonished his aroused heart. And he felt exhausted trying to figure out what would be the most effective way to use the 160 yen.

He owed every house something in the neighborhood of a hundred yen. So that meant that the hundred he had now would disappear within this night, and for the nine days from tomorrow, he'd have to get by with just sixty yen. Well, there's no helping it. Shall I go to the House of Ivy in Tsukiji? I know I owe them sixty or seventy yen for sure, and I do kind of like that woman Kokin. Her face isn't much, but she's built . . .

"Ah," he sighed and suddenly tossed his head as if clearing it. That's because suddenly everything beyond his feet grew dark, and it seemed to his imagination that, like a swarm of caterpillars, complex, white, undulating, supple figures were spreading before him: roundish or long and slender, big, little, some beautiful, some ugly. In a delirium he stood at the Ueno Hirokoji intersection and hailed a taxi. "To Tsukiji," he ordered, but then as they were approaching Manseibashi suddenly he changed his mind and yelled out to the driver's back, "Hey—no, take me to the Ginza, somewhere in the Kyobashi area." . . . He realized that before he did anything, he should attend to his empty stomach, accompanied with a cheery drink or two.

He could handle saké fairly well, but he was actually not much of a drinker, and at best, two or three carafes were enough for him. But it was his habit at times like this to drink strong Western whiskey to get drunk quickly, and so thirty minutes later he was occupying a chair in a corner of the London Bar on the Ginza. The seating in the place was in booths facing each other as in a third-class train car, with a table in between. The seatbacks were high and the spaces between the partitions were narrow, which was fine with him because he didn't like being seen by other people, and that's why he went there from time to time. However, that night the scene was quite lively, and there wasn't a single booth with both sides unoccupied. Sitting across from him were two men who looked like businessmen and a woman in Western dress who might be a typist. In fact it was because a glimpse of the woman's uncovered arms had caught his attention, that he took advantage the empty seat right across from her and happily wedged himself in. As he sat down, he could hear the woman say in German, "*Nein, nein, ich kann nur Whiskey trinken.*"

Sure enough, in front of the woman was a glass of whiskey. The two businessmen, one in a navy blue suit, the other in brown, had sandwiched the bare-armed woman between them, and the two of them were drinking cocktails. She had just finished speaking in German as Mizuno appeared across from her, and after casting him a glance as if glaring at him with her strong exotic gaze, she then quickly composed herself, stretched out her right hand on the table, and rotated her glass with her thumb, index, and middle finger. The salarymen undoubtedly had been chatting cheerfully, but now that an intruder had appeared they seemed to lose steam and just sipped their cocktails listlessly, as if not knowing what else to do. Mizuno tried to make himself as small as possible, uncertain whether he was doing something right or wrong. It was as if those three fingers surrounding the rim of the whiskey glass could see and couldn't very well ignore what was right in front of them, say, he'd done something utterly strange like ordering asparagus. Somehow I'm being bad, undressing these fingers and the palm of her hand as I gaze at them; in other words, it's as if the woman's whole body is completely nude; she is quite naked, lying here on the table right in front of my eyes . . . That's what Mizuno was feeling. They weren't particularly beautiful fingers, but that aside, the way they played with the glass bespoke a clever, experienced woman, and the way she crooked her little finger was amazingly attractive. This finger was—well, it would be strange to say "pert," but it was just like a leg, long and pliant. Beyond that, her palm, too, was long, and even though she didn't move it very much, from just the little way she gripped or released things, you could tell it, too, was amazingly supple.

The three of them were still silent, so it was hard to tell what her relation to the two men was, but on the face of it she didn't seem to be a "working girl." She wore no makeup at all, and she was pale, although her skin was dark. But its darkness had a smooth sheen, and the flesh of her arms was so nicely plump that it begged to be bitten into. Her clothing showed a quiet, purely German taste, and the subdued quality of the cloth harmonized perfectly with the color of her skin. The German she had been speaking before and her taste in clothes indicated that she must once have lived in Germany. She appeared to be in her late twenties. She was wearing a hat, so he couldn't see her hair well, but it seemed to be short and shingled.

"Hey, another whiskey." The woman finally spoke, and stirring the splendid flesh of her arm, she raised her empty glass.

"You're really quite something," Blue Suit said with a kind of vulgar, sycophantic laugh, seeming directed to his boss, and he looked up at the woman out of the corner of his eye.

"Really? I'm not, really."

"How much can you drink?" now Brown said.

"Oh, depending on how I feel, quite a bit."

"Well, I'd like to see you feel like 'wanting to,'" said Blue Suit, his nasty voice matching the vulgar laugh present in the look he gave her.

"I don't really get very drunk, you know. But when I *do* get drunk, I'm likely to end up passing out anywhere, even on the street."

"Wow, you're tough."

"But that kind of thing hardly ever happens. Only once, on Unter den Linden."

"In Berlin?"

"Yeah, and I got yelled at by a German cop."

At this point, the waitress brought the whiskey and the woman drank down three-quarters of it in one gulp. It could be that she was starting to get in the mood.

"What about you guys? Haven't you been nursing the same cocktails all this time?"

"Hey, aren't you drinking?" Brown said to Blue, nodding and urging him on.

"I am drinking. Doing it this way, I could drink a lot."

"What do you mean, 'doing it this way?'"

"Ha, it's coming out, that German training."

"Hindenburg, Hindenburg!"

"Why 'Hindenburg'? *Warum* Hindenburg?"

"Well, do you always take the offensive? Is it okay if we call you 'Miss Hindenburg?'"

"Make it 'Fraülein,' please."

"So—Fraülein Hindenburg, is it? But whiskey is strange considering your German training, you know. Shouldn't you be drinking beer?"

"I do, if it's German, but I hate Japanese beer."

"Oh, yeah? But they say that Japanese beer is at least as good as German."

"They may say so, but it's still no good. If you go to Shanghai, you'll find Löwenbrau, you know." She pronounced the umlaut very vividly.

This was strange. The two men and the woman didn't appear to have known each other before now. Had they just happened to meet up on the street? Or maybe they first began their conversation just now at this table? When Mizuno sat down at their booth, clearly they were only starting to feel each other out. And then Mizuno's curiosity was increasingly engaged as he realized that the woman was ignoring the two men and looking straight at him. It was just for a moment that she looked directly at him with dark intensity, but in that moment her black eyes opened wide and challenged him as if posing a riddle. When he looked straight back at her, she didn't flinch, but instead again opened her eyes wide and looked hard at him. A Japanese woman would have never stared like that. This was in fact the look of a Western streetwalker. So then what kind of training had this Fraülein gotten in Germany? "Hey, maybe there's some chance this girl is available."—At first it seemed an unachievable dream to Mizuno, but gradually he began to realize that it was not a dream. And this time he returned her look, his eyes filled with that intention, and the eyes that answered his gaze gave the same message. At first it was so unexpected that Mizuno was startled, and he blushed. But their staring match became increasingly insistent, and the two salary workers were left behind as the woman made Mizuno her companion in the conversation she conducted with her eyes.

"How about it, we haven't had dinner yet, but if you have no other plans, won't you come along with us?"

"Your treat?"

"Yes, of course. It would be the greatest honor for us to empty our wallets for you."

"*Danke schön!* I'll go anywhere with you." As she said this, she looked again at Mizuno. "Why don't you say something? I'm getting out of here with these guys, you know."—That's what her eyes said.

"Well, if it's settled, let's go, the sooner the better."

"Hey—the check!" Brown shouted enthusiastically.

"Now, there's no need to be in such a rush, I want another whiskey."

"But let's get out of here . . . right, Fraülein Hindenburg?"

"Why don't we make it 'Hinber'? 'Hindenburg' is too long."

"Never mind that—what are your names? Give me your business cards."

"Oh, how impolite of us. Here's mine—"

"I work in the same company, and we hope that from here on, our acquaintance will—" Brown and Blue both took cards out of their wallets and placed them before the woman.

"Ah, yes, so you work for an insurance company."

"And we'd like one of your cards, too."

"I didn't bring mine with me, but I was a typist at the German embassy. I'm on my own now."

"How about if you come to work at our company?"

"Anywhere would be fine, so I might just do that, you know. If you don't mind someone who drinks, do arrange it for me."

What fools they are. They seem not to have noticed yet what kind of a woman this "Fraülein" is. The woman is sending them all kinds of signals, and they're not getting them at all. A typist who drinks! They're probably thinking, what an interesting gal we've found, let's invite her to dinner, and have a good time! The woman knows this, and her secret contempt for them shows in her eyes: "What jerks!" Furthermore, the two of them look like they've graduated school not long ago, and so they probably don't have far to go to empty their wallets. The woman undoubtedly is thinking of them as rookies, and that's why she's been throwing all those sexy glances at me. So I should work my hardest to get her to switch from these novice businessmen to me.—Mizuno was sure that's how the wind was blowing, but if so, how should he proceed? He'd never before come up against a "modern girl" like this one. But, of course, he was drunk, too, so it would be terrible if his supposition were mistaken. "Modern girls" might exchange intense glances with men for no reason at all, and it might be premature to decide that the woman was wicked, just from her glances. If he were to insert himself into the situation carelessly, he might just get his ears boxed by that strong arm of hers . . .

Even though he was so shameless, Mizuno knew that he didn't cut much of a figure with women, so he didn't have much male pride. The two insurance company employees might not have had much on the ball, but all the same, they were quite a bit younger than he, and they were brimming with health and vigor like fresh, lively fish. Was the woman going to switch from them to him? . . . Huh, don't be stupid, no matter how much you think of yourself, take it easy, the geisha Kokin is the right level for me, why would this fancy "modern girl" have anything to do with me?

This is what he was thinking to himself when he felt something touch the tip of his foot. What the—he thought, and then it touched again . . . once, twice, three times . . .

"Well, then, come on with us—"

"Yes, it's probably a bother for you, but we would certainly like to have you keep us company."

"Well, all right—but I'd rather go to a good drinking place than to eat."

"Leave it to us, we'll show you a good time."

The two men had stood up and were urging the woman on, but Mizuno felt this thing on the front of his foot several times. Even without looking under the table, he could tell what it was because it was written on the woman's face. Her sharp shoes were pressing down on the big toe of his blue *tabi*-clad foot on its fine wooden geta. Was there some established Western way by which he could signal "Yes" or "No"? For example, he had heard that if a woman winked at him, and he winked back, she would immediately come over to him. But this was under the table: would it be all right if he pressed his foot back on hers? If he didn't do something, the woman might be angry or have contempt for him: "This guy seems to be interested in me, but even though I signaled him directly, he's not answering."—He hastily but timidly scraped along the floor with his geta, searching for the toe end of her shoe, but he couldn't find it. He was caught: he might run into one of the men's shoes, and if he stretched his foot out farther, he'd have to change his position. The woman drank down the last drops of whiskey and put the glass down on the table. Then she took up the squirrel-fur-trimmed coat that had been hanging across the back of the seat and stood up.

"Here—won't you help me on with my coat?"

"Wha-a-t?"

"Don't be such a lump—if you're going to be like that, then you're not qualified to be a 'modern boy.'"

The woman's beautifully taut shoulders, lustrous in the reflected light of the lamps, were turned toward Blue Suit, who stood and took the coat from her. Brown had gotten out of the booth a step ahead and was warming himself at the Junker heater placed in the middle of the bar.

"You sure have a great body; that's really rare for a Japanese woman."

"Really? Thanks." Her splendid arms slid smoothly into the sleeves and were hidden by them. The woman opened her makeup case, put on her gloves, and adjusted her hat in the mirror attached to the case.—That was the moment: Mizuno felt something pressing down on his big toe, long and hard. The woman was on the other side of the table from him and standing above him, so when he looked up at her, her face was hidden in the shadow of the lid of the case, but he suddenly realized that the lid was at something of an angle, and he could see her left eye alone, fully visible, looking down at him. He felt a jolt through his entire body. This was not the time to hesitate. I have to do something or other, quick, quick . . .

As if to say, "Don't be a worm!" she stepped on his toe again, hard enough to hurt. And then, moving her eye away and snapping the lid shut, the woman turned her back on him, while his foot remained paralyzed from the pain of his crushed toe. . . .

Until the woman had gone through the door with the two men on either side of her, he had hoped against hope that there might possibly still be some kind of chance, that maybe the god of good fortune would bestow on him some unexpected miracle, and he did not abandon all hope, but the three figures finally disappeared out into the street. . . . One minute, two, three . . . still Mizuno persevered, and sat watching so as not to miss a single customer coming in. Maybe she'd ditch the two men and come right back. He continued to sit there like that for the next thirty minutes, but the woman did not come back. There's nothing I can do, I let something terrific get away. What a dope I am! I thought I didn't have to do any work myself. I couldn't have been more of a dolt. Didn't I know full well from the beginning that it would come to this? And it's not that I didn't have the chance. The woman made the moves for me—how about this? This?—And yet I didn't do anything. I dropped the ball. Even after they went outside, if I'd run after her, I still would have had a chance. The woman seemed to be a professional with all the arts of understanding, as if I could leave it all up to her and everything would work out just fine. No matter how devilish she was, her sense of vanity would carry the day, and even if I did not attempt much myself, something more could have been possible. All the more because there wasn't anything cheap about her. Well, just think about it—where could you find anyone else like her? Her liveliness, her smart short hair, her face without heavy powder, her experience abroad. It's not that such a woman is not to my taste. Rather, I didn't approach her because I thought she'd probably not want to keep company with me, whether for money or whatever. And now I'm drowning in regret that I'll never get an opportunity like this again. Damn it—what a jerk I am!

Ordinarily he would get intoxicated from just slowly sipping a single gin-and-bitters, but this night he gulped down three glasses almost in desperation. And from time to time he would glance below the table and look reproachfully at the faint muddy signs of the shoes on the toe ends of his navy *tabi*.

"What's up? You're drinking quite a bit tonight."

Availing himself of the opportunity when one of the waitresses came to light his cigarette, he asked, "You remember the woman who was here earlier, don't you?"

"Yes."

"Where's she from?"

"Let's see—she's a typist somewhere, isn't she?"

"She come here often?"

"Not much here, but I hear that she often goes to the Monaco . . ."

"Where's that—Monaco?"

"Straight ahead in the Shimbashi direction, half a mile or so."

Hey—so I don't have to lose hope yet! I'll figure out the timing and go and wait at this Monaco. Depending on how things go, I might yet get together with her tonight.

The vision of Kokin was no longer in his head. All he wanted to do now was call back that lost opportunity, somehow or other.

I can meet her, I can meet her, before this night is out, I can meet her. From the moment I left my boardinghouse this evening, I've had a premonition that something good was going to happen. Maybe it wasn't an accident; maybe it was the god of good fortune who showed the woman to me. Some karmic connection made me stop at this bar, when my usual practice would have had me go straight to Tsukiji. And it was the same kind of karmic connection that had the woman come to this bar and seated her right across from me, when she always went to the Monaco. And then when we were put face to face, she immediately started coming on to me. That such a classy woman would indicate an interest in a man like me, who would otherwise never get a second glance from her—this just has to be fate. Probably the god of good fortune placed me in her eyes. And it just so happens that at this very moment I have 160 yen in my wallet. Everything's working out this way, just as I would want it to, and that means that Heaven has given her to me. Right—I must manage to seize this chance. If I can't meet her tonight, I will go to the Monaco every night. And if, despite that, I don't meet her, probably they know her at the Monaco, so if I ask, I could visit her house or write her a letter; there'd be some way to get in touch. It's bound to happen, if I screw up my courage. Somehow or other, within the next four or five days, I will see her again . . .

The woman left here a little past seven. If they were going to have dinner, that would probably take about two hours. So if at that point they go on to the Monaco, that would be around nine. Or maybe one of the guys would come up with some story, and they'd go stay at some geisha house or whatever. No, a woman like that probably wouldn't do a house. It would be a hotel room, or maybe she has a nest of her own. Somewhere in Kojimachi, or Azabu, or Akasaka, one of those quiet areas in the heights, a neat, cozy, little Western-style house . . . It would be good quality, tight shuttered, set up as if someone from an embassy or the Foreign Ministry lived there, and the light outside the entrance would be so dim that you couldn't even read the nameplate, and with the door firmly shut it would be as quiet as if the house were unoccupied. When you pushed the bell, a person like a Chinese amah would come and silently open the door. And then she'd say quietly *"Herein!"* in German. You'd follow the woman to the second floor, and there would be the secret bedroom. Your body would sink into the overstuffed easy chair; there would be the chaise longue, the double bed, the lace curtains, the mantel over the fireplace. . . . Gradually as drunkenness whirled around him, Mizuno wildly imagined this dreamlike scene, and it was as if he had become the hero of a dirty French novel. It was a dream that such a woman should make the rounds right in the middle of Tokyo, and that she would come trolling for men in the Ginza cafés and bars. Come to think of it, that meant Tokyo was quite a civilized place. He had never heard of such a thing, either in gossip or in the newspapers. At any rate, if word of it reached police ears, it probably wouldn't last long, so truly it was now or never. He'd have to move quickly.

At quarter of nine he left the London Bar and hurried down Ginza Avenue. Five minutes later he stood in front of Café Monaco. But before he could go in, there were the three of them just coming out, joking and chatting animatedly.

"Look at them—I knew it!"

Mizuno felt as if he would jump up, his body wound tight as a spring. Damn! This is really too close! I'd have missed them if I'd come just a little later, but to bump into them face to face like this means more and more that tonight is clearly quite out of the ordinary. Well then, I'm not going to run away anymore. I'm sticking with them no matter where they go. This kind of woman obviously will state her conditions openly in businesslike terms: "Well then, how much will you pay me?" Okay, let's finish our negotiations quickly. Come on, let me know what the deal is. I'll do whatever I can. For you, I'll sacrifice any amount, because there's no way I'm letting you go. . . . He didn't know where he was going, but just kept following them, as he continued to talk to her back. . . . Hello, hello, here, right behind you, here's a good sucker with quite a bit of money in his wallet, hey. . . . Isn't there some way to say something to let her know this? If I did, surely she'd come to me right away, now . . .

"Where are we? Tokyo? Yokohama?"

"We're at Unter den Linden."

"Hey, you can't fall asleep just because you're drunk."

"No, I'm going to lie down, really."

Brown and Blue both shouted "Hey!" at the same time. She had been walking arm in arm with the two of them on either side of her, but now all of a sudden she let her legs go limp and hung from the two of them.

"Hey, come on, no joking, in a place like this!"

"She's heavy, this woman!"

"*Natürlich! Ich habe* . . ."

"We know, we know, enough of the German. *Bitte. Auf japanisch!*"

"Hey, I'm impressed, that you can say that much . . ."

"Well, never mind, we'd like you to get up."

"Where is this, here? Isn't it too dark to be Ginza?"

"We're walking on one of the side streets. We're almost up to Yurakucho, over there."

"Well then, come on, drag me along just like this."

"This is hopeless, I've never seen a woman as much of a mess as this one."

"Hey, she's not really that drunk. She hasn't had that much to drink, you know."

"Doesn't matter—let's get her into a taxi."

The two men seemed to be quite overwhelmed. The three of them staggered along in a tangle for thirty feet or so through the dark side streets, and then Brown ran off to the main street to find a taxi, saying "Wait, wait here."

Oops, now I'm in trouble if I don't get myself a cab, too, Mizuno thought; and while he was thinking, a taxi stopped in front of the woman and Brown jumped out of it.

Blue called out to the driver, "Hey, take this baggage to Yurakucho Station for us."

"Oh, her alone?"

"Yeah, we're not going."

"Well then, am I going to get paid?"

"What'll we do, shall we pay ahead for her?"

"Do you suppose she has that much with her?"

The two men, working together, folded the legs of the woman, who seemed to have become dead drunk, and shoved her into the cab. Behind it as it dashed off, Mizuno ran at full speed to Yurakucho.

This day of greatly changing fortunes had been filled with worry and nervousness, as if he had picked up a jewel in his hand but then dropped it, but this was his last great effort. All would be decided by whether or not he could successfully get to the station by the time the taxi got there and the woman changed to the electric train line. This would be the final accounting of the day. . . . As he thought this, Mizuno ran for all he was worth. He was thin and rangy, useful for running, but he was wearing a kimono and cape, and besides, he spent all his time locked up in his room and got no exercise, so that when on occasion he did run, he immediately found himself panting. But when he had run two or three hundred feet and still hadn't seen the woman's car, it was his legs that began to give out. He'd stop from time to time, gasping and pressing down on his pounding heart, which seemed ready to burst at any moment. There was another problem: whether or not it was his particular constitution, when he ran hard enough to become short of breath, he would always get the urge to throw up. Although it happened even when he had an empty stomach, this night he had crammed so much into his stomach that it was even more urgent. As he ran, he gulped down the heaves that were becoming painful belches and threatening to erupt, but his breath became more and more constricted, and in the end his throat convulsed and he retched, vomiting the liquor and Western food he had just eaten onto the street. It was even comical: as he threw up, he could recognize each bit clearly—here are odds and ends of the beefsteak, there's the gin, that's the salad. He could imagine how it looked, his passage from Ginza to Yurakucho marked every several hundred feet by the remains on the pavement. He had a new worry: he'd eaten particularly fatty food to store up energy for the night's campaign, and he realized that he might be losing it all. . . . Probably the woman was from Yokohama, but how often did the trains run to Sakuragicho? Every five minutes? Every ten? . . . Supposing they weren't as frequent at night as during the day; could it be every ten minutes? If that was so, at best I mustn't be more than ten minutes late! . . . He should have been able to grab a taxi along the way, but the only one that passed just continued on even though he raised his hand. Maybe not another one went by, or maybe he was just in so much of a rush that he didn't notice any.

"One second-class ticket to Sakuragicho!" Just guessing, he bought the ticket and raced up the stairs to the platform at Yurakucho Station. For sure he was more than fifteen minutes behind the woman, but for no reason at all, as he climbed he had a feeling that she would be on the platform.

Sure enough, the woman was leaning at an angle on a bench as if she'd been thrown there, sleeping with her hands holding her coat together around her shoulders as if she were cold. Below the hem of her skirt there was nothing but the flesh-colored stockings, so that from a distance it could have been a man lying with his kimono tucked up behind him and a workman's jacket thrown over himself. From this angle, she was all legs. Five or six passengers passed back and forth in front of her in surprise, but Mizuno took no notice of them. Silently, without hesitation, he sat down beside the woman and slowly took out a cigarette from his kimono sleeve. Right before him were the woman's shoes on her feet. With her knees tucked together, they looked as if they would flip into the air.

"Huh, so these are were what were stepping on my blue *tabi* a while ago," Mizuno thought, and he gazed vaguely for some time at the shoe tips. Certainly, I've caught her but . . . And without a doubt I am now sitting side-by-side with her on this bench, but . . . now what do I do? Whatever I do, anyway, the woman *is* here. Whatever, I just wait until she wakes up. He forced down the grin that was bubbling up inside him. He, too, was drunk, but all the same, it was strange that he could behave as shamelessly as this. And then, when the woman wakes up, would she remember him right away? "Oh, you're here, sorry I was so impolite back there."—It would be great if she said something appropriate like that, but what if that earlier stuff was just a whim that she'd have forgotten in her drunkenness? He found himself hoping that he'd have a good long time to sneak the pleasure of having her collapsed dead drunk here at his side as he gazed at the blood vessels showing translucent in the arch of her foot through the stockings.

"Hello . . . hello, hello . . ." As the station employee came and tried to get the woman up, he looked suspiciously at Mizuno.

"No, it would probably be better to leave her as she is for a bit more. She's drunk quite a lot of whiskey."

"This lady—is she with you?"

"Yes," he said in a low voice, hoping against hope that she would hear him . . .

The train stopped hard at the platform. Great numbers of passengers were spat out, and as many were sucked back in. The sky after it roared away glittered with the illumination from the motion picture advertising billboards for the Hogakuza Motion Picture Theater. Above his head the lights signaling arrivals and departures blinked and changed color. These things all reflected meaninglessly in Mizuno's eyes. The cool night breeze that came from across Marunouchi touched the concrete floor and blew upward as if to scoop him up, and it felt good against his burning cheeks. Then, after an hour or so, around eleven o'clock, he began to readjust the woman's position, as her hips seemed from time to time to be about to slide down. Just as he was thinking it might be getting to be time for her to awaken, sure enough, leaning untidily just as she was, she touched her hat lightly with her hand and seemingly half asleep stood up unsteadily. A train for Sakuragicho just happened to come at that point and she staggered onto the second-class car. Mizuno followed her closely, with literally no space between them, and he took a seat just to the left of where she had plopped down, drawing so close that for all the world he looked as if maybe he was her husband. By good chance, the train car was nicely crowded. In other words, the seats were now full where the two had just sat down, and then another three or four people piled on and stood in a clump in front of them, shielding them from view from the other side. The woman was in a corner seat near the conductor's post, and she was leaning on one elbow, holding her chin against her hand, sound asleep again.

But how conscious was the woman anyway, to have stood up all alone even though she was supposedly drunk, to get on the train she was supposed to take and promptly find an empty seat? Was she completely unconscious, or did she vaguely know? With whiskey, unlike with Japanese saké, the body can stop working while the mind is still clear, so she might to some degree know what she was doing. If so, mightn't she be deliberately not showing that she was actually aware of Mizuno? She had sat for so long beside him back there but never once turned her face to Mizuno—wasn't there something suspicious in that? Mizuno remembered that when they crowded onto the train, he had pushed her shoulder a bit roughly from behind. Even assuming there had been no chance for her to turn around then, now the two of them were flesh partners, jostling against each other and feeling the hardness, arm to arm, hip to hip, separated only by their coats. Further, even though Mizuno was to some extent doing it on purpose, she could be pretending that she didn't realize he was forcing himself on her. Or maybe he should only think that she was used to a man's touch, that she slept every night feeling it, so Mizuno's arm was no more than the back or cushion of a chair. All the same, the amount of bumping was extreme. The woman's body became separated into three parts, her head, her trunk, her hips, and each swayed separately every time the train shook. When the train stopped with a jerk, her body would bend once to the right, and then snap back toward Mizuno with a bump. Sometimes she seemed about to bump into him, but then she did not seem startled and open her eyes but rather quietly sat there bobbing her head like a bobble-head tiger doll. Again and again, Mizuno felt the brim of her hat and the fur on her collar gently stroking his cheek. Gradually he became bolder, and when she bumped into him, he pushed back. As he did so, little by little he moved his arm around behind her. He imagined that she could perceive it like a bug crawling down her spine. The bug went around from her back to her hips, began to fumble around below her armpit, wound itself around the fingers of her left gloved hand. By the time they passed Kamata, most passengers had cleared out, and so he was quite exposed to the conductor, but by now he had forgotten all shame and decency, and the conductor, who could not have missed what he was doing, averted his gaze. In the end, under cover of the sleeves of his cape, he linked arms with the woman.

When they reached Sakuragicho, the end of the line, two things happened simultaneously: the woman disentangled her arm from his, and Mizuno pulled his hand back. The woman stood up and still without looking back at Mizuno headed down the platform ahead of him without hesitation, her pace much firmer than before.

"Hello, hello," Mizuno said as soon as they left the station grounds, running up behind the woman as she approached the stop for the city tram. As he matched his pace to her, he doffed his hat and bobbed in two or three obsequious bows.

"Um, I'm the man who met you at the London Bar."

"Oh, yes?"

"I mean, remember, I was on the other side of the table?"

"Ah, so-o" she said. Her "so-o" had a Western inflection. "Yes, yes, it was you, wasn't it? You're good, to recognize me."

"We've been together since the train. I was sitting next to you."

"Oh, my, I've had quite a bit to drink, and so—I've been most impolite, haven't I?" She had passed beyond the tram stop, so he had to run after her as he stuck close to her.

"Um, which way to where you live?"

"Where do you?"

"I—if it weren't a bother to you, I could see you home in a car."

"Ah, so-o—hmm, I wonder what I should do? I do, in fact, live in this neighborhood, but I also have a house over in Honmoku."

Mizuno had not come to Yokohama much, but it's not that he hadn't heard rumors of Honmoku, how far it was from the station, or what kind of area it was. And so he thought to himself, I certainly would like to have us go toward Honmoku.

"Well then, where are you going to stay tonight?"

"Let's see, which shall I do?—" She finally stopped, and as she stood she continued, "—I don't care which, you know, but I have two younger sisters at the house that's near here, so it's small and in kind of a mess."

"Oh, really? You have younger sisters?" Mizuno's attention was now drawn to these so-called younger sisters, too, and he began to think it wouldn't be bad to go there either.

"Yes, the three of us sleep in one room, and it's pretty tight. So I think it'd be better to go back to Honmoku, after all . . ."

"This residence in Honmoku, you're there all alone?"

"Yes, I've got the second floor all to myself, and I don't really have anything to do with the people below. It's quiet, the sea is right nearby, and it's a great place."

"Well then, let's see you to Honmoku. It sounds like that's the better choice."

"Hey, wait, wait a minute," the woman called to Mizuno as he was about to run to the taxi garage. "I hate taxis. You said a good car, so why don't you wait here for me while I make a phone call?" She quickly went into a telephone booth by herself.

Whether she was just ordering a car or perhaps had some other business to arrange, her call took quite some time. Mizuno was standing some thirty-five feet away, so he couldn't hear what she was saying, but when she finished, she again took her coin purse out of the vanity case and put some coins into the phone. He watched the movements of her gloved hands on the other side of the glass door, pressing the button of the case lid, working the metal fittings of the purse, so skillful and bewitching, and the memory of her palm and fingers lying on the table earlier came floating again into his mind. Yes, that's for sure, the woman is not bad, even as I watch her like this some distance away. There is none of the vulgarity about her that you'd expect of her profession, and she appears as honest as if she'd just come from some company office. I never keep relationships for long, but this time maybe I could enjoy her for quite a while. I could truly have made a good friend, and depending on how things go, maybe I could even make her my wife? . . .

"Sorry I've kept you waiting. They said it'll be coming right away," the woman said as she came out. "It'll be about five minutes," she added, pulling back the edge of her glove and revealing a sturdy men's-style watch.

5

It was already past midnight. The whole town seemed to have subsided into slumber, and the plaza in front of the station was empty. There were two bridges on the other side of the plaza, and on the far side of the river every house was shut tight. The woman watched intently in the direction of the bridge to the left. Five minutes had barely passed when a light appeared from that direction, approached the plaza, and without the woman's saying anything, a car stopped in front of the two of them. Silently picking them up, again it returned in the same direction and ran quietly along the dark streets.

Mizuno knew nothing at all about automobiles, so he didn't know what kind of car it was, but he could tell from how smoothly it was rocking that it seemed to be a very good one.

"Say, have you got a match?" the woman said, pulling out a German cigarette and tapping the end of it on the palm of her hand.

"There's one here—"

"That's pathetic—'there's one here.' When a woman presents a cigarette, a man's supposed to offer a light, you know."

"Oh, really? I see—I've never been with a 'modern girl' like you before. On that point, I'm even worse than those insurance company guys earlier."

"You saw that?"

"Of course I saw it. One of them wouldn't help you on with your coat, and you were sarcastic, right? After that, where did you go?"

"They invited me to go with them to A-One, but I like drinking better, so we went to a café."

"Café Monaco?"

"Yes, right—and when we left, we met you, didn't we?"

A snicker arose from the woman's nose, buried in her fur collar.

"Oh, so you realized it?"

"Did you think I didn't?"

"Well that's a surprise—so you were faking being drunk?"

"It wasn't a lie, but I wanted to get rid of those guys, and so I exaggerated quite a bit. But at Yurakucho Station I did doze off completely."

"And you were sleeping on the train, all the way to Sakuragicho."

"Don't be silly. How could anyone sleep when someone is tickling her?"

"Oh, I *am* sorry, that was rude of me. The fact is, I was the one that was drunk."

In embarrassment, Mizuno puffed at his cigarette quickly, but when he heard the woman snicker again, his cheeks colored.

"You don't have to apologize so much. Instead, tell me this: why didn't you respond to me?"

"Uh, then?"

"Right—didn't you understand what I meant?"

"It's not that I didn't understand, but I was trying to figure out what kind of signal it was. And then, I was a little hesitant—"

"Why?"

"Because I thought that if I were mistaken, I'd be in big trouble."

"You're a real goody-goody, aren't you?"

"Well, maybe I look that way . . . But at least I'm smarter than those two guys, because they didn't notice that you were signaling."

"When did you notice?"

"As soon as I sat down across the table from you." At this point, Mizuno began to take an intimate tone with her. "You were looking straight into my eyes, right? That's not the way an ordinary woman looks at you, I thought."

"Have you traveled in the West?"

"Nope, but I've heard that that's how they look at you in the West."

The woman chuckled and seemed to take it with good grace, but in her faint snort there was a slight echo of self-contempt.

He had absolutely no idea what direction Honmoku lay in, but as the car ran along, the sea was on his left and to the right he could see cheap makeshift shacks standing here and there like gap teeth. And in vacant lots everywhere, lines of destroyed brick pillars and parts of walls stretched like the ruins of an old castle, floating up indistinctly now and again in the darkness, illuminated in the headlights.

"Where are we, here?"

"Yamashita-cho—you can see the New Grand Hotel over there, right?"

"But what happened to this area? It looks like the aftermath of a fire. Was there a big fire recently?"

"This all is still left from the 1923 Great Earthquake—it's still just as it was, five years ago. Is this your first time in Yokohama?"

"Well, to tell the truth, it's, yeah, pretty much the first time . . . But you know, I'd heard stories about it . . . it's really awful, isn't it. If I hadn't met you and come to a place like this, I couldn't have imagined it in my wildest dreams . . ."

What the woman had pointed out as the New Grand must be the tall new construction in the direction their road was heading. Beyond it the road ran up into the hills and there was nothing that looked like a town to be seen.

"Where's Yokohama gone to?"

"This is Yokohama."

"But it's so isolated. Where's Honmoku?"

"On the other side of the hills."

"I can't imagine that there's such a lively spot on the other side."

"Honmoku's not all that lively, you know.—Before the earthquake, this area was the best place. It felt a little like being abroad."

As they passed beside the New Grand, the hills loomed up right before them on the road. There was a river at the base of the hill, and where it ran into the sea, he could see an old-style iron bridge. Just when he thought the car would cross the bridge and climb straight ahead up the sloping road, it turned left in front of the bridge as if to run straight into the sea. In the next moment, another bridge appeared and soon they came out into the middle of a broad plain that continued on the same level as the sea. They then continued in a straight line through an open space like a military parade ground.

"So you were here when the earthquake hit?"

"I didn't know about the earthquake; I wasn't in Japan at the time."

"You were in Berlin?"

"I did go to Berlin, but mostly I was in Hamburg."

"How many years?"

"About two . . ."

"Doing what?"

"I was married to a German man, and it was his decision to be in Hamburg." Her story came out bit by bit in response to his questions: how the German man had died, that her husband had left her quite a bit of property at his death and so for the time being she had lived comfortably at leisure, but now it was mostly used up, and so on. But it was as if she were talking at random, and he couldn't even guess how much to believe.

"Well then, you say you were at the German consulate?"

"Yeah, I was there, but only for a little while."

"How long?"

"Just a weensy bit," she answered noncommittally and continued, "But really—*do* I look like a typist or something?"

"Anyway, I can tell that at least you had a German husband, from your tastes. Anyone can imitate showy, modern ways, but it seems to me that to have your understated, sophisticated style, you had to have been trained by such a person. And it's especially clever of you not to use light-colored powder."

"I am dark, but I don't use light powder on my face or anywhere else, you know. And that's why anyone would mistake me for a secretary."

"That's why I hesitated, earlier. By the way, you—" Mizuno gulped hard and went on, "Since you seem pretty businesslike, how about discussing a business proposition?"

"Um, yeah, go on—"

"Tell me what you expect."

"Before that, there are conditions, you know."

Just at that point, the car stopped. He had been so absorbed in their conversation that he hadn't realized that they had passed through the open land, but he could see that the road narrowed from the point where they'd stopped and was lined on both sides with a cluster of small, squalid houses. He followed her as they went down some dark, dismal alleys and passed through others, making a number of turns one way or another, and finally came around to the back entry of one of the houses. The woman took out a key and opened the rain shutters.

The house was pitch black when they entered, but he began to be able to discern some shapes from the light of the streetlights outside that leaked in through the opened shutters. There seemed to be a kitchen sink and, at the other side of the wooden-floored room, sliding doors. Of course he couldn't tell anything about the room's arrangement, but from what he could see, he imagined that what lay beyond the screens were probably small six-mat and four-and-a-half-mat rooms and a tiny entrance foyer. Whoever was living downstairs, there were no signs of anyone waking up, despite the noise they were making.

"Bring your shoes and come on up—you have a walking stick too, don't you?" The woman closed the door from inside, and taking up her own shoes, she again passed in front of him and opened the sliding doors. "There's the stairway. I'm going ahead to turn on the light, so wait here a moment," she said as she went up the narrow, steep stairs.

The second floor was similarly cramped, but under the lights he found it unexpectedly bright and cheery. In the hallway at the top of the stairs, newspapers had been spread out, and on them were lined up a number of women's shoes of various kinds.

"I occupy the second floor. Want to see the bedroom?" As she spoke, the woman put the shoes she'd been carrying on the newspaper.

The bedroom was a little larger, maybe eight mat. A light with a cream-colored shade hung down from the ceiling, and on the floor was a faded figured green rug. A double bed occupied almost a third of the room; other than that the room was just about filled, with the decorative alcove closed off with a chintz curtain to make a closet, and there was also a small makeup table, an oil stove, an easy chair, and a bentwood chair such as one finds in cheap restaurants. Everywhere on the walls were pinned pictures of movie stars, but they were all German actors like Emil Jannings and Werner Krauss. But the most eye-catching thing in the room was the makeup table with a large mirror, in front of which were lined up perfume bottles, a bud vase, a French doll, and various makeup accoutrements, and standing amid the things scattered all in a jumble, the portrait of a plump German man in his forties, probably her late husband. As Mizuno looked around at all this, the woman took off her coat and put it behind the alcove curtain.

"Give me that match I asked for," she said, and she lit the oil heater. She picked up the kettle sitting on it and went out, saying, "I'll make some tea." From the next room, which backed onto the alcove wall, he heard the sound of running water.

Left alone to wait by himself, Mizuno felt his earlier intoxication completely dissipated. The room was nothing like what he'd been freely imagining as a scene from a French novel. Once when he'd gone to Karuizawa he'd met a certain sophisticated Japanese woman, and she'd invited him to the room in an annex that she was renting from a farmer family. It was just like this one. The woman was fine, but the room was a little depressing. If this is it, mightn't I feel really sad tomorrow morning? . . . He could still hear the sound of running water in the kitchen in the next room, and cups being washed and plates being set out. The woman, with her bobbed hair and stocking-clad feet stuffed into slippers, seemed to be working hard, bustling about diligently. . . . Oh, of course, this must be the way a German housewife would do it. Not what I'd expect: she might actually be a good housekeeper. She cooks, she uses the sewing machine, and that's how she keeps her man happy. . . . I don't know what conditions she'll propose, but from what we've been talking about already, we might even try living together for a trial period of a month or two. This might be the beginning of a new life for me, and at least it would be better than living with that blockhead who was my wife before. At any rate, this house is too depressing, so we could at least get us one of those new-style "culture houses" in the suburbs and hire a pretty little girl as a maid, if not a Chinese amah . . .

The woman came back carrying the kettle and, after putting it on the heater, again returned to the kitchen area and came back with the tea fixings.

"What are you looking at so intently?"

"I've been admiring your apartment."

"Why?"

"It seems to work well for you.—Aren't there any suitable apartments in Yokohama?"

"There are, but this is cheaper, you know. To live this way doesn't take much money."

The woman, too, seemed to have sobered up a bit; she sat in the chair facing him as she spoke. She was amazingly calm and collected, not at all the minx who was giving the insurance company men so much trouble earlier. Now that she'd removed her hat he could see that she had rather high cheekbones, and he was probably right about her age, around twenty-nine. Mizuno now felt no constraint; he grasped her splendid hand and pressed it down on his knee.

". . . I came after you from Tokyo on purpose. At this point even if you tell me to leave, there are no more trains, so there's nothing you can do but let me stay the night. Those conditions you spoke of—I'd like to hear them."

"We can call them conditions, but there's nothing complicated about it. It's just that . . . I'd like us to set up a period, say, a month or two or so."

"I have no objection, but even if you say a month, we can't very well meet every day, and so . . . well, I don't know how this would be, but, for example, if it were twice a week, we could establish which two days, from when to when . . . for the rest of the time, it goes without saying, you're free. What you do in that time, I don't want to know, and I won't even try to find out . . ."

"That's right—the time other than what we've promised is completely mine. And will you keep your relationship with me an absolute secret?"

"And you for me?"

"Yes, of course. Japanese men have a habit of immediately blabbing about things everywhere, but in the West, it's absolutely not done. They don't talk indiscreetly about things like their relationships with women even with their closest friends. And so you can rest assured that it won't get around."

"So in other words, you and I will be lovers just when we meet, and for the rest of the time we are total strangers."

"Yes, that's a good way to put it. If we meet on the street, or on the train, or in some crowded place, or if we're with someone else, we will never acknowledge each other."

"Yes, that's what I'd expect."

"We won't ask about each other's lives or real names. We won't write each other."

"Well, what shall I call you?"

"Isn't 'you' good enough? When we're together, there's no need for names. You are a man named 'you,' I am a woman named 'I.'"

"That's all for your conditions?"

"You'll keep them?"

"Yes, I accept them all."

"Then let's do it this way: we'll start with one month, and I'll have you come twice a week. . . . So let's try it like this, and if you don't like it, we'll end it after the first month. Okay?"

"Well then . . . what shall we do about payment?"

"How about 160 yen a month?"

"And . . . when should I pay?"

"Up front, of course. You'll hand it over when we've settled our contract."

Ah, yes, the bill is 160 yen, to meet eight times a month. Mizuno had started with just that amount, but he'd used bits of it here and there, so although he hadn't checked yet, he was sure he was around ten yen short.

"How would this be with you? I have about 130 or 140 yen with me now. Leaving out enough for the train fare I'll need to get back and some other small things, how about if I hand over to you all that remains, and bring the remaining bit when I come next time?"

"Well, let's see . . ." The woman looked down with a sly look in her eyes and continued, "I don't want to make things difficult, so it's okay if you bring it to me next time. You will be sure to bring it, right? In fact, tonight I don't feel like going on anymore—"

"Why not? That's a problem, you know."

"What's the problem? As long as you feel like coming, we can meet within the next two or three days, can't we?"

"But—that's—I mean, even though I came here specifically chasing after you—you're telling me to leave, at this late hour?"

"What do you mean, 'this late'? Dawn comes late but the trains start running around five, you know."

"Well then, can't we continue talking like this until then?"

"Yes, that would be all right; if you get sleepy, you just go lie down on the bed over there. I'm fine until ten in the morning. At ten, I'll get you up."

"What'll you do?"

"Don't worry about me. I don't mind staying up alone, and I can sleep on the easy chair."

What did she mean by this sudden switch in attitude? To be so finicky and not do business with me just because I'm a few pennies short of the contract amount? But if she got 120 or 130 of the 160 . . . what would she be losing . . . ? Setting aside any mental calculations of profit and loss, was she the kind of person who was uneasy if things were not exact, at least as far as money was concerned? To be such a stickler for the rules—could this be the German way, after all?

Mizuno couldn't imagine that she was toying with him. After all, he had purposely followed her from Tokyo. Now there was no more need to tease him, and given her straightforward attitude, she wasn't likely to take advantage of him in such a sleazy way. And from the woman's perspective: if she got rid of him like this, there was no certainty that he'd ever come back again. In fact, obviously there was a good chance that that's just what would happen. Surely the woman would not turn him away knowing full well that 120 or 130 was right before her eyes. Otherwise, why would she come on to him at the London Bar? Was she just drunk and having fun? The woman said she'd get him up at ten. Was that because she remembered that she had an appointment with someone at that time? Anyway, whatever the woman was really thinking, the result was that she *was* toying with him.

"Hey . . . don't be like that! . . . Come on, you . . ."

"Next time . . . next time you come."

"Why? How come you changed your mind so quickly?"

"I haven't changed my mind, but it's gotten quite late . . . and there's someone coming at ten." The woman smoothly pulled her hand out from between his. "I'm really hungry; how about you?—I'm sure I've got some black bread and sausage," she said as she stood up and went to the next room.

"Aah, I've been working so hard, and this is how it turns out."— Mizuno felt just like a dog that's had a piece of meat dangled right before his nose to make him keep running forever. She tells him, "Come, come!" and he races up panting, at which point she moves another couple hundred feet and says again, "Come, come!" So if he brings the promised amount next time, won't she just snatch it up and laugh at him, "You dope!" Seeing how it was working out, this was certainly not what he'd been hoping for. It looked as if something good would happen, and then nothing happened. The god of fortune had been making fun of him all along. I should have gone directly to Tsukiji yesterday evening; then I wouldn't have gone to all this stupid trouble, and I could have been together with Kokin already. . . . Now that I think of it, that's what I'll do now. If I give this woman the money and then she tells me, "Come the day after tomorrow," all my effort would have turned out to be worth nothing. Rather than going through all that bother, shouldn't I just plain give up and go straight off toward Tsukiji . . .

"Mr. Mizuno, how about reconsidering?" he said to himself sotto voce, imitating Kokin's tone of voice.

No, I'm here specifically for this purpose, so let's have it be the Fraülein. The woman has won, hooking me just when I was bored with outdated stuff like geisha. At any rate, for a writer, experience is everything, isn't it . . . especially experience with women. . . . The fact is, if I think of knowing this woman as a way of understanding this new era, then even if she deceives me and cheats me out of all my money, it wouldn't be a loss for me. After all, it would be a rich experience, and it could become some kind of material for a story. If I had gone to Kokin's, this money would have disappeared during the single evening, probably. And about now the height of my pleasure would have passed, and I'd be starting to feel regret and be thinking, "Hey, is this all?" Here, the fun is yet to come—I'm going to be having fun from now on. And who knows what the height could be? I haven't even gotten to the gate yet. If you arouse a man's curiosity this way, as much as possible, and build his anticipation, and keep postponing getting to the main stage, his excitement just gets deeper. And even as far as the money goes: if I go to Tsukiji it gets used up all at one time, and after that I'll just run up more debt. But here the money will last a month. Looking at it that way, how can I say, "Nothing good happened this night"? Far from it! . . .

But all the same, he'd really had to pee for quite a while. The fact was that the diuretic he'd taken yesterday afternoon had been working all evening and night, and after leaving for the Ginza he'd been to public toilets a number of times but he'd been holding it all this time, ever since coming to her second floor. That is, when he had asked earlier about the facilities, she'd said don't go downstairs because I have this, and she took out a Western-style white chamber pot. But Mizuno was afraid the vivid color of the methylene blue dissolved in the liquid would stain the bowl. A woman like this undoubtedly had a highly developed hygiene consciousness, and he had not wanted to be the object of depressing suspicions. So he had replied, "No, it's okay. I'll just hold it. I'm the nervous type, and so a chamber pot wouldn't work out," and he had endured as best he could. But now it was getting harder and harder to bear. What a stupid thing to do, I didn't have to have taken that medicine—he got all the angrier now; but considering all these awkward circumstances, he realized that the woman was right after all, and he should withdraw today for the time being.

"Well, how about it? Doesn't it look good, this *wurst!*" The woman placed several thin slices of sausage on a piece of black bread, and grasping the corners of the bread with her thumb and index finger and bringing it straight to her face, she inserted it into her mouth like a magician swallowing a sword. "Or if you're sleepy, just go lie down."

"Thanks—but I'd rather get our conversation settled. If today's no good, then what day would be better?"

"Well, let's see, today is Thursday, right?—I'm generally free on Fridays and Tuesdays, but this week is a bit full. How about if we make it starting next Tuesday?"

"Why wait until then? Tomorrow is Friday, so I could come tomorrow, right?"

"That's a bit . . . it would be a bit of a problem." As she said this she cut more sausage, her face infuriatingly calm and composed.

The bitch, she just keeps taking more and more advantage of my helplessness.—Even as he knew this with increasing clarity, Mizuno could feel himself being drawn into the woman's snare. He was always so poor, but he was the type who, on the rare occasion he had money in his wallet, would not be satisfied until he bought something, reasonable or not. And when he decides to buy, he is unable to contain himself until he does it. And so the salesman sees him coming and jacks up the price, and the higher it goes, the more desperately he wants it, and that makes the other party take even more advantage of him, and in the end he is forced to buy it at an exorbitant price. He didn't know if the woman had figured that out about him, but once he got started on this bargaining, he would be pulled on endlessly, without limit. On top of that he was worried that if he were strung along until next week, by then his 120 or 130 yen stash would be likely to have dribbled away. Already it had decreased by some ten yen or so just from yesterday evening. For now, it would work out somehow; but if he came up a hundred yen short, it would not be easy to make it back to 160. If he couldn't get together with the woman just because of that, what would he do? . . .

"So, are you sure it has to be next week?"

"Yeah, it just won't work for this week. I've thought about it but just can't find the time."

As he listened to the woman's words, Mizuno felt just as if he were a student coming to a language teacher for private lessons.

"Did you really like me that much?"

"What do you think?"

"If that's so, then be patient and listen to me. I'll be waiting for you next Tuesday, so come then. Anytime in the afternoon is fine. Pick a time, and I'll be there to get you at Sakuragicho."

"You're awful—"

"When will you be coming?"

"Oh, well, then save one o'clock for me. But if I'm a little late, will you still wait for me?"

"Whenever I meet someone, I always make it a practice to wait up to fifteen minutes. But at fifteen minutes, I take off."

Now that they had made their arrangements, there certainly was no way he could go off to sleep. Even though he felt he was being rushed out of the place, by the time he reluctantly left the house it was already close to five in the morning. The woman saw him off, saying, "I'll take you to the streetcar road." Outside it was still dark as night, and the stars glittered coldly in the sky that was beginning to get faintly light. Because the route was so labyrinthine, he didn't know where they were going. But as he followed her nearly half a mile in a direction that seemed to be different from the one they took when he came, suddenly from a narrow spot between closely packed house eaves, they came out on a road that was like a broad grassy plain.

"Look—that's the tram stop. Got it?—" The woman came to a halt.

There where the woman was pointing, two or three hundred feet ahead on the tram road, a red light glowed.

"—If you wait there, the one for Sakuragicho will come."

". . . Well, so this Tuesday—one o'clock in the afternoon of the twenty-second, right?"

"Yes, I'll be standing at the exit gate, wearing the same clothes as today." In parting, she briefly gave him her hand and turned back again into the close-covered alley.

The effect of the diuretic had been getting more and more urgent, and in the space between there and the tram stop, Mizuno finally relieved himself of his suffering. But when he got on the streetcar, suddenly the exhaustion of the previous evening hit him, and leaning against the window, he didn't even have the strength to think. He, who was so lazy he didn't have the stamina to sit at his desk a whole hour at a time, had probably never once in his life been so intensely active. From the time of his staring match with the almanac the night before, for the next thirty hours he had not had any real sleep. But although sleepiness was advancing on him, whether it was because he was so overtired, his whole body felt prickly, and somewhere in the core of his head he felt a throbbing pain. For love or money, he had no other desire than to get back as quickly as possible to his boardinghouse and comfortably stretch out his arms and legs. When he arrived at Sakuragicho, he sat in a fog until he could move to the train line. Soon, lulled by the heat in the train car, he fell sound asleep all the way through to Tokyo.

In front of the boardinghouse, he tumbled out of the taxi, but as he tried to make it up to the second floor, he encountered the maid who was sweeping in the vestibule.

"Ah! Welcome back—where'd you go last night?"

"Hey, I need some hot tea. Sorry, but bring me the hot water."

"Um, there've been several phone calls for you. They said that when you get back, let them know immediately, no matter what time it is . . ."

"Hmm? From whom?"

"Someone named Mr. Nakazawa—"

"Hunh, Nakazawa?"—Oh yes, that's right, there is that man . . .

"What should I do, let him know?"

"I don't care, leave me alone."

"But, you know, he's going to call again.—Yesterday he came to see you right after you left, and when I told him you weren't at home, he asked me if I didn't know where you'd gone out to, or how you were dressed, and lots of things like that. And then after that he kept calling all the time, and I was even awakened at two in the morning."

"I don't care! No matter how much he calls, tell him I'm not here."

"But, that's a real problem for me, I mean, . . . he's been just such a bother since yesterday evening . . ."

"That's why you shouldn't get involved with him. Whatever he wants, don't let him know!" Speaking over his shoulder, he climbed the stairs. But now, just as he was about to take his much-needed rest, he became filled with rage. That damn Nakazawa, wanting to know where the 160 yen has gone! It's not your money, and do you have to be so mush-mouthed just to support *The People*? Is that how you show your loyalty to the company owner? Instead of playing up to Harada, have some consideration for the artist! What does he think I am? Excuse me, but even if I'm skinny and dried up, I *am* a literary man! Your business relies on us! For a guy like you, doing something like this for yourself is a drug. You running dog of a capitalist! You journalistic parasite! . . .

When he got into the room, unable to hold himself together anymore, he took off only his jacket and *tabi* and was just about to collapse into his laid-out futon when something strange caught his sight.—On the desk, the almanac was still there properly, but beside it was a piece of paper with something written fine in pencil, spread out and held down by the ink pot, as if to draw his attention whether he liked it or not:

Mr. Mizuno!
We're in trouble! The company owner is horribly angry. He's furious, and considers you a swindler. When I got your letter and manuscript earlier, I came over immediately. But

you weren't home. Then I had no choice but to come back again now, at 10:00 P.M. You're not back now either. I don't know what to report to him. That may be all right with you, but please think of my position. As you know, I lent you that money on my own responsibility. If I can't find where you are, and it turns out that I don't get the manuscript, I will have to quit my job. I dare ask you: is this a way to exhibit your diabolism, to cheerfully make a low-salaried worker like me lose his job? Whenever, wherever, even two or three in the middle of the night, I don't mind, just so you call me as soon as you return. Until then, I'll not be sleeping a wink, I'll not go home, I'll just be waiting in the editorial office. If I don't get any news, I'll come again and again however many number of times I have to. I know it was terribly impolite for me to enter your room while you weren't here and write you a letter like this, and please forgive me for having caused you so much worry and irritation. Truly, please have pity on me. I am in tears.

I don't know what to do.

I don't know what to do.

"Hey, did someone let Nakazawa in to my room?" Mizuno glared angrily at the maid, who entered carrying the iron kettle. "To judge from this letter, Nakazawa came twice?"

"Yes, the second time was around ten. He said he wanted to check to see how much of the manuscript you'd written, so he wanted someone from the front desk to be present, and the master had no choice but to accompany him. Anyway, all he did was just look at the desktop . . ."

Damn, what an insolent guy! Trying to act like a detective! When he realized all his lies had been discovered, rather than being embarrassed, he was furious.

"You say someone else was present, but that doesn't matter—do you have the right to let someone into someone else's room while he's away? Tell the old man downstairs that I'm angry. And then, since I absolutely do not want to notify anyone that I'm back, be sure to let the front desk know I mean it. Okay? Have you got that clear?"

After the maid left, bowing and scraping, he poured out tea from the teapot and gulped down six or seven cups, then hastily burrowed into his futon and pulled the bed clothes completely over his head. He'd said not to tell them he was back, but he couldn't hide forever, and wouldn't Nakazawa come sometime soon? What—in this time of need, pull yourself together. Anyway, since clearly you can't do any writing at this point, we're going to have to fight sooner or later . . . Before he had time to adequately contemplate the implications, he felt his body sinking deeply, and within five minutes he was dead asleep.

After that, some minutes . . . some hours must have passed. Mizuno felt someone shaking his shoulder, and as if half in a dream, he heard a voice saying urgently, "Hello, hello." He began to realize that someone was trying to wake him up, but still he was so sleepy that not even duty could make him want to get up. But the voice gradually became more imperative and the shaking got stronger, so that in the end his eyes popped open, and in his foggy pupils was reflected the face of his middle-aged landlord.

"Excuse me for breaking in on you while you are sleeping, but please wake up for a moment . . ."

"Yeah, for what?"

"Well, a person from *The People*, he's waiting downstairs . . ."

"So, what did you tell him?"

"I told him you were sleeping right now."

"You said—you said what? You . . . I said that if anyone came, you were to say that I was out, I was so . . ."

"Yes, I was so informed, but he was here yesterday and asked me various things, and he seemed so terribly upset that I said, yes, sir, when he returns I will definitely let you know, and I accepted that charge . . . and so I just could not say that you were not home, sir . . ."

"Well if that's how things stood, shouldn't you have told me right off?"

"Umm," he said, not seeming the least bit abashed, and calmly looked at Mizuno over the spectacles on the bridge of his nose. His bland expression was extremely irritating, but the fact was that Mizuno was three months in arrears on his rent, so he really couldn't say much back to him. This guy, the master, probably had quite a grudge against him so maybe he had readily sympathized with Nakazawa. And maybe he thought that if he conspired with him to control Mizuno and get him writing good and hard, he'd be able to get paid. Okay, old man, here's something to learn: do something like this and just see if you get paid.

"Well then, is it all right, sir, if I tell them to escort him here . . . ?" As he said this, Nakazawa's footsteps could be heard in the hall.

"Please excuse me, have you awakened yet?—"

"Yeah," Mizuno said with a strangely excited quaver in his voice, collapsed on his side in bed, his knee on the pillow.

"Say, is it all right, would you mind if I came in?" To have the gall to come up to the second floor and then deliberately say something like that from outside the sliding doors—that was a trick no one but Nakazawa could bring off. At the threshold, where he now took the place of the departing landlord, he kneeled down and arranged his trousered knees properly for a bow, sneaking a glance at Mizuno to gauge his expression as he bent his head. Then, with his hands full on the mat as if he were a retainer appearing before his lord, he went on and virtually prostrated himself. Given how clumsy the man was, it did not work very well.

"Hey . . . I hear that you came several times yesterday."

"Yes." The face raised to him actually showed more than perplexity; Mizuno could tell that he was affecting a seriousness beyond a sense of gravity.

"Um, I did read your letter . . ."

"Ah yes, I did trespass while you were out, it was quite . . ."

"No, I was in the wrong. You'd be right to say I swindled you . . ."

"D-don't say that, it's . . . Last night I was out of my mind, and finally I wrote that stuff . . ."

"But it was pretty harsh, you know—'Your diabolism worked on a low-salaried worker like me,' right?—"

"Oh no, don't, that's awful!" Mizuno had been working at breaking down his companion's studied stern expression, but finally as he scratched his head Nakazawa said this and let loose with his usual cunning laugh. "That was . . . that . . . well, because I really was out of my mind."

Mizuno laughed.

"But then, you can't even imagine how surprised I was when I read *your* letter. To tell the truth, I am always praising you to the owner. I say, Mr. Mizuno is not the kind of untrustworthy man you think he is. That's how writers are, depending on their moods, sometimes they can't write what they promised, but it's not only Mr. Mizuno who's like that. After all, the owner realizes what kind of people creative writers are. To exploit them like a capitalist with his workers is absurd. To start with, the manuscript fees are too low for this creative work, so if it isn't possible to raise the pay, at least can't you respond with advances as a goodwill gesture?—I made this direct request for you writers, and made my own position extremely precarious. If you're too much of a stickler over each point, I said—so many yen for so many pages—well, then, it's just as if I'm going to them to collect rent. I say that every chance I get, but he's obstinate and still won't hear my advice. The owner may be fine with it, but it is painful for us men at the bottom of the heap. I'm getting to thoroughly hate being on the magazine editorial staff."

"If you hate it so much, why don't you quit?"

"Wouldn't I do it if only I could find another way to eat? You know, if I were the owner, I'd say, hey, I've gotten ten pages instead of the twenty, but waiting another day or two is no problem." Saying this, Nakazawa stopped with a kind of sly expression in his eyes, the kind he had when he told his usual dirty stories.

"By the way, last night, where were you going, anyway?"

"That has nothing to do with it."

"How about it?—They told me that you were all dressed up and restless when you went out."

"What the—I got the money from you people, and I wanted to take it to that moneylender I told you about, so I went out all set to just take a walk, but on the way back, I strolled a bit on the Ginza with the moneylender."

"Really? And then . . . ?" Nakazawa swallowed hard.

When it came to stories involving women, he was the sort of man who always set aside his magazine work and focused avidly on the tale. And so if Mizuno let himself get carelessly pulled into telling about the previous night's events, afterward Nakazawa would be able to exploit his vulnerabilities and toss off something like, "At any rate that's what I thought would happen, and that's why we couldn't very well lend you money." Mizuno realized this full well, and it's not that he couldn't dodge it nimbly, but the fact was that he was dying to talk about it with someone, so when he saw Nakazawa's nostrils flaring and heard him ask, "And then—?" he felt a grin surging up from the bottom of his stomach. Even if he'd not really wanted to say anything, it was already half out of his mouth.

"—You're not saying that's all there was to it, are you? What happened on the Ginza?"

"Well, you know there's this London Bar . . ."

"Yes, yes, there is—"

"By accident I happened to go in there, with the moneylender, you know—"

"Yes, well, forget about the moneylender, but . . ."

"No, I was talking to him as we drank . . . and there was this typist-looking woman on the other side of the table, a real beauty with bobbed hair, and at first there was nothing happening, but . . ."

"Ho-ho, so something did happen then?"

Mizuno snickered.

"That's mean, that's ugly, to laugh in that nasty way . . ."

"Well, she . . . that . . . under the table she started to play a strange game."

He didn't forget to always include that he'd been accompanying the moneylender. And changing the role of the insurance company men to the moneylender, from there on he went on telling the main plot, interspersing fact with fiction.

"Anyhow, how many times have you heard that bobbed hair 'street girls' appear right there on the Ginza?"

"That's surprising, isn't it, I'm pretty in the know, but . . . That's true, really?"

"True or not, she'd fully arranged a splendid house with that in mind, so isn't that great? The moneylender stupidly hadn't noticed, but *I* realized it from the very first moment. You said you've traveled in the West, and you must have admired the women, too, right?"

"So then finally you went on to Yokohama?"

"Yeah . . . I was supposed to be working on my manuscript yesterday evening, and I don't usually do such things, but faced with such an expression of intention, I couldn't very well remain silent, could I?"

"What kind of a place was it, the woman's house?"

"From the outside it wasn't much, but inside it was pretty spectacular. From the moment I sat down in the easy chair and looked around at the gorgeous room furnishings, I sort of felt like I was the hero of a French novel."

Nakazawa's eyes immediately lit up with envy. "What a great windfall that was.—And, in the end, did you accomplish your aim?"

"Of course," Mizuno said, suddenly straightening himself upright.

"But it's not cheap, I'd imagine, a woman like that? How much on earth did it cost?"

"Listen, as I just told you, that was after I'd given all my money to the moneylender, right?—So I had almost nothing in my wallet."

"Oh, yes, right." Nakazawa blinked his eyes as if he didn't know what to say.

"Fact is, I realized that if I'd known this was going to happen I wouldn't have repaid the money. I could have kicked myself. Of course, it was not money to be used in that way, but you find yourself saying, the hell with *The People*, and you forget responsibility and human feeling—it's frightening how you can get to feel that way, you know. When I think about it now, that was a real dangerous situation."

"Well, yes, that's good, but how much *did* you give her?"

"She said, 'Whatever you feel like,' and I said, '*Fünfzehn*!'"

"What?"

"She used German for all her negotiations.—Anyway, she got her training in the home country itself, so she was completely fluent, and even I couldn't catch more than half of it, but I generally understood the essentials."

"Well, then, I'm certainly not qualified—so how much was it, what you just said?"

"Fifteen yen."

"Really? Isn't that just the going rate?"

"It *was* a pretty 'reasonable price.'"

"Of course it was! Fifteen yen is not at all expensive. Even I could qualify—I should study some German and go out myself."

"Three-month intensive German course—you should walk around looking for advertisements."

"Three months is too long . . . one month—one week—mightn't they have something like that?"

Mizuno and Nakazawa both laughed.

"But, after all, there's the drinking, and the car, and the food and stuff, and before you know it, you're pretty pathetic if you haven't got thirty yen, probably."

"Yeah, it would take about that much. To tell the truth, it was forty yen." He said it easily, intending to lie with complete indifference, but Nakazawa, as might be expected, sat silent, with a strange expression on his face, and so Mizuno had to continue faking.

"That's what . . . that's why . . . from the time she was teasing me under the table, I was thinking, something could happen with this woman, so that's precisely why I left only a little money . . ."

"Oh? Well then, at that point you hadn't passed over all your money to the moneylender?"

"Uh . . . um . . . He said let's go somewhere and have a drink while we conduct our financial transactions . . ."

"Oh really? Then you went for a good reason, right?" Nakazawa's words sounded innocent, but the expression in his eyes said that he was egging Mizuno on.

"To be sure, I paid out most of it, and all that was left was a pittance. But no matter how nearly penniless I might be, I still have to have at least ten yen set aside separately, you know?"

"Ah, yes, sure . . . But I'd rather hear about what happened from there on, the part where it gets increasingly serious . . ."

"Her attitude . . . the way she flirted, how she showed affection—in everything, I don't know if you would call it German-style, but it all was Western, and she didn't seem like a Japanese woman at all. For me, you could even say that it was as if it were my first time . . ."

"Hey, just . . . just wait a minute! Don't go off on your solitary raptures—I want you to go into more concrete detail, for example, that . . ."

And so for the next thirty minutes or so, Mizuno constructed for his companion a scene from Western sexual history to excite Nakazawa as much as he wanted to be. He grew branches from the trunk, attached leaves to the branches, added flowers, as he went into exhaustive detail. Nakazawa listened enthralled, only saying, "Um, and then?" and "Ah, and then?" and occasionally licking his dry lips. The listener was so rapt that the intensity of the feeling was reflected back to the speaker; gradually Mizuno himself began to be turned on, so that in the end even he stopped thinking of it as a fabrication. And every time his companion let loose an envious sigh of admiration, he felt even more ecstasy and felt himself steeped in the same happiness. It was as if he were in actuality tasting that pleasure, and in the end, he became totally absorbed in sweet recollections.

"Hey, that's . . . that's enough . . ." Finally Nakazawa shook himself as if to sweep away the fantasies that were rising to overwhelm him.

"A bit more . . . there's a little bit more . . ."

"No fooling—don't joke with me! That's quite enough already . . ."

Mizuno laughed. "But *you're* the one who said you wanted more concrete detail."

"Well, you're right, but . . . you're awful, really! Last night while you were indulging yourself with such pleasures, here I was keeping a bleary-eyed vigil at the phone calling over and over!"

"I'm sorry, really, there's no excuse, I have no answer for you. But, you know, even when I think it over now, I don't regret it in the least. I may have given you bloodshot eyes, but it was worth it to me."

"There you are! There's nothing I can do with you!" Nakazawa said this with obvious petulance, as if he seemed disgusted at Mizuno's shamelessness, but at that point he did seem to come back to his senses, muttering, "This won't do, it's no good, to get all wrapped up in this dirty talk . . ." And suddenly scratching his head, he continued, "That's why I'm in such trouble, because this is always how it is. And then, somehow it's strange, but we're always talking at cross-purposes. Anyway, what *is* happening with the manuscript as a whole . . ."

"Yeah, well, it's still . . . I'm still feeling echoes of last night . . ."

"No, really—as I said before, I'm always making excuses for you, so when something like this happens, I've completely lost credibility with the owner. Whatever you used yesterday's money for, it's gone, so there's nothing I can do at this point . . ." As he talked, his face gradually returned to its original careful expression, and it cleared as if he had put on a mask. "The owner was already angry. He felt from your letter that he'd been cheated, and when I told him you'd then immediately gone out somewhere, he was extremely put out. Look, he said, I've been foolish to lend the money, and it's come to this, all this trouble he's given me. So I said, what, he's just gone out for a little walk; surely he's not taken the money and gone somewhere, and he'll be back soon, and tomorrow morning I'll bring the rest of the manuscript without fail, I'm sure he'll give it to me, and I calmed him down with stuff like that. I haven't gone to the office yet today, and it would really help if I could get it from you now, so how about it? At any rate, if you don't help me out, you should know at least this much: I'm really in trouble, you know . . ."

"Look, it's really kind of impossible for me to do it right now . . ."

"But I seem to remember that your letter said the remaining ten pages were done, you just had to fix them up a bit . . ." Having checked the desk already, he looked innocent as he closed in and threw his victim in a hole with no escape. It had been Mizuno's aim to look for a chance to provoke a rupture by picking a fight, but after the excitement of spending all this time talking about his encounter with the woman, he'd lost such an opening. Bit by bit he had argued himself into a corner, and for better or worse, he had to produce "truth" out of a "lie."

"Yeah, well, yes, it's done . . . It *is* done, but the parts I wanted to work on, I can't do them right now . . ."

"Well then, how many hours will it take . . . one? . . . around two? . . ."

"Let's see . . . No, don't know that I could do it even in two hours; no matter how fast I did it, even three hours . . ."

"That's excellent. Even if it takes three hours, it should be done before noon, so why don't I wait here until then?"

"But for you to do that would be a problem for me, you know . . . because I can't work with someone sitting at my side . . ."

"Yes, I imagined that's how it would be . . . And so, the fact is, I've rented myself a room here myself."

"Where?"

"At this boardinghouse.—Earlier, when I asked the landlord, he said that right below here, at the bottom of the stairs, room thirty was open. And so I decided to rent it for just half a month. In other words, by then you should have completely finished the manuscript." As he said this, Nakazawa calmly looked back at Mizuno, who was unconsciously glaring daggers at him.

"To have a watcher—that's a surprise. Is that what the owner said to do?"

"Yes, indeed. He said that if I didn't, he'd not feel safe. So it works out that for the time being, I'm to be your technical assistant—especially since, seeing that this Yokohama thing has developed, there's a danger of having you disappear into the clouds just like that."

"Hell, what are you thinking? That's just a one shot affair, because it's not a place I can go to twice."

"Oh no, not at all! We can't depend on that." Nakazawa continued, "Well, I know this is a bother to you, so I'll come back up in three hours—that is, at eleven thirty. Until then, please, I beg your indulgence. This finally helps me feel relieved." And again making an exaggeratedly polite bow, he went out.

"Damn, that was dangerous. I'm really in trouble if he finds this!" Without taking a moment to breathe a sigh of relief, he couldn't wait a moment to stick his hand into his inner pocket and touch the billfold that had started to slide down near his abdomen. He had been so exhausted that he'd forgotten to put it into the drawer when he went to bed. Anyway, that's great. Now there's a guy in this boardinghouse who searches through people's rooms while they're out, like a detective. On top of that, he even has the landlord as his agent. If I had innocently done something like putting this in the drawer, the moment he found it he could very well take it, saying, "I'll hold this for the time being." Dangerous, really dangerous!

Where should I hide it? . . .

Clutching it tightly to his chest, he threw back the covers and stood up. Then, keeping an ear out for people passing in the hallway, he went into the furthest corner of the room. Facing the wall and bending his head toward his chest, he held the money above his navel and counted out the bills in the wallet. Ten-yen bills: there were one . . . two . . . eleven . . . twelve . . . thirteen . . . fourteen? Hey, something's wrong, there ought to be fourteen, but . . . Hurriedly he counted them out again, but sure enough, there were only thirteen. Checking in his coin purse, he found a five-yen note mixed with eight yen and fifty-six sen in coin. That makes a total of one hundred thirty-eight yen, fifty-six sen—during the previous night, twenty-one yen and forty-four sen had vanished, disappeared. There was the taxi from Hirokoji to Kyobashi, the expenses at the London Bar, the second-class round-trip train fare from Yurakucho to Sakuragicho, the limo from Sakuragicho to Honmoku . . . that much he could clearly remember, but that shouldn't have been more than some fifteen yen, and no matter how much he tried to figure it out, he couldn't remember what he had used the nearly eight yen for. Even though he was stingy, he was careless, so this kind of thing happened all the time. Never mind seven or eight yen—there were times when he hadn't the slightest idea of what he'd done with something like a hundred yen. And so, he had a sense that he could account for a net 70 or 80 percent of the money he had as actually having been used by him, and for the rest, well, it had disappeared as completely as if he had thrown it into the ditch. . . . But, well, never mind, with this the woman would become his—if he could make up the additional twenty-one yen, forty-four sen, at some time, whenever. Forget about that for the time being—where should he hide this? . . . He took the thirteen bills out of his wallet, folded them in four, and clutching them in his hand, paced for a while here and there around the room, checking the window, worrying about chinks in the shutters. In the end he went over to the bookcase and put them in various books and then took them out, put them in, and took them out repeatedly for the next thirty minutes. At last he divided the bills into three piles and put them in order into Volumes 1, 3, and 5 of the English translation of Brandes's *Main Currents in Nineteenth Century Literature.* Then he penciled in on the edge of his notepad, "Brandes . . . 1, 3, 5." That's because, once before, he had completely forgotten the name of the book he'd used, and it had been the devil to find it again.

6

Once he had taken care of the disposition of the cash and realized that by some means or other he had to come up with ten manuscript pages by eleven thirty, just the thought of sitting at his desk made him feel sick. Ten pages within that time: given that one page was four hundred characters, that meant four thousand characters in two hours! Unless his head ran as fast as a sewing machine, there was no way he could work so quickly. Even writing a letter was not easy, yet creative writing required the writer to put out much more energy. A writer's craft required that he announce grandly, "Truly, I've never worked over a piece as much as this one," or "When I look it over, I see that there are a number of things I don't like, and so I need to work on it some more." At his usual speed, this much would take him two or three days. Given the current situation, it was all right with him if all he wrote was nonsense, but even to write nonsense required thinking time. To start with, he had absolutely no memory of what he'd written in the ten pages he'd already handed over to them, because at the time his only concern had been to extract the money out of them. All he remembered was the title, "To the Point of the Murder of the Man Who Wrote 'To the Point of Murder'"; he couldn't even remember the opening paragraph.

After all, he had started to write it some two weeks earlier. Then ten days or so passed, but he'd completely abandoned his work after running into Cojima on the night of the fifteenth, and it had stayed in the drawer where he'd stuffed it until the clerk came from *The People* on the evening of the sixteenth. So that meant he had written the tenth page during the night of the fourteenth, and for the three days after that—the fifteenth, sixteenth, and seventeenth—all he'd produced was utter commotion, with the Cojima incident, the matter of the money, and the Fraülein incident, and it felt to him as if another ten days had passed. Until now, when he'd been handing over five or ten pages every two or three days, he'd still have the last page or even half page with him, or if not, he'd at least have copied out the last line of the last page and would continue from there. But this time, far from leaving some margin—what words the last line ended with—not only had he not written anything, but he had completely forgotten whether it ended with conversation or narrative or something in between. Maybe he still had a page or two that he'd messed up in writing, he thought, so he searched through the desk drawer. It was so stuffed with paper trash that he could hardly get anything out, but in the back he did find two or three pages of manuscript paper on which some confused words had been scribbled. They had been rolled up into a baton and wedged in; he forcefully pulled them out and smoothed out the wrinkles. On the first was written,

To the Point of Murder: Part Two

or

Part Two: To the Point of Murder

Aha, so is this a memo for the plan? That's right, I must have written this down at some time—

1. We have here a writer with diabolistic tendencies. He publishes a story called "To the Point of Murder." Originally the whole of it was to be Part One. . . . However, out of necessity this current "To the Point of Murder" was separated off . . .

Otherwise, all he found were miscellaneous things written down and discarded, but nothing that might be of use to him for continuing writing in this time of crisis. Mizuno gave up scrabbling among the manuscript trash, lay down flat on his stomach, and then flopped over on his back.

In this posture, the desire for sleep that earlier had been an inexorable physical need again became overwhelming. For all that, Nakazawa, the jerk, was waiting in Room 30 downstairs, weighing on his mind, and he couldn't find the courage to drop off to sleep again. The boardinghouse landlord and Nakazawa both were now damn irritating; on top of that, the situation made him remember anew his uneasiness over "To the Point of Murder." Until now he'd forgotten about it because of that woman business, but clearly it was the most pressing need. In order to chase it away, obviously he had to just write the manuscript, quickly. . . .

To keep myself awake, let's get angry again at that jerk Nakazawa. It occurred to him that as the first step, he should get Nakazawa to tell him where the part of the manuscript he'd already sent had left off. The guy did after all always pass himself off as a faithful reader. He claimed that Mizuno's were the only manuscripts he read on the way to the office right after he picked them up; he said that he was delighted to be Mr. Mizuno's Number One Reader, and things like that. Mizuno had a recollection that there had been a time, before he thought Nakazawa was such a lowlife, that there was a party or banquet or something given by the owner, and he'd said some such thing. Mizuno thought it could just be an editor's flattery, but still, given how conceited he was and how he flattered himself, he also felt there might be something genuine in it. Even if he had just been talking nonsense after all, Mizuno could use it as the means to pick a fight with him.

"Even if he had just been talking nonsense after all—damn!" Mizuno headed down the stairs, talking to himself as usual. He opened the paper sliding doors at the entrance to Room 30, and there was Nakazawa, lying on his side, calmly smoking, his feet propped up on a ceramic charcoal brazier. His heavy glance seemed to suggest that he, too, had really been up all night without sleeping. Or maybe he had been fantasizing about the story Mizuno had told him about earlier, that scene out of a dirty Western novel?

"What do you think you're doing, anyway?"

At Mizuno's question, Nakazawa started in surprise and sat up formally, as usual smoothing his trousers over his knees. He'd been leaning against a cushion, and he pushed it toward Mizuno, who was still standing.

"Well now, that story about the woman . . ."

Mizuno had been almost joking, but at this he bit back his words and sat down haughtily on the proffered cushion with an expression of extreme irritation. And then he did not speak immediately. The fact is, his head was all fuzzy, and he didn't know what to say.

"I'm really disgusted, you know," is all he said, and nothing more.

"Yes?" Nakazawa tried to prompt Mizuno to continue, but not knowing what the issue was, all he could do was present himself as extremely embarrassed.

"While I'm out, a guy ransacks my room, and he doesn't find the manuscript I'd started to write. There are some notes, but things are really a mess."

"Yes. Well, I did step into your room while you were out, but—"

"Nah, I'm not saying that *you* rummaged around, but . . ." He continued even more aggressively, "Things like this happen, and that's why I hate to have people come into my room just whenever they want. It's not simply that I'm eccentric. It's that something that looks like trash to someone else might be extremely important to me, you see. Actually, I'd kept copies of pieces of the pages I gave you the other day; in fact, two or three pages were practically complete, and there was an outline draft, and they were bound together; anyway there were enough to piece together . . . , but, hmm, it's really strange," he said, deliberately making it seem as if he were saying the last part to himself.

"That is a problem, I can see. . . . No, it's truly a problem for me, too."

"But it's not enough to say, 'Gee, it's a problem,' is it?" he said, hectoring him. "You read it and should know how it ended, shouldn't you?"

"Yes—well, only—anyway, I was really flurried this time, and I wasn't in a position to look at it along the way, so . . ."

"But the time before—you didn't look at it that time, did you? That's how those typos got printed as is and made such a mess. You bear some responsibility for that, you know. Such an attitude reflects on me, too—even when the writer's had fine inspiration come boiling up, it all goes to naught. And that's especially because I'm different from the rest of the crowd. You're surely no fledgling reporter, so shouldn't you understand the nature of important writers? . . ."

As if he couldn't bear this reaming out to continue anymore, Nakazawa said, "Well then, anyway—" and he started to rise, "—any bit earlier we can make it, the better, I think, so let me phone immediately. Your dissatisfaction with me as an editor is quite justified, and I will accept your rebuke later when we have the time for it."

Mizuno listened to Nakazawa's footsteps leaving the room, and he thought, here's the plan: I send him off as an errand boy to the company, and while he's gone I cover my tracks. Then he immediately rethought it: there's no way I can get out of it at the moment and go to Honmoku. And as he continued to weigh the various considerations—the money he'd hidden between the pages of the books, how much money he still had to come up with, how to spend the time until the next Tuesday—he completely forgot about the manuscript.

Just at that point, Nakazawa came in, saying, "Sorry I've kept you waiting. Luckily it's not yet gone to copyediting, but they were just about to do it, so I've had them send the office boy with it. He'll be here within the next fifteen minutes."

When he'd returned to his own room, Mizuno resigned himself: there was no way he could escape. Rather, he should just write as much as he could, no matter what, and as the pages mounted up, it would naturally become the way to raise cash by the next Tuesday. But first things first: at this point he was unbearably hungry. In desperation he rang the bell long and hard to call the maid, and he had her bring some cakes immediately. He drank tea and ate, and drank and ate, and before long he'd finished it all. Forbidding Nakazawa entry to his room even when he brought the manuscript, he forced himself to sit at the desk, planning to have eight or nine pages done by noon.

Secretly he had been worried, but now that he read it over again, he was impressed with himself: it was unexpectedly well written. He thought, if I was able to scribble out that much at that time, and it was as good as this, then today if I only set my mind to it, there's no reason I shouldn't be able to come up with something. But try as he might, he couldn't squeeze out a single line. The best he could do was pick up his pen, put it down, check the condition of the pen nib . . . The other day, too, he had gotten stuck at this same point and then got sick of thinking about it. He attempted to calm himself by thinking that being impatient wouldn't do any good. This has been worrying you all along, so it might help to just look at it for a while, he thought; and then he stood up and went over to the bookcase. He took the three Brandes volumes out, lay down on the floor, and again carefully turned over the pages into which he'd pressed the bank notes, sighing and muttering to himself, "Tuesday, Tuesday."

Before long he was remembering the shape of the woman in the train the night before, and how drunk he had been, and he began to feel just as though the tatami beneath him, warmed by his own body heat, was the woman's skin. As he kneaded and stroked it, he became aroused, and finally he even felt that he was in the rocking train car. But the outcome was that he fell sound asleep.

Someone called to him and he awoke, immediately remembering, "Oh, that's right, Nakazawa's here." He sprang to his feet, and then saw that the three Brandes volumes on which he'd been pillowing his head had collapsed, and he had drooled on the cover of one. He quickly piled them up again, and while carefully pressing down firmly on them, he called Nakazawa in.

"I really needed that sleep—my head's all clear now," he said to forestall any comment from Nakazawa, and he quickly stretched out his hand to take up the pen. Thrusting it toward his companion, he said, "Listen, I'm sorry to do this to you, but be my secretary for a while. Let's do it by dictation. Come on, you'll do this for me, won't you?"

Not unexpectedly, Nakazawa looked glum, but then, since he'd asked so abjectly, he couldn't very well refuse the proffered pen. Maybe it was because he'd had that little bit of sleep, but when Mizuno started speaking out his nonsense, somehow the sentences followed one after another, and in only an hour and a half, some four pages and two lines were done.

"You'll let me off with this much for today, okay? I mean, for me to have done this much after a night like yesterday's is quite an accomplishment. No, that's right, you've put a lot into it, too. Thanks for your participation.—Hey, how about dinner, since I've not eaten yet either, you know."

Mizuno went on chattering with a kind of excitement, impelled by the momentum of dictating. And while Nakazawa sipped his cup of tea, once again he started in with that account that could have come from a Western sexual history. Of course, he was just inventing randomly as he went along, but he generated quite a bit of heat with the hope that he could re-create it right before his eyes.

"When you create with such energy and tell it to me, we could get it down on paper with quite a bit of progress." Nakazawa urged him on, sitting glued to his seat, and not until three o'clock did they finally set out.

At times dictating, at times picking up his pen and writing it out himself, he worked even through Sunday, not allowing Nakazawa to get away from delivering on his promise. In Mizuno's gut, the result didn't matter at all. All he wanted was to have delivered forty written pages by Tuesday morning, including what he'd handed over already, as a result of which once more *The People* would have to pay him 150 yen. Mizuno found Nakazawa strange. Without knowing Mizuno's hidden agenda, he still seemed satisfied just with the unprecedented progress of the work, and the salacious stories Mizuno interspersed here and there to entertain him. And then, whether or not it was because Mizuno had this secret impetus, he found the resulting work as he went on to be not all that bad.

By Monday morning he had begun to write the thirty-fourth page, and when he realized that he had only five or six pages to go, his brain began to work even more sharply. He was too impatient to write it himself, and thinking to attack it in a single stretch, he again began to dictate. At 4:00 P.M. he had exactly forty pages. The payment from *The People* should be there by five. There would be someone at the printing plant until five, too.

"Well now, I'm going to take a break at this point," Mizuno said leaning back on the tatami. He took out a cigarette, lit up, stretched out his legs and lay back on the floor spread-eagle. "How about it—why don't I wind up for the time being? There's quite a bit piled up for now, so why don't you just deliver it to the printing plant at this point? They could do the copy-editing quickly and show it to me right away, and that way I can keep up the momentum.—Oh, yeah, that's right: I'd have some business with the accounting department. Listen, there'll be no problem this time because I'll tell them to pay me just for what I've handed over already. Come on, let's go out now and get something good to eat. It's been a while since we've done that, and you must be tired out from all this stuff."

"I'm okay, anything is fine, but you—you've put out quite an effort for me. If I'd done as much, I'd be really proud of myself. The story's been getting more and more interesting, and . . ."

"While we're all full of energy, let's go somewhere and spend the night out—you know, to replenish our strength? You've been pushing me hard, and I've had only this boardinghouse food. My body can't go on like this."

"I'll keep you company anywhere, but the London Bar would be dangerous!" Nakazawa said with a laugh.

Mizuno laughed, too. "Yeah, they might catch *you* this time!"

Nakazawa laughed again and left in good spirits, but he was back within the hour. They decided to go to Komatsu, an eel restaurant. Nakazawa showed signs of inebriation immediately, but he manfully continued to raise his saké glass. This was just what Mizuno had been hoping for, and he continued to ply him with drink. Nakazawa's speech got confused as he sank into drunkenness, and instead of addressing Mizuno politely as usual, he started mixing familiar terms and slang. He left their work far behind and starting mumbling about "London Bar" and "Fraülein." Mizuno watched him with detachment and worked on a scheme to get rid of him.

In the alley that led to the main street, Nakazawa stopped to relieve himself. Mizuno suddenly raced out to the boulevard and immediately grabbed a passing taxi and piled into it. Behind him, Nakazawa seemed to realize that Mizuno had gotten into the taxi, and he stumbled after it.

"What are you doing—get going!" Mizuno yelled at the driver. When he turned to look behind, he saw Nakazawa running, trying to catch up, his arms spread wide.

The driver asked, "Where to?" but Mizuno had no idea of his destination. He finally noticed in what direction the cab was already running, and he said, "Shimbashi." From there he could immediately head for Yokohama tonight just as he was.

The station clock showed that it was still about seven. Was it so early, he wondered to himself, and took out his own watch. It read past seven thirty. Two or three days earlier he was sure he had checked with Nakazawa and synchronized his watch to Nakazawa's. But maybe, he thought, Nakazawa had pushed it up thirty minutes to trick him into finishing his work faster; Mizuno reset his watch. Okay, now that he'd come this far, he could leave for Yokohama from here. But he had no idea of how to spend the time until noon tomorrow. He wondered where he could go to kill some time, and slumping against the waiting room seat, he began to calculate mentally just how much money he actually had in all. There were the thirteen bills he had taken from between the Brandes pages, and there was the 150 yen he'd gotten just a while ago, and then there was the small change of eight yen or so from what he'd had the other day. He'd used about fifteen yen at Komatsu, and then the taxi fare. It ought to be more than he'd need, but he wondered if he was in fact sure that there was that much. He put his hand in his breast pocket to check out the thickness of his wallet, got worried, and went into the washroom to examine it again more carefully.

He did then realize that he had more than enough time and money, and he began to feel like strolling around Ginza again for a while. There was of course a chance that he'd be caught by Nakazawa, who undoubtedly would still be wandering around there, so he did feel a certain hesitation, but he'd deal with that when the time came. As he ambled over, he imagined he could take the high ground by saying something like, Hey, I've been looking for you, and ply him with more drinks. It was the time of the long nights of early winter, when people crowded the evening streets. As he thought about Nakazawa—It's not impossible that the guy could be somewhere around here—he passed by the London Bar. This made him feel like going to see how things were doing at the Monaco. He might just run into Fraülein's friends there. In truth, he couldn't stand waiting until tomorrow.

Monaco was jam-packed. He was sober and ordered a glass of plain soda water and found a place to sit in a corner. As he casually looked around at the other corners, he saw that there was a woman with Western clothes. The Western clothing was quite noticeable, and it caught his attention. Mightn't it be Fraülein? But even though there was something familiar about her face, the instant he shifted his gaze, he realized that the middle-aged man beside her was Mr. T. I., a fellow writer. So that meant the woman must be M, he thought. She seemed not to have noticed, so while he knew her by sight he pretended not to know her. Oh, yes, that's right, if I go to Tiger, this is the time of night Mr. I. N. is likely to be there. Of course his all-important Fraülein was not there.

Until now he hadn't thought of wearing Western clothes, but when he imagined the woman who was to be his companion, he started to feel that he ought to try it himself. The next thing he knew, he was standing in front of the show window of a certain store, contemplating the showy plaid and homespun fabrics displayed in it, cloth that might do for an overcoat.

"So—one garment, thirty-eight yen?"

Western clothing seems to be pretty inexpensive, he thought. The next store's window showed Western accessories. Flesh-colored women's stockings brought up her image sharply to his memory. He looked at them for a while and then plunged into the store. He began to feel his usual impulse to buy things he had no need for. At first it occurred to him that he might get the woman a present, but then he realized that it would be better not to, in case it didn't fit her taste, and he gave up the idea. Suddenly a walking stick caught his attention. The one he was carrying was one he had bought on his return from a summer stroll he'd taken three years ago, but it was quite cheap looking. After much back and forth, he finally chose one made of black euonymus wood with an ivory handle. Seventeen yen fifty sen. And then, two linen handkerchiefs. Somehow these things left him still feeling unsatisfied. As he was looking at women's gloves, he began to desire a pair for himself. And then he realized that he had made no provision for his Western suit. He kept wandering here and there throughout the store, but whatever his eye hit upon now seemed a waste of money, and he felt overwhelmed.

He left the store and thought about the walking stick, given his new taste for Western clothes. It was totally unsuited to the kimono he was wearing. What a cheapskate he was; after buying something, he'd always go on about how expensive it was or how there must have been something better than what he got. On the other hand, he was vain and weak willed, so he was often sucked into buying things he didn't like even though he was looking right at them.

Well, it mightn't look good with a kimono, but if he were wearing a suit, it wouldn't be bad. He slipped it out of its yellow knit bag and gripped it in his hand again. He tried twirling it. The sculpted bulldog head fit his grip pretty well. He decided to toss his old one away somewhere. Where should he—no, rather, *what* should he do tonight? He could go to Yokohama after all and spend the night somewhere until daybreak, right? He'd been so hounded by work for the past few days that he hadn't really been able to sleep well, so if he didn't sack out totally tonight and rebuild his strength . . . With a nasty, sly smile on his face, he turned his feet again toward Shimbashi. Planning to get rid of the walking stick, he turned into the darkness along the river across from the Hakuhin Building. For no particular reason he put the old walking stick into the new bag and hurled it into the river from the dirt embankment as he walked along.

He settled deep into a corner of the leather chair in the chilly waiting room and noticed unhappily that his wooden clogs weren't of very good quality. As he raised his face, his gaze collided with that of a woman who seemed to have been watching him from a seat across the way. Who was this woman? He had a feeling that he'd seen her before, somewhere. As he looked hard at her, trying to remember, the woman, too, seemed to be looking back at him. It took him five or six minutes to realize that this was his former wife. She had been his wife, but to run into her at this strange time, in this strange place, and given that even when they lived together they never communicated very much and they'd had no contact at all since separating two or three years earlier, she came across to him as a totally different person. She seemed to have aged considerably and looked so plain. He'd heard a rumor that she'd married someone else somewhere. Word had it that she'd had enough of being a writer's wife and had married a completely different kind of man and was living somewhere in the country. She hadn't been very strong from the start, but her color was even paler now, and she looked more worn out. Undoubtedly she'd had some hard times with Mizuno, but she didn't seem to be living happily now either . . .

At that moment, the woman picked up the small cloth-wrapped package at her side, stood up, and came toward him.

"It's been a while," she hailed him, a faint smile playing around her mouth. Her expression held something sad and ironic, definitely not kind and friendly.

"Yeah, it has been," Mizuno said, similarly wary, and he nodded without taking off his hat. By now she was standing in front of him. The seat across from him was empty, and she seemed to be trying make up her mind whether or not to sit down. It was as if she was waiting for Mizuno to say something to her.

"How are you doing these days? . . . Same as usual?"

"Yeah, I'm still the same. . . . How about you?"

"I . . . I'm not in Tokyo these days."

"So where are you?"

"I'm tucked away in the country."

"Where? Somewhere far?"

"Yes . . . no . . . not too far . . ."

"Around Kamakura, right?"

"A little more . . . it's about two and a half hours by train," she said with hesitation, and then clarified, "In Odawara."

"So you come into Tokyo from time to time, do you?"

"I hardly ever do. Today we, um, had a little business to do, so we came together, but on the way there was somewhere else to go, so we're meeting here."

The woman's "there was somewhere else to go" clearly should have included "for my husband," but the words were deliberately ambiguous, and with her embarrassed expression and bitter smile they seemed to convey some special meaning. She turned and looked behind her at the wall clock that showed nine thirty-five.

"He's supposed to be here at ten."

"Well then, we still have some time, right? You could sit down here with me, couldn't you?"

"Thanks . . ." There was something a little stupid and gullible about the woman, but also an aura of sweetness about her. She sat down docilely as she was told, and as she pulled her wool shawl around her shoulder as if chilled, Mizuno had an unexpected sense that he was seeing a vision from the past.

"Are you waiting for someone?"

"Me?"

"Yes."

"Nah . . . I came here with nothing particular in mind, but it's still early, and I was trying to figure out where to go."

"Are you by yourself now, too?"

"Yup—ever since then I've been living on my own."

"That's probably best, maybe, for someone like you."

"I don't know if it's good or not, but I just don't stay long with any woman, so there's nothing to do about it. What about you—the guy you're with now, is he good to you?"

"Well, he is easy to be with, but . . ."

"What's he do? Business?"

"No . . ."

"Company man?"

"No, something completely different."

"School teacher?"

"No—he's a Methodist minister. After you, I became a Christian, you know."

"Huh, so you're a minister's wife, are you? So then you're living happily off in the country."

"Not all that happily." The woman laughed sadly with resignation.

"But you must be happier than when you were with me . . ."

"Well, yes, that's true."

"So then, you're happier, aren't you?"

"Just because it's better than when I was with you doesn't mean I'm happier, you know—because being with you was way worse than 'unhappy.'"

"Wow, that's quite some way to put it. But I think that there's no way people can be happy in the ways they hope for, and we just have to put up with what we get. There's no end to what we desire . . ."

The woman was silent and seemed to nod. Mizuno's attention was caught by the graceful bend of the full-fleshed nape of her neck, as her ear bent toward her shoulder. Her hair was dry, faded, and lusterless, but far from wasting away from her troubles, she was instead well endowed for a woman of her years, and fuller than she'd been before.

Was this a sign of her apathy, or could it be that she didn't even realize she was actually satisfied with her current situation, regardless of what she said? From the line of her back that he could glimpse beneath her wool shawl . . . this body, all 120 pounds or so, drawing breath beneath the lined black satin obi wrapped around the cheap quilted kimono—this was once my "wife." I had found the fleshiness of her body attractive, and then I came to hate it. All there was to the body was plumpness, but no elasticity. There was no vitality to it. As if the goodness of this easy-natured woman inhered even in her flesh, he could feel it in touching her. Her flesh was asleep. And so, what on earth could this woman mean by "happiness"? What kind of "happiness" does a woman like this pursue?

"Why did you become a Christian, anyway? There must have been something you felt, right?"

The woman snickered lightly, as if she felt she was being teased.

"Yes, why?"

"No special reason."

"So—do you believe there is a God?

"I don't really know.—But I've been told that I'll come to know in time."

"By the man you're with?"

"Yes."

"Well then, it's not God—it's the *man* you believe in, right?"

All the woman did was shake her head from time to time, or smile forcedly, or say "yes" or "no," and she didn't speak very quickly. But at the same time she didn't seem to mind talking to him, and she stayed at his side. When he remembered how in their married life they had never talked together, side by side, for half an hour like this, Mizuno felt unexpectedly sentimental.

"So then, if you continue this way, isn't that true happiness? And if you complain, you'll be punished." As he said this, he felt his eyes burning. He wanted to add, "You should let him be as good to you as possible. I'll be standing in the shadows, thinking of you and wishing you the best, too." But he thought if he did, tears would come welling up.

The woman stood up with a light exclamation and looked in the direction of a man in a suit who had just come into the waiting room. The man was a couple of years younger than Mizuno and wore strong glasses—indisputably a minister type.

"That's Mizuno," the woman seemed to have said, because the man glanced sharply in his direction, but just as he thought they might be coming over to say hello, they went in front of the ticket counter and passed right through the gate as if time for the train was pressing on them.

Mizuno watched them walking away from him and continued to sit blankly on the bench. From his youth he'd been accustomed to a life of wandering, so he was not likely to be feeling sadness at this late date. But all the same, the station made him feel a kind of belated nostalgia for travel, all the more intense on such a cold evening. He found himself thinking that this was the wrong person to have come across at this bad time. He had separated from his wife with no lingering regrets, so it was as though she was just someone he'd run into along the road. And yet for some reason, on this particular night, a feeling of homelessness flooded into his heart. No matter how much he tried fantasizing about the Honmoku woman, he kept coming back to an elementary melancholy. In his mind's eye he saw reflected clearly the husband and wife sitting companionably side by side in a corner of the train car as they headed for Odawara. Surely the man, with his pale, swollen face, was taking good care of her. His good-heartedness, too, had something saccharine about it, and that made him appropriate for the woman he was with. At least he was a better fit for her than Mizuno had been. He didn't know what kind of life a minister led, but it must be a peaceful existence without many needs beyond prayers and sermons. He imagined the little thatched-roof country home they must be living in. Behind the house an orange grove spread on a hill to the south and a little brook meandered along the flank of the hill. Every morning the wife would go out the back door and faithfully fill the bucket at the well. At noon she would sit on the veranda that caught the sun so well and do her sewing. In the evening she would stand by the gate and await her husband's return, while off in the distance the violet pleats of the piled-up Hakone-Ashigara mountain range soared into the misty evening sky. He felt faint envy at these scenes as he wrote them in his heart, of the couple at their evening meal or murmuring together in bed. It's not that he wanted to try a life like that. His nature was so constructed that even if he could find pleasure in living such a life, it would not be temperamentally suitable for him; that's what made him feel lonely. In all the years of his life from his student days when he was in his early twenties until now, he, too, had experienced a home life, but only for three short years. Just that once had been enough for him. I'm not the sort of man to have a wife and home ever again, he realized, and at that point he was done with it. And so although he'd sent his wife away and was living in a boardinghouse—and although ordinarily he took it as a point of pride that this was a consequence of his devotion to his vocation as an artist—why tonight had he gotten so weak? Come to think of it, not just tonight, but recently from time to time, he'd been feeling this way. Maybe it was a sign he was getting old. When he was younger he'd never felt so unmanly, and if on occasion he felt it coming on, he'd immerse himself in the pleasures of drinking and women, and that would completely distract him. But now the reverse was happening: it seemed to be trying to prevent him from just that pleasure. . . .

Ten thirty: for him that was just the beginning of the evening. To return early to the boardinghouse and crawl into bed at this hour was the most dangerous thing he could do because he'd spend a sleepless night.

"Saké, that's what I need—saké." With that in mind, and as a way to kill the time, he ducked under the curtain of an *oden* stall near the station.

7

It was after eleven when his eyes opened. By good chance he'd slept deep and well, but maybe because he'd drunk so much the night before, he felt a dull ache in the back of his head. He pulled himself out of bed and raised the blinds on the window. As he gazed upward he could see the back of the building next door beyond the glass doors. A large concrete chimney soared into the bright, clear sky, and white clouds floated quietly above the roof of the eight-story building. The color of the sky, the shapes of the clouds, and the cheery sunlight met his eyes and, surrounded by the moist warmth of the steam-heated room, he realized that, early as it was, spring had already arrived. He found himself imagining the successful accomplishment of today's pleasures. When he'd missed the chance to go to Yokohama last night and wandered into this hotel at one in the morning, it had been gloomy and on the brink of rain. He had prayed that it wouldn't rain tomorrow, and this weather bode extremely well. . . .

"All evil deeds require a day with a perfectly clear sky for their working." He didn't remember when it was that he'd taken this as his motto. Among the things to be considered evil deeds were deceiving people, stealing money, indulging in dissipation, and such like, but as long as the weather was good, he felt remarkably free of the pricks of conscience. Was it his physical constitution that made him so susceptible to the influence of the weather? Or could it be that a man living such an isolated life, like he was, would be given to bouts of depression if he wasn't always surrounded by bright colors? For his entertainments, too, as much as possible he preferred daytime to night. Something like last night, where he'd had that unimaginable encounter with the woman, had made him into quite a sentimentalist, but that, too, was the working of "night." If it had happened on a morning with weather like this, he would surely not have felt so off balance. Look at that blue, blue sky! That sunlight! I've got nearly three hundred yen in my breast pocket and that classy woman waiting for me! Am I not fortunate?

As he lay in bed with these thoughts running through his head, he had a sudden realization: I have to get a shave. In fact, he'd shaved just the previous morning and it hadn't grown out much. Usually he let it go for two or three days, but the woman was so stylish that if he weren't perfectly smooth in the Western style, she might tell him he was a boor. Even with this gorgeous weather, she'd be put off if he looked scruffy. Since he'd had the leisure to do that stupid shopping on the Ginza last night, he should at least have gotten himself a Gillette.

He called the bellboy and asked him, "Say, before I take my bath, I'd like to have my face cleaned up—do you have a barber in the hotel?"

"Well, actually, we don't have a barber . . ."

"Might you have a safety razor?"

"We don't have razors either, but they probably have them at the Marunouchi Building. Shall I go see if they have them?"

"Yes, get me a Gillette as quickly as possible."

He handed the bellboy a five-yen bill, and then, jumping out of bed, he paced back and forth restlessly in the room, going over to look out the window now and then, checking on the state of the weather. So—I'm at the very top of a four-story building. Those guys down there below me are a different kind of animal. That Nakazawa, my ex-wife, they're just maggots in my sight! He made as if to spring up into the air, and whirled around on his heel two or three times.

He had to be on the train by twelve, and if he was to grab a bite to eat, this was the time to do it. Impatience rushed him along as he plied the Gillette in the Western-style bath, and he found himself pulled back into those same old fantasies that came boiling up, brought by thoughts of the pleasures that were about to be his. He had to arrive at Sakuragicho by one. And the woman would be standing at the exit wearing what she had been wearing the night before. And then—? And then what should they do? Wasn't there something sensational they could do? But that house in Honmoku was too wretched a place. Wouldn't there be some place more elegant, brighter, grander, something more suitable for making love to a woman like that? Or even better—should he bring her to this hotel? . . . As he lay in the tub looking up and watching the soap bubbles running down his arm, he idly played out fancies—let's do that, and then we'll do this. . . . Eventually, he was quite in a trance, seeing clearly before him things that were not there; then he came to with a start and went back to scrubbing himself briskly. This just won't do. If I keep wrapping myself up in delusions, that alone will exhaust me. Until I meet with the woman I mustn't think about it. I must diligently wash myself, fill my belly, and run off to Tokyo Station. For the present, that's what I should pay attention to. Even as he thought this, and knew that time was passing, his mind would not work as he willed it to; he warned himself, "It's late, it's getting late," but kept endlessly pursuing his fantasies. Grappling with so many daydreams, he couldn't brush them aside as they pressed in on him one after another.

"Oh hell, I'm in trouble—I've only got fifteen minutes till twelve!" He hastily grabbed for his kimono without even drying himself properly and, while dressing, pushed the bell on the wall.

"My bill! Quickly! I'd planned to go eat, but there's no time. Hurry up and bring the bill right away!"

He had put his overcoat on over his damp body; he was dripping with sweat but had no time to mop it with his handkerchief. Not waiting for the bellboy to come, he went down to the lobby by elevator, settled the bill and, without even checking the change, raced out of the building.

"Say, here's your walking stick!" The bellboy came running several hundred feet behind him, shouting and brandishing the bulldog-headed cane he'd bought the night before. But all he did was half turn around momentarily and gesture as if to say, Never mind—I give it to you, it's yours! He ran all the way to Tokyo Station. The plaza in front had never seemed as huge as it was today. He'd seen the building right ahead of him as he turned the corner from the hotel, yet no matter how much he ran, it was still off in the distance. He'd have to manage to get there and then go to the train entrance at the far end of the long, long building, and then make it through the long, long underground passageway and go up and down stairs. He was filled with rage just to think of that interminable path until he arrived at the long platform—how inconvenient they'd made the train stop! As he ran he felt his throat seizing, and he spat out bits of undigested material left in his stomach from the night before.

Luckily, he made it just before the train left the platform. At this time of day there were few passengers in the second-class car, but few as they were, when he entered his eyes were met with a flickering, incomprehensible burst of red, white, all sorts of bright colors, and he stared despite himself. They were perhaps the wives or daughters of some foreign embassy: a seventeen- or eighteen-

year-old mademoiselle who seemed to be going to see someone
off on a ship or meeting one, because she had a big basket of flowers standing in front of her; a young woman around twenty who
could have been her sister; and a fiftyish woman who might have
been their mother. Accompanying them was a fatherly, elegant
older gentleman and a boy around thirteen or so. They made up the
larger part of the passengers, with only two or three additional
Japanese in the car. As the train began moving, the women continued their bright chattering. It was his considered opinion that
no matter how beautiful Western women were, they always smelled
of soap—better to see them in the movies. But now, so close to
them in actuality, he couldn't help being excited. Additionally,
the Honmoku woman and these "hairy foreigners" were connected
in some inevitable way. In just another hour, she'll be mine, he
thought and felt a strange joy welling up in him. With no other
impetus, he felt that the visions he had conjured up not long ago
in the bath were appearing right before his eyes. Come to think of
it, these Westerners are strange creatures. Even the women move
with amazing power; they stuff themselves with butter and beef,
anything fatty and oily, develop their bodies as much as possible,
and then they wear all this exciting clothing. Women's ways are
fully dedicated to presenting in the mind one idea only—how to
stimulate—in the most effective, appropriate, and intense way. A
man's nerves are gradually desensitized as he becomes more and
more accustomed to something he sees all the time, so the woman's presentation must become increasingly intense to be able to
arouse him. For her to go out publicly on the street in full daylight
in outfits like this is far more stunning than if she were walking
around naked. Their clothing is not for the purpose of keeping
out heat or cold . . . its function is to draw attention. This is of
course what Tolstoy was attacking in "The Kreutzer Sonata," but
setting Tolstoy aside, surely the general run of men burn with

passion morn till night. In fact, when you look at it this way, that's precisely what the will to live stems from. "It's a waste not to live. Life brings us these beautiful creatures; in order to get my hands on one of them, I'll work with all my energy, make as much money as I can . . ." This must be where Western men get their entrepreneurial work ethic, their vitality. The woman's clothing is the propeller that makes them move. After all, wasn't it that Honmoku propeller that got me to churn out thirty pages in only four days? . . .

When they got out at Sakuragicho, he shouldered his way through the line of Westerners as they made their way down the platform, and feverishly raced down and then up the stairs of the underground passage. And then, his propeller—the Fraülein's green hat—there it appeared, amid the crowd at the exit gate.

"Ah, there she is, she's there!" He was just about to raise his hand to her when the woman acknowledged him, and then after signaling him sharply with a powerful glance, she turned on her heel and went ahead to wait for him at the station exit. There was a distance of thirty or forty feet between them as he was about to go out the exit gate. Maybe because he was looking at her from a distance, he suddenly felt something like a light disappointment. Certainly her clothing and accessories were just as they had been, but somehow they gave a different impression from the time before. First of all, it was strange, but today rather than looking like a typist, she'd turned completely into a streetwalker, no matter how he tried to see her. It wasn't that her makeup was different. She still looked fresh and unmade-up. So what could it be? There are women who give a completely different impression in daylight and at night. Was she one of them? Or was it because he'd been drunk at the time? No, rather, could it be that today the woman must be sober, and when she gets serious, her demon's skin is stripped off? . . . What is she, this kind of woman? This person

I've been chasing feverishly in such utter confusion—wanting to make that guy Nakazawa envy me, getting all messed up myself in the process, cranking out thirty pages in four days . . .

"It's exactly one, isn't it—you are quite punctual." The woman spoke, looking at her watch, as he came up to her.

"Have you been waiting long?"

"I got here three minutes ago." As he vaguely watched out of the corner of his eye the line of foreigners troop past the two of them and start to get into an automobile, she then prompted him, "Well, what shall we do at this point—go to Honmoku?"

"That's all right with me. . . . What do you want to do?"

"Either way . . ." It was her usual curt, perfunctory tone. Mizuno began to get an increasingly strong sense that he was making a fool of himself. The scene was just what he'd been anticipating all this time, but it looked like it was going to end pathetically. She says, "Either way," so should I tell her, "Well then, please excuse me, I'm just not as interested in you as I was before." But if he did that, she might just calmly break it off herself: "Oh, yes? Well then, that's just the way it has to be." . . . But even as he hesitated, he didn't feel like retreating, since he'd come all the way out here. Oh, come on, don't say anything, and let's see what amusements develop. Don't be such a sap, whining about how pathetic it is. Come on. It's pretty good anyway, isn't it? Seeing this body again, these arms . . .

"Hey, let's go somewhere interesting."

"Fine with me. Where?"

"Don't you know some good place?"

"Can you row a boat?—I'd like to go out on the ocean."

"No, that won't work. I'm no good at any kind of exercise, boating, tennis, all of them."

"Well, then, let's go driving out in the country."

"But we have to have at least some general destination in mind. Shall we go to Kamakura by car?" Bit by bit, he was entrapping himself. "At any rate, no matter where we go, I need to get something to eat . . . there must be some great place you know in Yokohama."

"Why don't we leave right away, before that? Wouldn't it be better to eat in Kamakura?"

"That's a bit cruel, you know. I haven't had anything to eat yet today. I was worried about being late, so I rushed off to get here as soon as I got up." Mizuno said this deliberately joking, and the woman snickered in amusement.

"Well, then, we'd better go to the station restaurant."

"Instead of that—what do you like? Shouldn't we go to a place you like?"

"I'm not hungry right now. I could have a drink, though."

"How about Chinese? They say Yokohama is great for that."

"Oh ugh, no way!" The woman screwed up her face as she spoke. "Do you really eat filthy stuff like that?"

"Don't worry—it's all right, since it's all fully cooked."

"No—there's no way I'd eat it. It stinks, and it's dirty, and unsanitary . . . totally barbaric!"

"But didn't you say you'd been to Shanghai?"

"Sure, I was in Shanghai, but I never once ate even chop suey. I always stuck to Western food. So let's go to the station restaurant—that'll do."

She spoke as she continued steadily climbing the stairs, and Mizuno followed her. She opened the door to the second floor restaurant and lightly called out, "Hi there!" as if she went there all the time.

"Welcome!" Mizuno felt that the waiter was looking at him with an expression that said, "Oh, great, she's brought another peculiar guy to chew up today!" so he tried to be unobtrusive. The woman took off her coat, revealing those luscious arms.

"What will you have? Are you here for a meal?"

"He'll eat, I'll drink. Now, what shall I have? What've you got in cognacs?"

"Hennessey, Martell, that's about it.—For the Hennessey, we've got the Extra."

"I hate Hennessey. Give me the Martell." The woman went on like this, with all this sophisticated knowledge Mizuno didn't have.

"What is this stuff, this Martell? Is it different from whiskey?"

"It's cognac, is what it is."

"Cognac, is that a kind of brandy?"

"Yeah."

"That's strange. Didn't you say that you only drink whiskey?"

"When? When did I say that?"

"At the London Bar, when you caught those insurance company guys, and you said it in German. *Ich kann nur Whiskey trinken*, you said."

"I was just saying stuff to intimidate them. I pretty much like all Western liquor, but I hate Japanese saké—it makes your mouth smell. Don't you go drinking Japanese liquor today!" And the woman, with another slight gesture, crooked her little finger as she lifted her glass. "How about it? Want to try it?"

"Well, maybe I'll have some whiskey . . . ?"

"But try this. Japanese don't know the taste of brandy. When you get used to drinking it, it's much better than whiskey."

"For all the show you make of German—isn't brandy French?"

"Yes, but if you go to Germany, you find some things that are better than French. The Rhine wine they make in the Rhine valley is much tastier than French wine. Real drinkers say it's the best."

"Does that liquor come to Japan, do you suppose?"

"It does, but what you get in Japan is no good. If you don't go to the Rhine and taste the real thing there, you'll never know how good it is." Starting with her lecture on liquor, she went on to talk nostalgically about her memories of the Rhine region. Mizuno kept her company and tried what she was drinking but couldn't tell at all what was good about it. Because he was taking all this strong alcohol on an empty stomach, drunkenness came upon him quite quickly. "Get drunk fast, get drunk fast"—Mizuno drank as if he were praying this magic spell. The drunker he got, the more beautiful the woman came to appear. Her presence was so splendid, so classy, she looked as she had recently at the London Bar, like the vision he had created in his mind ever since then, not inferior to that diplomat's wife and daughter . . . hey, that's right, hasn't she been getting to seem that way bit by bit? Isn't that one of the great things about being drunk? Right? How about it? He wished he could give Nakazawa a glimpse of this. "Say, Mr. Mizuno, you're doing really well! You've finally caught her—"

"Hey, what about what you promised?" The woman suddenly spoke, as if she could read in his eyes what Mizuno was dreaming.

"Uh . . . ah . . . anytime is okay, I've got it with me."

"Well then, pass it over to me now. 'Payment in advance,' you know."

Mizuno saw that the woman's hand and pocketbook were now under the table, and so he took the bundle of bank notes out from his breast pocket and put his hand under the table like hers.

"It's all there, sixteen bills, right?"

"Right—*danke schön!*" Under the table, the clasp of the pocketbook snapped shut. At the same time, a flirtatious smile floated over her cheeks.

"How much do you make a month anyway?"

"How much do you think?"

"Between five hundred and a thousand yen?"

"Well, whether or not that's what I make, anyway I need a thousand a month for living expenses."

"What takes so much, lots of clothes?"

"My clothes are pretty low key, and generally I just buy the material and make them myself, so that doesn't take much, but there are after all the luxuries. Cars, for example—I spend around a hundred yen a month on limos."

"That *is* quite a luxury—but, you know, I spend a couple hundred or so a month myself," Mizuno added, deliberately expansive.

"You sure ride a lot. Isn't that extravagant of you, too?"

"I need it for work. For a woman it's a luxury, but for a man it's a necessity.—But if you need a thousand yen a month, well then, your former husband must have been pretty well off."

"Western men think it's perfectly normal for their wives to spend a thousand yen. And so in the West, if they don't have money, they can't get married. A Japanese man marries even if he's poor, and he leaves his wife in a miserable state. I think that's terrible. And it's the woman's fault if she goes to be his bride."

"You're right—it's her fault. They operate on the principle that love covers all poverty."

"If it were me, I'd have to get a thousand yen a month just for spending money."

"So if someone gave you that, you'd marry him?"

"I'm not saying that I wouldn't if he didn't, but Japanese men are hopeless."

"There are exceptions among Japanese men, you know. I for one like a woman with expensive tastes."

"Really? But if you tried having me as your *frau*, you'd regret it, you know—because I'm willful, wild, hard to control."

"I like a woman like that . . . makes being good to her worth the effort. It would be great to try having a wife like that at least once. Give her all the luxury she wants, let her buy whatever she wants, eat whatever fancy foods she wants, let her do whatever she wants, let her behave just as she desires—I've always dreamed of getting myself a *frau* like that. But of all the Japanese women I've seen until now, not one has been worth it. Maybe there is one, but I've never bumped into her. That's why even now I'm all by myself."

"Oh yeah? You're not married?"

"I have been, but I wised up and got rid of her, two or three years ago.—I've been on my own ever since. I intend to hold out until I can make my dream a reality."

Under the table he felt the tip of the woman's shoe touch him. On top of the table she stretched out her hand and arms as if to excite his sense of touch. As his stomach filled, a different appetite came bubbling up. His whole body was impatient. The three or four feet of table between them became an unbearable hindrance . . .

"I love your arms . . ." When they got into the car, he took the woman's hand as if he'd been eagerly waiting just for that chance, and loosely swung her arm back and forth. "When we met at the London Bar that time, it was your arms that seduced me. They are truly magnificent, truly!"

"Everyone says that, that my arms are great—"

"They *are* great! It's a pleasure just to swing them like this. I'd like to make them into a toy and swing them forever."

"If you want, make me into a toy."

"It doesn't bother you? To have me hanging on you so much like this . . . ?"

"Not at all—I like having guys hanging on me."

When Mizuno was young, he had, like all literary-minded young men, talked often about "platonic love," but he'd never actually had the experience of true spiritual love. He was a kind of woman worshipper. But as is the case with men of this type, because they dream of a woman as so beautiful, so nearly like a goddess, when they encounter the reality they always feel disillusioned. For a man, when a woman loses her divinity, there is nothing else but for her to become a plaything. For Mizuno, the women with whom he'd been in any relationship approaching romantic had all been nothing more than toys. It was something like love, but not real love. He didn't know what real love was, so he didn't know how it was different, but at any rate it surely was not this tepid thing. As a poor man envies a rich man, he vaguely imagined that true romantic love would be such that the pleasure would be shared mutually soul to soul, that there would be rapture to the depths of his soul. It was ridiculous that he should be near forty and still be thinking such things, but although he'd touched the skin of many women up to this day, he'd never touched the "heart" of a woman. And he realized that it was not the woman's fault but rather some spiritual element lacking in him, and that sometimes made him sad. He'd just never known a love that could raise him from the earthly plane to a heavenly realm. He didn't understand ecstatic joy, a state of self-abandonment. And he would gradually age, and finally die without having tasted it. That dissatisfaction was always in his head. Every time he got another woman, he was in a fever: this time will do it, this time . . . And these days he'd been getting sloppy: when he was in his cups he'd even delude himself so that no matter who he got his hands on—a geisha, a prostitute—he would "fall in love" for no reason at all. With the energy of drunkenness he would elevate some worthless woman to the status of an ideal and pile on nauseating flattery, play up to her, tease her, sigh deep sighs, and do such stupid things that even he could hardly believe his own acting. But however clever his performance was, nonsense is nonsense after all, and true intoxication was hardly likely to bubble up from such love. As drunk as he seemed to be, somewhere at the core his heart was always stone cold sober. Whenever he started to heat up, immediately he heard a voice coming from himself, insulting him, and his passion would sputter out and disappear. . . .

"Do you really feel that you could become my toy for me?"

"It's not that I'd be doing you a favor. Although you are swinging my arm like crazy . . ."

"No, what I'm talking about is not arms."

"Not just arms—you could make any part of me your toy."

"Being a toy is complicated, you know. I've made a number of women into toys before now, and not one of them was able to do it completely. I think you might be able to do it, but . . ."

"What is it, that you're looking for?"

"Do you think you can truly get me totally drunk? Theater, nonsense, anything would be fine, however you do it, could you pretend and make it seem to me like real love? If you could do that, I'd pay you as much as you want . . ."

"Well then, give me your order. What kind of woman do you want?"

"Are you saying you could become any kind of woman?"

"I'm pretty sure I can. If I couldn't, I wouldn't be able to make my living as I do, you know." The woman spoke with full confidence, in tones that showed a fundamental understanding of her profession.

Before long, the car passed through the town of ramshackle houses, with the sea spreading out broadly on the left side. In the hillsides on the right, raw red scars gouged the earth, still left from the landslides during the earthquake. These things swept through his field of vision. As the car raced on, he could feel his heart pounding along with it.

"The man I was with, that German man? He had some unusual tastes, and he had a number of orders for me."

"Orders . . . ?"

"For example, he liked to hear a woman crying—not wailing out loud, but sniffling along quietly, as if she were whispering. . . . He said that gave him pleasure."

"So you did what you were told?"

"I sure did. I cried really well for him. There's no woman who cries as well as you, he said to me, and as a result he was very good to me. When I cried particularly well, afterward he'd be in a great mood, and he'd buy me a new dress or other stuff."

"The guy sounds like some kind of pervert."

"All men are perverts. Some of them are even weirder, but for the most part I do what they order, if it's not too off the wall. One man told me he wanted me to be a deaf-mute."

"Why?"

"He said that hearing people talk bothered him. He was extremely moody, but shy on top of that, and he said to me, I don't need to hear you, it's enough for you to be a silent toy."

"That's impressive—he knew just what he wanted. Of course he was a Westerner, right?"

"Right. Japanese men don't have very complicated needs. They're pretty conventional and boring. 'Love' is a kind of theater, and it doesn't work if you haven't thought out the plot."

"Well then, I'd like to have you work out a plot for me."

"Just what kind of woman do you want me to be?"

"When I make love to a woman I always feel regret afterward, and I get sad. Even right in the instant, I've never been so carried away that I lost track of where I was. I always feel somewhere that this is not real love, it's a fake."

"These days there isn't any such thing as real love. We're all acting, you know.—What it comes down to is, you're just not good at theater."

"Could be. But it also depends on the actress."

"I'm a fabulous actress, you can rely on that.—And I'll write you a script that will always interest you, with turns and changes."

"Turns, and colors . . ."

"It'll be Technicolor."

Mizuno placed the woman's hand flat on his knee and fiddled with her ring and middle fingers as if making a twisted paper string.

8

Mizuno spent the next four days in a totally different world. The chains that had bound his life so far were sundered on that day, and from then on, like a book with blank pages, he became a void. During that time, what they did, how they did it, where they spent the time—from the day the two of them went by car to Kamakura, he was ceaselessly riding in something, continually shaken back and forth, always running. In his youth he had done quite a bit of wandering, and he recalled that there had been times when he stayed for three or four days straight in the pleasure quarters. But by the time he reached thirty-five or so, inevitably he had settled down a bit, and even when he did overindulge, he exercised a certain degree of control, for he no longer had the physical stamina he'd had in the full flush of youth. But this was now, and while he was dead tired, and even in danger of collapsing on the street or even dying, still he continued to be dragged along, covered with dust. Those four days were for him a literal "world wrapped in darkness." He felt that he never saw the light of day the whole time. When he set out for Yokohama on the morning of that day the sky was blue, but after that the only sky was the woman's body, the sun after that was her smoldering eyes. When they got to the place where they were to stay the night in Kamakura, the woman said there was no way they could stay there and they should return to her place instead; by the time he was dragged back to Honmoku, it was past midnight. When she opened the rear entrance in the dirty little alley and he went up to the second floor, what surprised him was how it had been set up. The woman pinned back the divider curtain and showed him the fully mirrored display alcove wall. . . . Stimulants, anesthetics, liquor that would drive a man wild—she brought them all out and said, "I've got lots more to make sure you won't get bored." The next morning, he handed over to her all the surplus money he'd brought, and it's true that he pressed her to let him stay another night, but day and night got completely turned around, and he didn't know when the next day came. Sometimes he slept and when he awoke the woman would be doing something in the next room, or she'd have gone somewhere to make a phone call, always busy at something. And then she asked him, "Oh, you're awake? Did you have a good sleep?" and she would once more work her magic on him. From time to time she changed the color of the lights, and with the red or purple or yellow, she became different women. The woman to a man, the man to a woman, like an animal, like a god—every time he slept some, the plot and scene changed. On the evening of the second day he returned to Tokyo and pawned his plated watch, managing to get fifty yen. Of course he did not stop at his boardinghouse, but he could see even in the face of the clerk at the pawnshop, where he was known by sight as a frequent customer, that somehow he had changed. It amazed him that the clerk remembered. He did feel that he was a completely different man, and it seemed to him that it would be natural if someone didn't recognize him. That evening he again crawled into bed in a room at the Marunouchi hotel and slept like the dead until the morning of the day after the next day. But as he slept, he continued to be assailed mercilessly by fantasies. The red woman, and the purple, kept chasing him forever. He was driven crazy with a feeling that every possible joint ached, and even as he slept on, he sensed that his body was rotting away completely.

He was intensely tired, but he didn't feel it all that much the next day, but in the second and third days the exhaustion gradually spread through his body. By the morning of the third day he could feel the result of the shocks of the day before the day before even more strongly in all his joints. Why then did he want to go back to see the woman again when he got up from the bed? Where in his body did he still have that much strength? Did he value so much the promise that they were to meet this day, too? Was it that he hated wasting the money he'd already spent? Or was this the continuation of the dream that had assaulted him for two days and two nights?—Rather than finding the woman loveable, he thought of her as frightening. Being with her meant not entertainment but that he was going to be severely whipped all over his body. Imagine a person at the top of a tall building or on the edge of a cliff: his body twitches and he wants to throw himself off. That's very much what the feeling was like for him. But at the same time as he found the game terrifying, he was strangely enough dragged toward it. So half unconscious he called the clerk, paid his bill, retrieved the bulldog-head walking stick he'd left behind the time before, and staggered into the elevator. When the iron folding gate clattered shut, enclosing him in the box, he instantly thought of a prison cell. He felt as if the two of them were all alone, just the two of them, in a box like this. Suddenly the elevator started to drop from the fourth floor. Feeling his head swimming, he clung to the walls with both his hands.

Because their agreed-upon meeting time that day was 4:00 P.M., the underground passageway at Sakuragicho was already dark. The lips of the woman standing at the ticket gate struck his attention before anything else. She was wearing a squirrel-fur coat with a bag hanging from her hands. It made him think of a whip.

"Exactly four, you're right on time today," she said, repeating her earlier comment. "Are you okay? You're looking a bit pale," she asked smugly.

No matter what she asked, Mizuno said almost nothing. Silently he went where the woman was going, collapsed where she lay down. His body was like a piece of taffy or a lump of clay. . . . "You've gone mute; that's good," the woman said. Then as if tearing off clay, she pried open his mouth with both hands and poured liquor in. He drank and drank but didn't get the least bit intoxicated. Nor did he get excited. All that happened was that he got a headache, his face grew more and more pale, and his strength flagged. Thereupon she smeared a mysterious white butter-like massage cream over his hands and feet. He began for the first time to feel some sort of stimulation. At once his clay-like dead flesh revived.

"Well then, until next Tuesday, and in the meantime do something about your pale face."

By the time he left her voice, tinged with derision, behind on the second floor and went down the stairs, it was six in the morning of the next day. Although the woman had said she was good until noon, he went out the front as if fleeing. Where he was going, how he made it, he couldn't say, but at any rate he managed to get to the terminus at Honmoku and returned to the station by streetcar. All that was left in his breast pocket was enough money to get him back to Tokyo.

"To Yushima," he said as he got into the small cab and then dropped onto the narrow seat as if collapsing and fell asleep.

How much time passed? From time to time in a state between sleep and awake, he felt a thump and the car swerving left or right; but finally it seemed to have stopped somewhere, and he heard, "Hello . . . hey, hello . . ." The taxi driver put his head out the window and asked, "Hey, where do you want me to let you off?"

"I'm going to Yushima."

"We're at Yushima. Where are you going to?"

"Where are we? Where is this? Part way up the hill?" All he could see with his sleep-fogged eyes was the eaves of one house after another, and he had absolutely no idea of where they were. The echo of the trembling earth as a crowded streetcar raced by right before him reverberated in his ears.

"We're right at the very top of the hill."

"Well then, go another two or three blocks, and there should be a barbershop on the left side, and the baker . . ."

"Yes . . ."

"At the corner of the barbershop, there's a mailbox, and at the corner just before that, there's a hardware store . . . turn left there. And the third building on the right is a boardinghouse."

By the time the car stopped in front of the boardinghouse he had finally roused himself. He told the driver, "I'll pay you in a minute, so wait here a bit," and just like that he went straight up to the second floor. He got his futon ready by himself and crawled in, and then called the maid.

"Oh, you're back?"

"Sorry, but there's a taxi waiting at the gate . . ."

"So, you're going out again?"

"That's not it. I haven't paid him yet, so tell them at the front to take care of it and have them put it on my bill." The old man will probably grumble about that again. There's no way he'll be happy about paying it for me, so I'd better get into bed before he shows up. . . . Before he even had time to finish the thought and while the maid's footsteps were still echoing in the hall, he immediately fell sound asleep.

But his sleep was unexpectedly short, and around eleven his eyes popped open. He'd left Yokohama about six, so it must have been around eight when he got here. He'd slept only three hours. However soundly he'd slept, and the sleepiness still remained, still he'd awakened at eleven, as was his habit. He was much more tired than when he'd collapsed on the hotel bed the time before, but this time he didn't feel it that much. Then his whole body had hurt, but this morning the pain was gone as if swept away. There was no dull ache in the back of his head; instead, his head felt quite clear. It's just that his body seemed to have gotten too light, and—shall we call it the will to live, or his vital energy—something fundamental and crucial was completely gone from him. Mightn't this be what it felt like to lose a quart of blood? He was lying down so he was okay, but if he stood up and tried to walk he was sure he'd be staggering. At any rate, the fact that he didn't feel tired was eerie. The exhaustion the time before had reached its height on the third day, so this time it would take even longer and not reach the crisis point for a week or more, probably. The only thing that bothered him at this point was that his mouth was extremely sore because he'd been forced to drink so many different things. Maybe if I have a smoke, he thought, and stretched out just his hand from the bedclothes and fumbled around the pillow— at which point he felt not his cigarettes but something dry that rustled. It would seem that while he was sleeping the servant girl had brought several letters and two or three days' worth of newspapers that had come during his absence. He quickly pulled back his hand, scrunched up his neck and burrowed even deeper into the futon.

Undoubtedly there could be nothing good in the letters that had come while he was away. From what he'd touched, he could tell there were five or six of them, but most were probably from

Nakazawa. He must have been wondering where I'd disappeared to ever since I left him at Nihonbashi, and when I'd not shown up for two days, and then three, the guy must've gone crazy and wildly sent me one letter after another. They would be marked "ASAP— Confidential" or "Extremely Urgent!!!" written in red ink and double circled. Just to see the hasty, furious writing on the envelope would tell the content of the letter without reading, and when he thought of the pile of them pressing in on him at his pillow, he didn't feel much like extending his neck again. But of course he couldn't stay like this forever; at some point he'd have to pick them up, and once he did that, he'd certainly want to read them. Wasn't there some way he could bury them without reading them? . . . With his head still pulled in he just put out his hand once again and touched the letters. There were only three. One was in a rectangular Western-style envelope; the other two, Japanese. *The People* used smooth, waxy paper, so these would seem not to be from them. He resolutely brought the three letters into bed, and letting in just a little crack of light as he first took up one of the Japanese envelopes, he fearfully turned it over.

The printed address identified the sender as "—— Prefecture —— County —— Town Library." This was most probably a form letter "Requesting a Donation from the Author." The other, also printed, was from "*Queen* Editorial Department," maybe a commission for a manuscript from a women's magazine. The remaining one, the Western envelope, had the addressee's name written in pen and no return address. This was most likely from some reader he didn't know, he thought, but nevertheless he slit it open. It held only a little piece of paper, maybe one inch by two inches. It was a clipping from somewhere: "Nakajiro Cojima (35), formerly a reporter for *XX* women's magazine, was discovered dead by passers-by near dawn yesterday around 6:00 A.M. at a spot some distance from his house in Urawa, Saitama Prefecture. Murder is suspected, and a major investigation is currently under way." Aha, this must be a clipping from my story. No, wait, it's not—the layout is different from *The People*'s fiction column. Well then, is this an article from a newspaper? No, mightn't someone have printed it specifically as a malicious joke? This must be Nakazawa's work. . . .

He gradually made the opening in the covers bigger as he continued to read, and before he realized it, he brought his head out to look at the clipping in full light. He noticed that on the back was written in pencil, "November 26 *Tokyo Asahi Shimbun* morning edition article." He opened the *Asahi* newspaper that lay beside his pillow. At the bottom of page seven was a small headline: "Former Women's Magazine Reporter Killed." It was indeed that very article. He lit a cigarette and as he slowly, calmly, smoked, he reread it. But no matter how many times he read it, it was always the same. Without a doubt it was printed there just that way.

"Hah, so I'm a fortune teller." He gave a brief ironic laugh. That his prophecy had come true did in fact make him want to crow. For a moment he remembered Cojima's face in the shadows and the white monkey jumping on the screen in the movie *Chang*. But strangely, that was not enough to make his heart beat faster or to change the color in his face.

He continued to puff away at his cigarette as he thought, even though it had gone out. Then he lit a new one and again gazed at the printed page. "Nakajiro Cojima (35)"—so there was no doubt, the man had been killed. The article made the fact unassailable. That singular, ambiguous presence had vanished from the earth. But in the face of this somehow immutable fact, it was met with no commensurate serious, appropriate response at all. In the case of a murder article, if it has great social value, it is mentioned in especially large type, covering two or three columns, so it catches people's attention. But to have such a small headline and do it in such a writing style—one or two people might see it, hardly any would read it fully, and even if they read it, they'd immediately forget it. Cojima's death counted for nothing more than the impression the article gave. In other words, it was a death on the face of the printed page. From that perspective, it was the same as a death in a novel. No, in fact the reporter who wrote this article probably didn't even use his imagination as much as a novelist would. He might have merely pushed his pen mechanically, no more than if it had been the most ordinary, pedestrian work. All the same, that even the phrasing was the same as his was strange. Maybe there was a standard pattern for such things, so that it would come out like this no matter who wrote it, but somehow when he read it he felt that it was from his own story. Surely the newspaper wasn't making fun of him, but given how accustomed he was to using various models in his stories, the separation between reality and made-up stories was not as clear as the average person might think. Whether he died in real life or in a story, there wasn't much of a difference, he found himself thinking.

But who had sent him the clipping, the sender of the Western envelope? Since it was from this morning's paper, he must certainly have cut it out very early and dropped it in a mailbox somewhere in this neighborhood. The postmark wasn't clear, but it has to be the work of someone in Hongo, or Shitaya, or Koishikawa, or maybe Kanda. Could it be Nakazawa after all? This business of deliberately using a Western-style envelope—there's something fishy about it. If not Nakazawa—it could be the doing of the Shadow Man, the man who killed Cojima.

The sliding door opened and the servant girl brought in lighted charcoal for the brazier. Usually he joked with her, but this morning, he affected a cool, calm pose.

"Hey, when did this letter come?"

"It came this morning."

"When, this morning?"

"It was just a little while ago. When I brought it in to you, you were sleeping, so I left it there."

"Hmm . . . so it was after I got back, right?"

"Yes."

"I suppose Nakazawa came while I was away?"

"He did come."

"About how many times?"

"Once."

"Once?"

"Yes."

"Just once?"

"Yes."

"That's really strange. When did he come?"

"Remember three or four days ago, you went out together? It was morning of the next day."

"That was it—he never came again?"

"Yes."

"And phone?"

"He didn't call."

"No one else came?"

"No, no one else."

This was getting stranger and stranger, and why? When he was coming by all the time pressing and pestering him, Mizuno was exasperated and disgusted, but now he felt uneasy to be hearing nothing. This Nakazawa—had he finally just had enough? Or had he taken the blame and resigned, or been fired? That would be too bad. If he had caused Nakazawa to lose his job, he couldn't say that he felt no remorse. But whatever the situation with Nakazawa was, it shouldn't all end just like this; whether another editor took his place or something, there should have been some sort of hard negotiation over a conclusion like that. And so it was quite strange that there hadn't even been a phone call. Had they all given up on him, from the owner to the employees, and tossed him out? At any rate, to have gone so completely silent was no trivial thing. There had to be some sort of story here.

"When Nakazawa came, how did he look? He must have been angry, right?"

"Well, now, I don't really know because I didn't see him."

"Who answered the door?"

"I don't know who answered, but when the visitor was told you were out, he asked if the landlord was home, and he spoke to the landlord and then left, I heard."

Hmm, so that's it, they told the old man something. If I ask him I can get a sense of how things stand, but it is a pain to have to talk about something like that with him. Shall I phone and try to check it out indirectly?—No, wait, wait. If they've gone silent, I should pretend I don't know anything and just leave it as is. Whatever, for sure I should send something off quickly. By this time, the damn old man may have already informed against me by phone. He might have taken it upon himself to give play-by-play reports on me: "He returned this morning," or "He's sleeping now," or "He seems to be getting up." They might be discussing me: "So he's awake?" "Yes, he's up." "Well then, I'm coming right over. Don't let him go anywhere." "Right, I won't let him get away this time. I've got him caught tight, so come over quickly." And then pretty soon some editor will come racing over, his veins standing out in rage . . .

With this as his secret guess—even somehow feeling extremely entertained about it—Mizuno ate his lunch with composure. But an hour passed, and then two, yet the phone did not ring and no one came to visit. Maybe the old man would intervene if he made a show of going out, he thought, and tested by putting on his coat, deliberately clomping down the stairs, passing by the front desk, lingering at the shoe cabinet, and then starting to leave by the front;

but the old man just opened the glass sliding door a little, glanced out, and said nothing. So he left intending to go to the bathhouse, clutching his soapbox, towel, and bathhouse pass in the breast of his coat, and had a good long soak for a least an hour. He returned feeling refreshed for the first time in quite a while, but still no one said anything. A bit drained by the steam, and maybe because his body was comfortably warm, he felt the several days of accumulated exhaustion hidden deep inside him gradually lead to a sensation of lassitude that spread over his whole body, and just as soon as he threw himself down on his futon, he again fell into a deep sleep.

When his eyes opened in the evening, his head felt heavy. This morning his whole body had seemed to be floating lightly, but that clearly had been only temporary, and, as if he'd developed a fever while he was asleep, now the heavy dullness of a sick person spread through his hands and feet. His stomach seemed not to be working right, and he realized that the lunch he'd eaten that long ago was stuck in his breast undigested. He felt like a lump, like he might just stay in bed like this. His eyelids seemed swollen, his face bloated. He took out the hand mirror he'd stuck in a corner of the bookcase and looked at himself. His color was bad, his cheeks were in fact even more sunken in his emaciated face, and his lips were dry and chapped. At this point, shall I go get a shave? . . . Oh yeah, what happened to that safety razor I got, I wonder. I'm sure I put it in the pocket of my coat, but . . . He stood up, went over to his Inverness coat hanging on the wall, and searched around in the inside pocket. His hand touched the flat nickel box that held the Gillette. He thought about it and realized that most of the money he'd made up to this point had vanished without a trace, and all he had left was this Gillette and the bulldog-head cane, but he was lucky to have not forgotten at least this much and brought them home. He sat in front of the bookcase again and clicked the nickel case open and shut, assembled the parts of the razor and took them apart, while all the time in his head totally different fragments passed as dreams. Then suddenly he remembered those three volumes of Brandes, and taking them down from the bookcase, he flipped through the pages. It would have been great if even a five-yen note had slipped out for him, but Brandes was not likely to produce such a stroke of luck, and of course such a fine thing was just not going to happen. . . .

Their next meeting was the coming Tuesday, but if he didn't have even train fare to get to Yokohama, it just wasn't going to happen. So he had no choice but to write some more manuscript pages. But he wondered if there wasn't some way to compromise with *The People* without losing face. The company has fought with me, and the manuscript fees they've paid so far have come to nothing, so maybe I should try to get in touch with them. If I meet them halfway, maybe even if they grumble a bit they'll actually be relieved. I should try phoning them first to see how things are going. No, wait, if I call first that would be a surrender. If I show weakness they'll be sure to apply all kinds of limitations and conditions: We won't pay you this time until you deliver a complete manuscript, or We're going to keep an even closer watch over you. I should probably continue to hold out and let them blow off steam. . . . But if I do that, what about the cash for next Tuesday? . . .

He kept praying they would call as he went back and forth to the head of the stairs, trying to make up his mind. Finally he couldn't stand it anymore and went down to the phone. But for some reason, it just rang and rang, and although he called several times, no one picked up at *The People*. He called the operator and argued with her until finally she tried and got someone. He asked, "Is this *The People*?"

The person answered, "Yeah"—a blank voice he didn't recognize.

"Is Mr. Nakazawa there?"

"Yah, so who are you?"

"This is Mizuno—Mizuno."

"Yah, Mr. Mizuno—"

"Yes, if Mr. Nakazawa is there, please get him to the phone."

"Yah, your business?"

"Well, it's something I can't explain unless I talk to him directly . . ."

"Yah, yah, well, hold on."

He seemed to be an office boy or something, and after going away for a moment, he came right back on.

"They say Mr. Nakazawa left about twenty minutes ago."

"Well then, anyone else's okay, would you get me someone from the editorial department?"

"All the editors are gone."

"Now that's a problem—how about Mr. Harada?"

"Mr. Harada isn't here either."

"Isn't there anyone there? Anyone would do."

"No one's here."

"Ah, I see. . . . Well then, I'll call again, but tell them tomorrow that at least I called."

He'd said Nakazawa had left around twenty minutes ago, so at any rate it was clear that he hadn't been fired, but if that was so, then it was even stranger that he'd not come by the boardinghouse at all. For that matter, the office boy's tone had been distinctly unaccommodating, so somehow the situation was different from usual. If the company had been in an uproar searching for his whereabouts, and that had caused the owner to fly into a rage, there was probably no way that even the office boy wouldn't have gotten a faint hint of it. And then he hadn't been surprised when he said, "It's Mizuno," and there was that "Your business?" Under ordinary circumstances, he would have dashed away to let the

owner know, but for him to be so calm—call it vague, disconnected?—wasn't it almost as if he'd been told, "If Mr. Mizuno
calls, don't engage with him." Might he even have been ordered
to treat him almost as if saying, "The company has no need of you
anymore"? If he was right about this, things were going to be a bit
tough from here on. He would have to go out, face the owner, hang
his head, and maybe even proffer a written apology; otherwise
things might not get fixed up.

Well, let's give it another day, he thought, and went to bed
early that night. It was a measure of how tired he was that even
though he'd slept quite a bit during the day, he could still sleep so
much. His eyes opened the next morning at eleven. He stretched
out his hand and felt beside the pillow, but there was nothing
but the newspaper, and not a single piece of mail this morning.
He didn't really have many friends, so it was not unusual for him
to get no letters, but—was it because he'd done something bad?—
he'd felt ever since the phone call yesterday that he'd been cast
aside by the world, and he felt strangely desolate. He'd expected
Nakazawa to show up, and nothing had come from him. He
tried at least to catch the maids and joke with them, but even they
seemed to be distancing themselves from him, and he wondered
if they'd been warned off by the old man.

"Say, come on in, sit down here." The maid had brought his
lunch tray in and seemed to be in a hurry to leave when he called
her to stop.

"Do you want something?"

"Your coolness is quite irritating.—Come on, guess where I've
been."

She snickered.

"What are you snickering about?" She snickered again. She's
laughing at me, he thought; she left as if she was fleeing.

In the afternoon mail there was a single piece of mail. It was another Western-style envelope, unsealed, and there was no return address. What emerged from it was a printed card with the following formal message:

This is to inform you that despite all medical treatment, my father Nakajiro died after a long illness this month on the twenty-fifth at 10:00 P.M.

The funeral will be held on the upcoming twenty-ninth (Tuesday) from two to three in the afternoon at Yanaka Funeral Hall.

Cojima Teruo

It was quite a delay to have a funeral on the twenty-ninth for a death on the twenty-fifth, but then, the body probably had to be sent to the metropolitan police headquarters for examination and autopsy. Since he'd gotten this notice it would be bad if he didn't go to the funeral and offer an incense stick, but what kind of karmic connection was there between them, Mizuno wondered. What were Cojima's survivors thinking, to have sent him this announcement? Where would they have heard of an association between the dead man and himself? Had they found Mizuno's name in Cojima's address book or something like that and sent it without a thought? But they'd never in their lives exchanged letters, so probably Cojima wouldn't have written down Mizuno's name and address in his book. So maybe someone had suggested it to the family and ironically, on purpose, had had them send it. Mightn't there be someone who planned it as a nasty joke, just to see how this Mizuno presented himself, coming to the funeral . . .

He took up the morning newspaper, scattered around on the floor, and opened it to page seven. To tell the truth, he had been a bit worried yesterday, so he had covertly looked for articles about it, but the news of Cojima had appeared only in the morning edition of the twenty-sixth, and there were no follow-up articles in either that day's evening edition or the next day's morning and evening papers. Of course that might be because it wasn't deemed newsworthy enough, but given that "major investigation for the criminal presently under way," there was nothing about whether the criminal had been arrested or, if not, whether they had some general clues, or a grudge was suspected as the motive, or it looked like a robbery, or it could have been a mistake—there was absolutely no report on any such circumstances. Until just ten days ago, Mizuno had been so hideously tormented, to a degree that he himself now found almost comical. Yet now that his obsessive thoughts had become fact and Cojima had been killed, maybe because the incident with the Honmoku woman had in the meantime gotten sandwiched in, and their contact seemed to have petered out, he didn't at this point seem to be frightened or even regard the situation as very serious. The fact was that he did have this tendency to try as much as possible to bury his fears. All severely neurotic people fixate on and fear utterly ridiculous things even though there is no rational object. But they can be distracted, so if they get good at being able to turn their feelings around, then also for no apparent reason their fears and worries can quiet down and go away. Mizuno knew that about himself, and he had a suspicion that it was precisely in order to forget about Cojima that he had made such a big deal about the Honmoku thing and had gotten so intensely involved with it.

But as he looked at the showy death notice lying here right before his eyes, there was no way he could prevent the hidden fears he had pushed down beneath his consciousness from gradually creeping stealthily upward to the surface of his heart. In his childhood, when he walked on dark roads and the like, he would hear an eerie scratchy noise behind him, following him all the time. If he would turn around, he'd see what it was, but the child didn't have the courage to do that, and while he forced himself to feel calm by thinking it was the rustling of the leaves or the wind passing through the tops of the trees, it became a sound that couldn't be the wind. And even as he came to realize that it was without a doubt a shape-changing fox, or a badger, or a bogeyman, he tried anyway to drown it out with his own footsteps or fool it by humming a tune. But as he hurried his pace along, the sound behind him got closer and closer, came right up to his shoulder, and in the end a giant monster big enough to pierce the clouds suddenly stood in his way, right before his very eyes. The child shrieked wildly and fell on his bottom. Mizuno had been getting the feeling recently that there was a black shadow stealthily dogging his footsteps. Having no news from Nakazawa, having that strange exchange on the phone with *The People*, with the boardinghouse old man glaring at him silently, the maids treating him brusquely and not willing to joke with him at all—in essence, being treated as if the whole world had by agreement cast him aside. . . . And although his own behavior had exhausted all goodwill toward him, that might not be the only reason. Mightn't there indeed be some other larger, more nefarious reason? As of now, it hadn't taken the form of direct suspicion, but suspicious glances were being cast his way from everywhere, and couldn't that be why everything around him had gone quiet as the grave? . . . Mizuno's head, try as he might not to think about it, at some point had become filled with this black shadow. There was no way he could make his nerves turn in any other direction. He tried every which way to recollect disembodied bits of Fraülein's flesh, her arms, her feet, her body, and tried to immerse himself in those imaginings, but before he realized it, the woman's phantasm turned into Cojima.

If people truly were suspecting him, who was the person who started the rumor? The relationship between himself and the models in his stories—once Cojima was dead, there could have been hardly anyone who knew. If there were, it was only one or two. For knowledge of it to spread around their world, for it to have changed the attitude of the maids in the boardinghouse, there had to have been someone who set afloat the whole issue of the model in "To the Point of Murder." If the situation had progressed to that point, it would have reached the ears of the police and the newspapers, yet why hadn't there been any direct contact from any direction? Or maybe while he himself was unaware of it, his personal life was quietly being investigated. That would be no surprise. Since he last met with Cojima on the fifteenth, someone could have known generally about his whereabouts. The most problematic part would be his activities surrounding the twenty-fifth when the crime had occurred, but if it got to court, he would be able to present the Honmoku woman as his witness. . . . He'd promised to keep their relationship secret, but hell, if it came to that, surely she wouldn't deny it. . . . No, wait a minute, if her own prostitution activities were made public, she'd be guilty of a crime, too, and so she'd probably put Western-style self-interest right up front and cruelly pretend to know nothing. . . . She did, after all, seem to have such a mercenary aspect to her. . . .

At this point his face suddenly paled when he realized that if he were to be taken into custody today and were questioned about the events of the night of the twenty-fifth, he would inevitably have to explain that he was at the woman's house in Honmoku. Then the prosecutor would ask, "Who was the woman whose house you were at?" And he would not be able to answer that question. He didn't know her name. "Well then, what about her address?"—That would be the next question. But he couldn't answer that either. "Well, at least you must know how to get there, let's have you take us there."—Even if he were asked that, it was quite doubtful whether or not he could take the prosecutor to the woman's house. He had been there three times so far, and each time he'd been there for at least three or four hours, once for more than ten hours, so he knew the inside of the house well. He also had a fair sense of what the outside looked like. But when he thought hard about it, he realized that he had just a general sense of the neighborhood—he hadn't the slightest idea of where to turn from the streetcar road, or what number on what street it was. In addition to not knowing much about the Honmoku area, whenever he'd gone or returned home, it was always dark, late at night, or very early in the morning. It's not that she insisted on it, but that's just the way it worked out. And usually they'd go as far as possible by car and walk the rest of the way, but it wasn't clear where the car had stopped. To be sure, if he could figure that out, the woman's house was only two or three blocks from there, and he imagined that if he just walked around aimlessly he'd find it. But they'd gone in and out of so many identical squalid little alleys, that without actually going there and trying, he couldn't even guess whether or not he'd figure it out. If he didn't find it and could only wander around here and there, he would be even more suspicious to the prosecutor. You don't know where she lives, you don't know her proper name, and you've just been enjoying yourself recently with her as a "contract mistress"? I've never heard of something so crazy. Do you actually know *anything* about her?—What could he answer? She knows German, she originally had a German husband, she once lived with her husband in Hamburg—that's absolutely all he knew. And since he had only her word for it, could he even trust that? Other than that, she frequented the Café Monaco on the Ginza, and the waiter at the Sakuragicho station restaurant knew her—he could offer that, but what would he do if neither Monaco nor the waiter knew where she lived? Even supposing they knew, if the woman firmly denied a relationship with him, was there anyone who would testify that he was in fact at the woman's house on the night of the twenty-fifth? The people who lived downstairs from the woman on the second floor—would they question them? But since they'd never met face-to-face, it would probably be difficult for them to say positively who was on the second floor that night. "We heard a man's voice and woman's. That's all we know." That's probably all they could say. So the next time they met, it was essential that he note down the street and number of the house. But that was tomorrow, Tuesday, at the same time as Cojima's funeral. Furthermore, he was to meet the woman at one o'clock, and the funeral was from two to three, so he'd have to give up one or the other.

Of course, he didn't have a close relationship with Cojima and therefore had no obligation to go to the funeral, so it would make sense to give that up, but he had no little desire to see how it went. If he met with the family he might learn more of the circumstances of Cojima's murder, what's happened since, whether there is any information about the murderer, things that you wouldn't know from the newspapers, and he might be able to get a general sense of how they regarded him and learn why they had sent him the death notice. He didn't have a wide circle of friends, but he was more or less connected to the literary world, and there might be a few faces Mizuno knew at the funeral. He wanted to see what the attitude of the whole crowd was toward him. But now he worried again about the Honmoku situation if he did that. He had no special need to have it tomorrow at one, so it would be all right to move it a day later, but he had no way of letting her know. If he were to break their agreement even temporarily, what on earth would she do? She said she wouldn't wait more than fifteen minutes past the appointed time, so having to wait just that much probably wouldn't make her too angry, but then there'd be no chance to arrange the next assignation. The next meeting after tomorrow would be Friday, but if he didn't say anything, would she be there for him at 1:00 P.M. at Sakuragicho? If she used to-morrow's breach of promise as grounds for cutting off their con-nection, that would be horrible. So obviously it would be better to go tomorrow, wouldn't it? The funeral lasted until three, so maybe he could meet her at Sakuragicho at one, tell her the situation then quickly go back to Yanaka, and then, when the funeral was over, maybe he could return to Sakuragicho? Of course by then it would be late in the day and not the best situation for checking out the Honmoku route, but the next day he could investigate at his leisure in the daylight. Depending on how things went, if he told her honestly that this was a special case where he needed her to vouch for him, he could appeal to her generosity.

He got this far in his thinking, then suddenly he had another thought: one thing I could do would be to go to Honmoku to-night and see what happens. If I go now, it's questionable whether or not she would be home, and even if she was, if she'd see me, but even if she weren't home, I could leave a note for her, and that would be good enough. After all, if I go out alone and by good chance manage to locate the house, that would accomplish one part of my objective.

Gradually he came to the conclusion that this was what he should do, and so he took up his pencil and worked on a draft of the note to leave:

Tonight something came up suddenly to make me have to change our appointment. It is for that purpose that I have suddenly come to visit you here. "I" am the man who has been meeting with you on Tuesdays and Fridays. The man who has been calling you "Fraülein Hindenburg." I appeal to you to not blame me too harshly for selfishly coming to visit you at a time that is not our appointed time. In other words, some crucial business has just suddenly popped up,

so there is absolutely no way that I can get to Sakuragicho at
one o'clock tomorrow. Accordingly, I'd like to make it 5:00 P.M.
Please be sure to be at Sakuragicho at that time.

As usual, he wrote and rewrote it over and over again. And
then, after that, he added:

As you can see, there is a name printed outside the margins
of this manuscript paper. This is the name of a certain writer.
I can leave to your imagination, without explaining, the relationship between that person and myself. Details when I
see you tomorrow.

Then, thinking it was better to let her imagine without his
writing anything, he erased it again. And then he wrote on the front
of the envelope, Fraülein Hindenburg.

9

He wanted to go while it was still light, but he always lingered and killed time between making a decision and executing it, so it was after four when he finally left the boardinghouse. Before he left, he gathered together the same ten volumes of Brandes he'd been using, tied them up in a bundle, took them to a used book store in Morikawa-cho, and got enough for train and car fare to Sakuragicho. By the time he did all this and got there it must have been around seven. To get something to eat as well, he went up to the station restaurant.

"Good evening, are you alone tonight?" the waiter said. Using this as his opening, Mizuno asked where the woman lived, but the waiter gave only an extremely vague answer: "Well now, the lady seems to have a number of houses here and there."

"No, there's one in Honmoku, right? I'd like to get a general idea of where it is."

"Really? Have you ever been there, sir?"

"Of course I have, but she brought me to a part of Yokohama I'm not familiar with, and it was always late at night, so I didn't know where we were. We went by car, and after we got out, we walked some more, but I couldn't tell clearly where it was that we got out."

"How about if you try asking the driver? It was a taxi in front of the station, right?"

"No, not there. She said she hated taxis and called one from a garage somewhere."

"Well then, it'd be a cinch to ask at the garage."

"I don't know what garage it is. The woman called on a public phone, and about five minutes later, it came from somewhere in the direction of that bridge over there."

"Hmm," the waiter said, cocking his head. "Then if you aren't lucky, it'll take some doing to find it."

"Why?"

"That woman's pretty cagey. She's always prepared for times of emergency, not to get her ass caught—she does come here from time to time, but she's never let slip her name."

"Yeah, that sounds right, she's never told me her name either."

"If she wasn't so secret, she'd catch the cops' attention, and she wouldn't get good customers.—That's the way the round-eyes do it, you know."

"So she's come here with different kinds of customers?"

"Yeah, she's brought 'em. Other than you, there have been two or three Japanese, but the general run are foreigners."

He talked quite a while with the waiter, but it was useless, so it was with a fair degree of hopelessness that he got into a taxi in front of the station.

"Let's see—I'm going somewhere in Honmoku, you know? In a kind of grassy field-like place there's a street that the streetcar runs along?"

"Yes, yes . . ."

"It has to be somewhere in that area."

"About how many stops before the end of the line?"

"If I knew that much, I wouldn't need your help . . . in that area, isn't there a part where all kinds of squalid little alleys twist in and out and all around? . . ."

"Let's see—"

"Oh, never mind, just take me there, and when I see it, I might be able to figure the rest of it out."

Where he got out seemed possibly not to be the wrong place, but when he entered into the alleys, he realized that it would be no easy task to hunt out the house that he was looking for. First of all, since he'd not even seen a nameplate on the house, there was no way he could ask for it directly. Furthermore, all the houses were of the same construction, so there were no landmarks to jog his memory. They'd always gone in by the back door, so he had no sense of what the front entrance was like, and if he went around to check out a couple that might be it, someone might mistake him for a prowler. After wandering in and out for quite a while, he finally found a hardware store and asked them if they knew of such-and-such a woman who rented the second floor of a house nearby.

"Um, a woman with short, bobbed hair?" A man who seemed to be the owner asked from inside, although he looked doubtful.

"Yes, that's it, she's around twenty-eight or -nine, and she wears Western clothes and looks like she works in an office."

"I've never seen a woman like that. A woman like that, she'd sure stick out in a place like this . . ."

"Yes, I suppose . . . I'm certain it was around here, but . . ."

"Are you sure you've not got it wrong? 'Cause this isn't a place where a woman like that'd live."

He had two or three other conversations like this, but no matter where he asked they all agreed that they had no knowledge of her. Even if he had the wrong alley it didn't make sense that he was completely off. He was sure that the house was near, some-where in the general area. So it was pretty strange that there was no one who had seen her. Actually, she'd had him wait on the second floor while she went to the public bath in broad daylight or went to use the public phone. That made him realize that his way of asking had been wrong—when she had gone out in the day-time, she'd been wearing a light bath kimono under a tight-sleeved coat, and a hat like a man's soft hat, and at first glance she must have left the impression of a tough young houseboy. After all, the waiter had said she was wary, and she would have done her best not to stand out in the neighborhood. So there was no reason they should know, when he asked about bobbed hair or Western clothing. That's right, I should look for bathhouses. If I ask there, they could possibly know. He then walked around looking for bathhouse chimneys and hit the mark.

"Ah, yes, that woman does come in from time to time. They say she lives five or six houses from here, on the second floor of the Tanakas'. If you ask there, they'll surely know."—The second bathhouse he stopped at told him this. He found the house and went around to the back, but the door was closed. Yet without a doubt this was it. He went back to the front lattice door and tried gently to open it, but it was locked and inside was dark.

"Um, excuse me," he called out, but no one answered. It was as silent as if it had been vacant for some time. As he ventured to continue calling out and knocking on the door, he could hear a sleepy-sounding voice respond with a single "Oh." The paper of the inside sliding door became light, and a man came out wearing a padded kimono.

"I'm sorry, but I've got something to ask. . . . Is this where a twenty-eight-or-nine-year-old woman with bobbed hair is rent-ing a room?"

"Huh? . . . You are who?"

"I've visited the woman two or three times, and I called at this house. She didn't let me know her name, so if you ask me, I won't know it, but . . ."

"We don't have such a woman here."

He continued standing there with the light at his back, so Mizuno couldn't see his face well, but the man kept looking him up and down suspiciously.

"Who is this woman you're asking about?"

"Well, I don't know what her name was, but . . . it's really strange, but I could swear that somehow it was this house. . . . I don't suppose . . . um . . . you've rented rooms here before?"

"We have rented but . . . these days there isn't anyone here." To surmise from his tone of voice and his attitude, sure enough, this was the place, but maybe he thinks I'm a detective come to investigate. Since he's playing dumb, there's no point in continuing to press him, and besides, after all, the woman might be staying somewhere else tonight, so she probably won't be coming back.

"Oh, I am so sorry for the trouble I've caused you." So saying, he left by the front and at first went a couple of hundred yards away, but then he snuck back to the rear entrance. When he tried the door, it slid open. What's this? It's not closed from the inside, so mightn't she be coming back at any moment? Since the woman always firmly closed it when she returned, right now there was no one on the second floor. He thought to himself, maybe I should try to imitate her footsteps and go up to the second floor, but he hesitated to go so far, and instead took out the letter he'd brought in his breast pocket and put it on top of the step into the vestibule, leaving it where the woman would have to see it when she took her shoes off.

Now that I've figured out where the house is and delivered the letter, I can go to the funeral tomorrow at my leisure, he thought, feeling that he'd accomplished his objective. Thirty minutes later he was bumping along on the Tokyo-bound national train line.

But once again he began to worry: what if it was actually the wrong house? Then the woman wouldn't get the letter. Not just that: as the waiter had said, since she guarded her secrets so jealously, then even if she did read it, wouldn't she pretend she hadn't? If so, then he shouldn't wait until five to come but should come first at one to make sure. And then, she's likely to be quite irritated to find he was playing detective and arbitrarily invading her privacy while she was out. Mightn't she even use that as an excuse for cutting off relations with him? Since the woman didn't even want to know his name, he could be sure that she wouldn't want to be involved in the matter that so worried him. That being the case, he'd made a serious mistake in using manuscript paper with his name printed on it for the letter. That alone was already a big enough slip to draw her ire. . . . In the end, wasted effort or not, he'd have to go to Sakuragicho at one tomorrow or he'd not feel safe. To have gone all the way to Honmoku tonight turned out to be useless, but there was no helping that.

That's what he said to himself. Nevertheless, the next morning he continued to worry. There was surely an 80 or 90 percent chance that the letter had gotten into the woman's hands. Maybe she'd not be much put off and figure that anyway he wasn't going to be there, so she wouldn't be waiting there at one. But Mizuno left the boardinghouse anyway at eleven thirty and was at Sakuragicho at the appointed time. The woman was waiting at the exit, exactly where they'd agreed, looking for him to emerge from the underground passageway. And even before he exited, she started to walk to the public phone to call the car as she always did.

"Hey, wait, wait," he yelled, running to overtake her.

"What?"

"Today I have . . . it's not a good time for me."

"Oh really?" The woman stopped in front of the phone booth. "So shall we cancel?" The woman spoke briskly, with no trace of regret.

"No, I don't mean to cancel, but . . ." You didn't see my letter, he was about to say, but corrected himself. "I have a funeral for a friend at two o'clock, so I can't make it before five."

"So—let's make it at five."

"That's okay, right, you will be waiting for me at five?"

"Right, for sure—until five fifteen."

"The fact is, I came just now, specifically at one, you know, because I thought it would be bad for you to be kept waiting and not have me show up."

"Thanks for the effort. Since I'd leave after fifteen minutes you needn't have worried about it."

"Well, excuse me then, I have to get to the Yanaka Memorial Hall as quick as possible."

"Bye-bye—" The woman briskly headed for the station plaza; but as he watched her moving away from him, Mizuno suddenly felt curiosity welling up in him. He couldn't keep himself from saying something, and ran after her.

"What is it?" The woman heard his footsteps and turned around.

"You—didn't see my letter last night?"

"Letter?"

"Yeah . . ."

"Addressed to me?"

"The fact is, I brought it myself last night, to the Honmoku house."

"Hmm—so who did you give it to?"

"The back wasn't locked, so I opened it and tossed it in and left."

"I don't know anything, nothing about it.—You didn't talk to the people downstairs?"

"I did talk to someone, but he said they didn't have anyone like you."

"Well then, didn't you get the wrong house?"

"Could be."

"Don't you think it's likely?—What did you write?"

"Just what I told you now."

"That's all?"

"Oh—and I was worried so that's why I came." Secretly he was nervous that she might be irritated, but she didn't show any particular signs of it.

"That was a silly thing to do, two wasted trips," she tossed off, laughing, and got on the streetcar.

Would it have been better if I hadn't asked, after all? When he was back alone, Mizuno immediately again began to feel anxious about it. What he did in one moment he regretted in the next. His life was a succession of such moments, and in this case he should have considered the consequences of the act, but instead he was just carelessly carried away by the impulse of a moment. Could it be that she hadn't seen the letter? Was the house last night the wrong one? There was no way he could believe that, but all the same, the woman's manner was so completely offhanded. Even supposing her skill at covering up lies without showing a sign was so well developed from long practice, could she so calmly feign ignorance? Couldn't it be precisely because she hadn't seen the letter that she was waiting at one o'clock? . . . No, she definitely did see it, but maybe she knew my temperament, so she thought I'd do this, and that's why she came here? . . .

As if a little bird had told him—although there was nothing to show it might be so—he had a premonition that this would be the last time he saw the woman, that although she'd said she would be there at five, he couldn't trust her. This was a woman who prided herself on strict observance of promises, so if she said she'd come, she'd come, surely. But it could be that in her heart she had decided this was it, she was going to end their connection, and this was just a way of letting him down easily. Somehow he felt he was right. Maybe the woman had read the letter after all, and she was angry that he had broken the agreement. He had unilaterally corresponded with her; he had used letterhead paper with his name printed on it. If she had even the slightest literary interests, she might already know his profession. She would know that a relationship with a writer was something that might get out, and she might have started privately to be on her guard. Or at a deeper level, she might have begun to intuit that she might be getting involved in some sort of incident. . . . As he mulled it over, he realized all the more that beyond skipping the funeral, he should have done whatever he could to keep the woman from getting away.

It was around three by the time he got to the memorial hall. As he gave his business card to the receptionist, he was apprehensive about how he would be received, so he presented it cautiously. But no one had an expression that said, "Aha, this man?" Maybe because it was late, he could find no one he knew as he looked around the room. The woman sitting at one end beside the casket must be Cojima's widow. He quietly advanced and bowed his head before the photograph. And then he looked up at the portrait with close attention. The half-length portrait of the man in his frock coat captured the sense of "Shoe-Leather" well. From that perspective it was a photo that brought back memories. He picked up a stick of incense, and over the incense burner, offered it once, twice, three times. At which point, "Hey," someone tugged at his sleeve. He turned around, and saw that it was Nakazawa.

"Hey . . ."

"I heard from the receptionist that you were here, and came right over. It was kind of you to make this trip, busy as you are."

"No, not—are you one of the funeral officiants?"

"Yeah, well—they said that there might be some people from the literary world, and I was asked to greet them. By the way, would you like to give your condolences to the widow? I'd be glad to introduce you . . ."

"Thanks . . . But in the midst of all this, I hesitate . . ."

"It's probably okay, since the service is mostly finished. . . . Anyway, this unexpected misfortune is such a pity that even if it's a bother for you, won't you meet her and offer her some comfort? It was really good of you to come. No one would ever have thought that you would take the trouble to come. Didn't you say there didn't seem to be much of a connection between you and the deceased while he was alive . . ."

"That's right, there wasn't, but I did use him as a model and . . ." Mizuno laughed artificially, but Nakazawa didn't join him.

"If you were to give her your condolences, the whole family would feel honored, too. How about it? Is it too much trouble?"

"Of course it's not a bother, but, you know . . ."

"Well, then, come this way," Nakazawa said, and without asking anyone but taking it upon himself, he went up to the widow.

"Madam, this is Mr. Mizuno, the writer. He hates dealing with people and rarely goes anywhere, but today, knowing the situation, he came specifically to see you . . ."

The widow started as if embarrassed and stood up politely, bowing her head as she looked down, but at the same time, she threw him an upward glance and glared at Mizuno sharply as if to tear him apart. And then no sooner had she taken her seat again than her face began to tremble, she pressed her handkerchief hard to her eyes and suddenly burst out weeping wildly.

This is dangerous! Mizuno instantly felt. This woman knows something. She ought to have used some stock phrases expressing something like gratitude for friendship with her husband during his life, but instead she looks at my face and without a word bursts into tears. This is utterly strange. Come to think of it, there was hatred burning in her eyes as she looked at me just now . . .

"I'd like to . . . I mean, I'm truly . . ." Even under different circumstances, Mizuno wasn't very good at those polite phrases, but he thought that he had to do something to retrieve the situation. Yet that's all he could come up with before getting stuck. After standing for a few moments he finally came out with the words Nakazawa had just used: "It's truly such an unexpected misfortune . . ."

"Absolutely. It would be one thing if he'd died of illness; we could accept that, but . . ." Nakazawa inserted himself from the side with that same solemn expression he used when he was pressing Mizuno for a manuscript.

"It is natural and right that you cry. Especially since Mr. Cojima was not the sort of man to incur enmity from anyone . . ."

Unable to help himself, Mizuno turned to Nakazawa and asked, "Have there been any clues since then?"

"No, they say there's still nothing."

"When exactly did the incident happen?"

"They're saying it was probably between ten and eleven on the twenty-fifth. Anyway, they say that road is terribly dangerous."

"Oh, really? So it could have been robbery?"

"Nothing was taken. Isn't that right, Madame?" While the two were talking, the widow had completely stopped crying, but when he looked at her pale face, Mizuno felt his own face go pale.

"Yes, it was his monthly payday, and so he had money with him, but none of it was touched, so . . ."

The widow spoke for the first time. Her voice was strong and clear, untouched by the crying she had been doing until then; she spoke in sharp, staccato phrases, and as she spoke she continued to glare fixedly at Mizuno.

"Yes, yes, that's right . . . the twenty-fifth was payday," said Nakazawa, sounding as though he were prompting her, "so from that perspective it must have been a grudge, mustn't it? After all, since it was Mr. Cojima, it probably didn't have anything to do with a woman . . ."

"Maybe he hid something from me, but I do believe there was absolutely no way it could have been.—And even if there were a woman, to have been so hated by another person for that reason . . ."

"Was there anything unusual in his attitude recently?"

"Yes . . . I mean . . . it didn't have anything to do with a woman, but he did say that he was in quite a state of nervous exhaustion, and that he couldn't help feeling that someone was trying to kill him."

"Really? When?"

"Let's see . . . it might have been the night of the fifteenth of this month. He would go to the movies on the Ginza or things like that, and when he came home late, he didn't always talk about how dangerous the road to home was, or how it was too isolated and he was thinking of moving to Tokyo, but that night he talked about how it bothered him, and when I asked him why he was talking about it, he said that somehow he felt that he was going to be attacked by someone sometime soon."

"Hmm," Nakazawa said portentously. "Generally, Cojima was not one to worry about such things. Somehow, he must have gotten a hint from somewhere."

"I thought it was strange too, and when he said it I wondered if there was some particular reason, but he said no, there was nothing specific, that he hadn't done anything that would make someone feel malice toward him; it's just that somehow he had a premonition. So I said, then we should leave such an isolated place and move to the city as soon as possible, and that's how it was working out; he'd planned to do it before the end of the year, but ultimately it wasn't in time, and that's how all this happened . . ."

"Hmm, from what you say, he said these strange things on what day this month?"

"It was the fifteenth."

"The fifteenth . . . so he went to Tokyo on the fifteenth." Nakazawa said this with a very matter-of-fact expression, looking straight
into Mizuno's eyes as if to uncover the facts. "Might something
unusual have happened to him in Tokyo? If so, you, Mr. Mizuno,
would know human psychology better than I, but . . ."

"Well now, yes, maybe something did happen . . ." Hold it—
wait a minute—why tell such stupid *lies*! Why don't you tell him
the truth: that you went to the moving pictures with him on the
fifteenth, that you walked on the Ginza, that you returned to
Hirokoji together in a taxi, and that you felt you could see death
in Cojima's face? What a dolt I am! I've dug my own grave!—
Mizuno was always just too smart for his own good. That being
said, he had been led on to some degree by Nakazawa's pompous
presentation, but given that he was an inveterate liar even in
trifling matters, this tendency has appeared inadvertently at a
very important time. Just when a careless man should be most
careful, he gets panicky and so confused that he could throw his
life away.

"There must have been something, for sure . . ." Nakazawa
persisted. "Especially if he was late in going home, maybe he met
someone he knew and was told something that upset him, or encountered something out of the ordinary, it could have been
something like that? . . . How about it, the powers of imagination
of a writer could see it's not inconceivable, is it?"

"Such things do happen."

"Maybe a clue could come from some such unexpected direction. That he said he had a feeling he would be killed—it's as if it
wasn't some vague, groundless fear but something with a deep
actual connection to the facts of that night, wasn't it? . . ."

"Hey, hey, stop playing games—are you trying to scare us?"
Mizuno ached to seize the chance and cut him off with a light,
joking confession like, "The fact is, that night there was this and

this," but whether or not he knew, Nakazawa didn't respond to that and only went on ponderously with things like, "If only we knew whom he met that night," ignoring Mizuno's lead and giving him no opportunity to get back in.

When he left the memorial hall he returned right away to Tokyo Station, but in his head he now was turning over something other than meeting with the Fraülein—unraveling the strange puzzle Nakazawa had tossed to him. On the whole, Nakazawa ought not to have been on such close terms with the dead man that he would have been asked to be part of the funeral team. He had once said himself that he had helped with editing *Humoresque* magazine, but at the time he had known Cojima only slightly. It was fishy that today he was being such a busybody at the memorial hall and so overly friendly to the widow. I know that the guy has been bitter toward me recently. Come to think of it, today he ought to have said something about the manuscript, too, but he said not a word. I was resentful, too, and so I made no excuses, but for him to be silent, well, there had to be something deep behind it. Maybe he used my distress over that "model" issue to frighten me with his strangely ominous tone of voice, while inside he was shouting with joy. If so, then this has to be who sent me that clipping, without a doubt. But would his revenge be accomplished just with terrorizing me, or would he not be satisfied unless I were actually trapped in the crime, that's what worries me . . .

But that was not his only uneasiness. When he got to Sakuragicho at five as arranged, the woman who was always there and should have been standing at the exit gate was nowhere to be seen. Ah, my earlier premonition hit the mark, he thought. If she were coming, she'd surely be here already. She decided not to come today after all. In the vain hope that she would come, he waited fifteen minutes, twenty minutes, finally an hour, but as he was about to go to Honmoku again, he realized it was pointless, and there was nothing to do but turn back in a daze, after all. And even on the train going home, the woman and Cojima became all jumbled together, keeping him in a state of excitement with various fantasies. He couldn't help thinking that the sudden disappearance of the woman and the problem of Cojima were somehow connected. On the surface of it, there seemed to be no connection between accidentally meeting the woman at the London Bar and the Cojima incident, but you couldn't categorically say there was none. Somehow there was a behind behind the behind, and he had a feeling that from the beginning the woman's ensnaring him might have been a service she was offering to the Shadow Man, who was manipulating her. Mightn't he have been pulling the strings? Come to think of it, it was strange that a stylish, modern woman like her would notice a man like Mizuno, who didn't look like he had much money, even if it was all business to her. And all this secrecy: insisting on secrecy in everything, not revealing her name; that was fishy. And their meeting specifically on Tuesday and Friday—maybe that too was part of a deep plot to ensure that Mizuno's activities were hidden from the rest of the world on the night of the twenty-fifth. Damn! Finally I have fallen into the Shadow Man's trap. Even as I warned myself not to get caught, I didn't see that the woman was part of it, and I inadvertently got taken in . . .

Don't be ridiculous! How could there be something so stupid? To enlist a woman and kill an innocent man just to entrap me—who in the world would go to such complicated trouble? These are all my crazy delusions.—Mizuno tried to think of these fears as completely groundless, as if it were something like a lie, but if that was so, then why did the woman disappear? Speculating further, Mizuno didn't know if suspicion had fallen on him, but didn't the rest of the world find him problematic? And because the woman knew his name from his letter last night, mightn't she be avoiding getting involved? Or it was not impossible to interpret it as the workings of Nakazawa's maliciousness. In other words, because he had been forced to listen to Mizuno on his amours, he had picked up the woman from the Monaco or somewhere and had made a secret deal with her—such a thing could happen. If so, Nakazawa could have told her something like, "The man's going to be arrested for murder soon, and if you don't get away quickly, you're sure to be called as a witness!" Maybe he scared her with something like that.—At least these imaginings were more realistic than the others . . .

10

From then on, days of ennui and idleness continued for Mizuno. Nothing more came from *The People*; the maids at the boardinghouse looked at him strangely, and every morning when he stretched out his hand beside the pillow, there was not a single piece of mail. Until now his solitude had been of his own choice to avoid social contact, but now that he was cast aside by the world like this, his life was unsettled rather than calm. He could understand if he had withdrawn deep into the mountains, but to be on the second floor of a boardinghouse right in the middle of a great city and still be all alone put him in a state of vertigo where he felt his body was floating in space. At least if he had some money that would be okay, but if he went out for a walk, he didn't even have streetcar fare, so he could do nothing but lounge around his room all day. When he sometimes went out into the hall, the inn people all scraped furtively past him, as if they were trying to avoid him. Maybe it just felt that way to him, but that's the only way he could see it. In front of him they were quiet as death, but behind his back they always seemed to be gossiping and whispering. Gradually these rumors would get bigger and bigger, and eventually they might come to the ears of the police, and a detective would come to visit. But even a visit from a detective would be welcome, rather than being ignored like this. Maybe he could appeal to them: "I used so-and-so as a model when I wrote such-and-such a story, so there's no real need for an investigation"? . . .

On the other hand, he couldn't forget the business of the Honmoku woman, so when the next Friday came, even though he knew it was hopeless, he managed to scrape together the train fare and set out for Yokohama. The day of the funeral had worked out as it had, but the woman had taken prepayment for a full month. It had been premature for him to decide that he'd been cast from her memory. Maybe that day she'd gotten suddenly ill and couldn't come. So he imagined, but this, too, was a vain hope, for there was neither hide nor hair of the woman. When he returned discouraged in the evening and opened the sliding doors to his room, his heart suddenly leaped in his breast. There was a business card sitting on his desk. He had had a visitor while he was out.

On it was printed, "*The People* Jiro Watanabe." Hey, I've never heard of any Watanabe at the magazine, but why didn't Nakazawa come, I wonder. He called the maid and asked her, "This business card? What's it about?"

"Yes, well, soon after you went out, that person came."

"Around when?"

"It might have been around one."

"Didn't he leave a message?"

"Nakazawa was going to come, but he was busy and couldn't get away, so he'd come as his representative—"

"He didn't say that I should phone when I returned?"

"Yes, um, he said that in the evening around eight he'd come again—"

This is not about the manuscript; it's something else, he felt instinctively.

As promised, at eight o'clock this Watanabe showed up. Sure enough Mizuno had no recollection of him; he seemed to be a couple of years older than Nakazawa, around thirty-five or so. Even though he was only a representative, the man had an impressive presence, and as if he'd been instructed by Nakazawa, he stopped outside the room at the sliding doors and made a perfect, deep bow and then, with a subservient smile playing around his mouth framed by a handle-bar mustache, he said, "Pleased to meet you . . ." and again bowed politely.

"So you're Watanabe . . ."

"Yes, that's right. . . . It happens that Nakazawa was supposed to come, but recently he's, uh, helping out in the advertising department, and because he's busy, I've been deputized to come in his stead."

"That's what they said, and I hear that you came earlier. Unfortunately I was out for a while, and I apologize for not being here."

"I am much obliged."

"Well now, we can't talk with you out there, so come on in here.—You've been at *The People* for a while, but I don't seem to have run into you . . ."

"Ah, yes, that's right. I joined the editorial department about a month ago.—Anyway, I'm glad to meet you."

As they talked, the man appeared to be constantly looking around the room with sharp glances. He was a full-bodied man; in that, he somehow resembled Harada, the editor-in-chief. He gave an expansive impression and had a reassuring tone that might cause other people to relax their guard, but counter to appearances, there was an unexpected tension and nervousness in him. Every time Mizuno said anything, he would respond in Nakazawa style, "Aha, I see." He kept his head lowered, seemingly modest, but he continued to throw out an endless line of comments about the literary world: rumors about the literary establishment, conditions in the publishing world, magazine sales. He never came out with why he was there.

"Well, whatever you say, with the general economy so sluggish these days, things are not very good in the publishing world, either. They say that if bad times come, magazines and things like that will still sell well, but it's all a matter of degree, and recently even magazines hardly break even, so, well, we should just take it a step at a time . . ."

"How's *The People* doing?" He had no choice but to play along with Watanabe.

"Yes, well, thanks to you all, *The People* is somehow managing to stay afloat, since we can get good manuscripts from various intellectuals."

"Well, of course, that's because *The People* pays well for manuscripts. . . . In the case of fiction, you can't very well take price into consideration, but it does after all help provide an incentive for working hard at it."

"Yes, it could very well tend to be as you say, to some extent. The things you write, Professor (here, he used 'Professor'), are all quite good, but especially the one you did just recently, the one entitled 'To the Point of Murder,' that one I myself personally believe is a masterpiece among masterpieces, truly a masterpiece . . ."

"Yes, yes," said Mizuno who had been listening to him perfunctorily, but then finally he couldn't stand it anymore. "Well then, what's your business today?"

"Yes, well, um, what it is—Nakazawa should have come out himself to say it, but as you know, there was that situation between you, and it's a bit difficult to ask it, but . . . well, Professor, how do you feel about it? . . ."

"No, well, you know, there's no reason for me to feel anything about it—since I met with Nakazawa not long ago at a certain place and the two of us discussed our feelings about it quite a bit."

"But you said those things about people arbitrarily coming into your room while you were out and messing things up, and how it made you lose your manuscript, and what with being so enraged . . ."

"Wha—at? That's because it interfered with my writing, and I was really irritated, so I just said it in the heat of the moment. Writers are extremely self-involved people, and to have such a thing happen is a serious disruption, you know."

"If you'd said that, he'd have felt much better, but he said that he had no recollection of touching your manuscript, and it was so unexpected that he was really upset. But because it was certainly a mistake to have entered your room without permission, he was terribly embarrassed."

"But when I met him just recently, he didn't seem that way. The man is sneaky; maybe he wasn't so embarrassed that he would say something about it. . . . At any rate, I was at fault in that incident. I think that what I did to *The People* was inexcusable, and so far as a manuscript is concerned, if you commissioned me, I'll happily write it anytime."

"Oh, right, the fact is, about the manuscript . . ."

"Yes, the manuscript? . . ."

"That's, it's, well, it's truly hard to say it, but . . ."

"Yes, yes, what about it? . . . Come on, don't hold back. You're saying you don't need any more of it?"

"Yes, no, well, we'd certainly like to get more of it, but, um, well, the editor-in-chief told me to ask, in general, about how many pages are yet to go, and what's the plan going to be."

"That's funny, to ask such picky things . . . To tell the truth, since I've dropped the story in the middle, I've lost all interest in it, and I don't want to write any more of it."

"What a pity, when you've done so much splendid . . ."

"No, that's it, and since I probably don't have anything more for that story, I thought I'd start again and write something new for you since I've already gotten an advance payment . . ."

"But according to what Nakazawa says, Professor, haven't you already collected material and made a complete plan for it? To be perfectly honest, 'To the Point of Murder' seems to have become something of a topic of conversation here and there, so it would be good if we could have the continuation, you know."

"Popping up as a topic recently? Is that really so? You know, it came out quite a while ago."

"Yes, well, again recently, apart from its literary value, it seems to have become a topic in quite a different sense, but . . ."

Mizuno was startled and looked at his companion, but Watanabe was quite calm as he spoke.

"Yes, well, ever since that recent murder, people have felt quite a bit of curiosity about that work, and have wanted to read it . . ."

Aha, so that's it—they want to cash in. That damned owner—first he gives up on me, and now suddenly he wants the sequel and sets an employee on me just for that. Okay, okay, if that's how it is, I'll make him pay: he has to put aside my recent debt, and he'll have to give me a new advance, and if he doesn't like it, he can forget about it—shall I propose that to him? Whatever happens, it's not bad for me. Cojima's murder has brought me good luck—isn't fate amazing? And just when things looked so dark. What the hell—if it'll bring me money, I might as well write the damn sequel . . .

"Oh really? That's the first I've heard of it . . ."

"Well, but what with the model for the guy in the story's getting murdered recently . . . that Cojima . . . wasn't he actually the model?"

"Nah, you put me on the spot when you ask so baldly. All I can do is leave it up to the reader's judgment."

"Well, I didn't notice it myself, but aren't they saying that the name 'Cojima' was actually in it? And didn't they say that at the time you wrote it, Professor, you said when the story was published, you had a premonition that the man who was the model would be murdered . . . ?"

Mizuno laughed. "Well, sure, I said it to Nakazawa, as a joke, but what with its coming true, I've felt real bad about it. But is that general knowledge?"

"There wasn't anything in the newspapers and magazines about how it was too bad about Cojima, but everyone is whispering it— that you, Professor, wrote the story and didn't you kill Cojima with just the same feeling as the protagonist in the story . . ."

"Th-that's just it! That's why at the time I was so worried that I almost had a nervous breakdown. That people would think so!"

"Huh? People surely wouldn't seriously think that, but if they did, that would be interesting, wouldn't it? Especially since you, Professor, are a diabolist, and . . ."

"Oh, right, and that I didn't kill him could be a lie, too, right?"

"But how about it—when that murder incident came out in the papers? You must have been just a little surprised, right?"

"Strangely enough, I wasn't surprised. I felt that the premonition had hit the mark. But now in fact I've gotten to feeling that things are a bit eerie."

"How so?"

"Even if the rumor wasn't entirely serious, it might reach the ears of the police. And I've wondered if a detective might show up before long . . ."

"Yes, but wouldn't it be even more interesting if a detective did show up to investigate? Maybe one's been here already?"

"Don't even joke! Maybe other people would find it entertaining, but what a mess it would be for me."

"Wouldn't that degree of mess be fun? It would even make the sequel sell better, wouldn't it?"

"Oh yes, I see—I'm being held in detention, and it's free advertising for *The People*!"

"But wouldn't it be a good experience for a writer? How about it—why not try going to jail?"

"They'd be willing to pay a manuscript fee?"

"For certain, I can make them do it. They can pay it out of the advertising account."

Mizuno laughed. "So you'd rather that I go to the police? 'Could be that I killed him, so anyway, put me in jail, please'—right?"

"No, I'm not joking. It would be strange if you barged in yourself, Professor, so you should have someone else do it for you. Then they'd come for sure. I don't know if they'd actually arrest you, but even if they detained you for one or two nights, the experience would have its effect, you know."

"It's all well and good if it's only a night or two, but what if they investigate deeper and decide I'm the criminal—what'd I do then? In any case, all things being equal, once the judge thinks you're it, you're ruined."

"And if you, Professor, became the criminal, the sentence would accordingly have to be severe because it was premeditated, and that would undoubtedly mean the death penalty."

"If so, no amount of manuscript payment would be enough, would it?"

Watanabe chuckled. "But *The People* would cheer—'The work the writer bet his life on!'—and everyone would be talking about it."

"When people like you get your journalist nerves in motion, there's no helping the poor writer.—No, it's irresponsible for you to say it's a joke or not serious, because there are cases where it has hit the mark. There's the example of Cojima, and . . ."

"But really, how about it, Professor, couldn't you make the world believe for a while that you could be the murderer? . . . The fact is, the owner asked me to explore this with you and see if you would do it."

"You've got to be kidding! What the hell, this is just crazy . . ."

"No, from the company's perspective, anything that sells magazines is great, so they're quite serious. . . . On top of that, they believe that to be under suspicion like that would not harm your reputation. . . . Just say I were the judge: if I had done research into your works and your proclivities, it would be natural, Professor, for me to think logically that you were the criminal. Anyway, we'd like you to agree at least not to resist being picked up by the police for questioning . . ."

"So you're saying that *The People* staff members would spread the rumors everywhere?"

"Not just spread the rumors—we could help by handing you over to the police . . ."

"Aha—then you are . . ."

"Yes, you probably realize by now . . ."

". . . a detective." As he said this, Mizuno watched Watanabe take a business card out of his pocket.

"As you have surmised, I am. Accordingly, I really do apologize, but at any rate, I actually would like to question you a bit . . ."

"Why, yes, of course, whatever you . . ."

"Of course I do not suspect you in the least, Professor, and so it's quite a bother to the police, too, but the clamor of rumor has been quite intense, and so we could not just ignore it, and . . ."

"Yes, yes, I can certainly understand your position. Your consideration in this case . . ." Mizuno's voice started to rise, but he spoke fairly calmly.—"Well, then let's see, I'll put on some tea, and we can do our questioning quietly."

"No, well, to do it here is somewhat, what shall I say . . . I'd like to have you come with me . . ."

"Ah, yes," Mizuno said clearly, sounding almost refreshed. "—You mean, go now, right away?"

"Yes, I'm sorry it's the middle of the night, but . . ."

"Oh, now, no problem, we writers are up all night and sleep late in the morning, so anytime at night is just fine. But I'd like you to get me back by morning, okay?"

"Well, yes, we don't hold you people for no reason at all. You must have a lot of work to do, and it would be terrible if we interfered with that."

"Oh, don't worry about that, but . . . It's funny—at first when you came here you said you were from *The People*, and it turns out in the end that you're their booster after all."

Watanabe laughed. "At any rate, it's unprecedented for us to do this for a mere suspicion, and so the newspapers will probably make a lot of noise about it. But anyway, as you said just a while before, everything is experience for you, so this is worth trying at least once."

As the detective said this, Mizuno responded, "Well then . . ." and nimbly stood up, making his preparations to go. Taking his wallet, which had only two yen in it, out of the desk drawer and putting it into his breast pocket, he threw on his cloak.

"Sorry to keep you waiting. Shall we?" He left first and headed down the stairs, intending to look around for the maid just as he always did when he went for a stroll, but strangely he couldn't repress a bitter laugh, as if he were embarrassed or wouldn't acknowledge that he'd been defeated.

"Ah—you've called a taxi for me," the detective yelled into the office by the entrance.

"It has arrived," the landlord said, opening the sliding doors; he stuck out his head and looked at Mizuno as if he found him loathsome.

"It's gotten much colder. The temperature's dropped remarkably tonight." As the car started off, the detective lit a cigarette.

"Um, I suppose you've got a good heating system? I don't mind being kept awake, but cold would be a problem."

"Yes, of course; we'll make sure you're not cold."

"I've heard tell that you use torture to force confessions, but you aren't going to treat me that way, are you?"

"That was an uncivilized practice of the past, but these days it's completely gone, and all the more for a person like you, Professor . . ."

"So it'll be all right, really? I'm not just physically weak, but on top of that I've gotten to be quite a coward. I can't even trust myself if I were tortured—who knows what I'd say just to avoid pain."

Watanabe laughed heartily.

"No, I really mean it—it's no laughing matter."

"Well now—we're here. Let me guide you." The detective started off first, and after making two or three turns along the corridors, he put his hand on a door, and making a polite bow, he said, "Here, right this way, please." But there was somehow a trace of derision in his politeness. At the same time Mizuno could hear the sound of footsteps from behind, and another man, wearing a blue suit, came in, seeming to push him in as he did.

"Yah, so it's you, Mr. Mizuno?" He spoke in quite a friendly manner. He was pale and thin, with a rough complexion and sharp features. Mizuno had no memory of meeting him and didn't know why he would be addressed so intimately as "Yah, Mr. Mizuno."

"To have made you come out so late is quite an inconvenience to you . . . ," he continued, but for some reason Mizuno couldn't respond as easily as he had before. Maybe for one thing it was because the man had a strangely unpleasant expression, but for another, it could have been the depressing color of the walls in the cramped, gloomy room. Watanabe appeared to be an underling, and when he carried a chair in, his superior first sat down arrogantly and pressed Mizuno, "Here, take a seat."

"Well now, we know this is sudden, but the reason we had you come here right away tonight is that story you published recently, 'To the Point of Murder'—we've got a few questions to ask you about it. The crux of the problem is the protagonist of the story, the murderer—his philosophy of life, and how that might intersect with the author's outlook on life—that is, *yours* . . ."

"Of course, that's how we amateurs think . . . ," Watanabe, the subordinate, chimed in as if to encourage Mizuno. "We figure that there must after all be some correspondence between the author and the main character, right? If there weren't, then I should think that the author couldn't really describe the character's psychology in much detail . . ."

"Yes, well, that does depend on the work, but in general I'd say that there are two types of writers: one who hides himself completely when he writes, and one who wants to be writing himself—not that he doesn't write about people other than himself, but who ultimately is explaining himself, whatever he writes . . . in a word, what we might call the objective writer, and the subjective writer, you know."

"Well then, Mr. Mizuno—which type are you?"

"I believe myself to be the subjective type."

"So that means that your story, 'To the Point of Murder,' represents your own state of mind?"

"Absolutely. I know that in this case it would be more strategic for me to say it doesn't, but that would negate my artistic stance completely, so . . ." Without looking around, Mizuno heard the sound of a pencil behind him whispering smoothly across paper. Clearly someone was taking down his words.

"All right. So anyway, the protagonist expresses his view of life in a number of ways, in various places, doesn't he? For example, 'This world is total nonsense' or 'I've never loved anyone but myself, and that's just my nature,' or 'The pricks of conscience are just a kind of neurosis'—could we say that such statements do represent your own opinions?"

"Quite so."

"And then, the author describes the protagonist's character like this: 'He is an extreme nihilist.' And he says of the character's situation, 'Because that's the way he is, he has no close friends; his life is solitary and he's treacherous.' We could also take this as the author explaining himself."

"Yes, that's quite right. But I want to clarify one thing: surely I'm not the only person in the world with such opinions or life views. The reason you don't see other people confessing truthfully, 'This is the kind of man I am,' honestly and publicly, is that people would call them evil, and they would exclude them from society. So they're terrified they'd be persecuted if they confessed that openly. There's nothing I can do if society calls me evil—but I will not lie about myself. In actual daily life when I'm dealing with people, I do tell lies all the time. But when I take up my pen and work creatively, I expose myself bravely and frankly even if it goes badly for me. In that respect, I believe I am more honest than most of what the world calls 'good men.' That is my way of working to be a man you can believe. And that's where I take my pride as an artist."

"But now, that's a problem—when you say this, how do we know that you're not just pulling the wool over our eyes? We don't know what to think. You say you tell the truth—but that's in your artistic life. And then you say that when you actually deal with other people, you lie all the time. So in other words, it works out that you push everything that's awkward into your art, while in everyday life you're playing a wolf in sheep's clothing. Well, we don't know about art, and we don't need to know about it, but we do need to know about your real life. So in fact, as we investigate you here like this, we can't distinguish what is the truthful artist and what is the lying social man. And what are we to make of what follows, what I just quoted from your story: '—As he felt his creative talent fading, he came to think that he would have to put his thoughts into action in the real world?' or 'If he felt his creative inspiration totally fail to bubble up, he would have to do that thing, or he would feel too lonely and empty'—what about that? Are you actually feeling that your talent is *in fact* really fading?"

"Ah, that's exactly where the real me and the protagonist in the story are different. I do not feel that my creative talent is flagging, and if nothing else, this story I've written, 'To the Point of Murder,' is proof that my creativity is not failing. If it were, then like the protagonist, I might feel the desire to turn thought into action. But happily or unhappily, I'm not there yet."

"That's just the point, you know: to be honest, we really can't tell whether this very story is good enough to be proof of your talent or if it shows that your inspiration is in fact already running out. As you probably know, the literary world didn't regard it very highly. There were quite a number of people who said it was a failure, actually . . ."

"Whether public opinion says it is good or bad is not the issue. Setting aside their judgment, what's important is whether or not the writer himself has given up on his own talent."

"Yes, yes, in other words, it's a matter of whether you feel in your own heart that it's a problem for you. And, as I was just saying, since we have no way of telling whether it is the truthful you or the liar you, we can't tell the true state of your heart. There doesn't seem to be any way to make us able to trust your words. . . . How about it? Isn't that where we are? You said that in order to disarm your conscience, you deceive people, lead them on, and little by little pile evil deed on evil deed to desensitize your nerves. Don't you see? It's just natural: we can't trust what a man like this says."

"I agree, in principle . . ."

"You agree in principle. And in this case?"

"In this case I want you to believe me. After all, I am speaking about my own talent, and I'm doing it with all my confidence and honesty as an artist."

"But who can say that isn't a lie?"

"Who can say it isn't the truth?"

"Well, yes, there we are, still running around in circles. And so we're fools to keep questioning you like this. So let's try getting at it from another direction. Let's say you are identical to the protagonist, and let's say that you've brought your thoughts into action. In other words, you've killed this man you've written about, this Codama or Cojima. You've been extremely clever to hide all traces of the crime, but let's say you draw suspicion because by chance you'd published this story earlier, and you're called before us and we question you. In that case, wouldn't the answers we get from you be exactly the same as the answers we're getting from you now?"

"They might come out the same."

"So let me reword it: we proposed this hypothetically, but you would still give the same answers. Whether or not you're the perpetrator—there's no way for us to know, since we can observe only from the outside. Right?"

"Maybe it would seem to come out the same. But there's something unreasonable in your assumptions. Supposing I truly had the will to carry this out—I'd not be very well likely to write a story that would draw suspicion . . ."

"But the opposite could just as well be true, you know. Why *would* a person who was going to murder someone write such a story? Precisely to make us think as you just suggested. Even if we're not that cynical, it could be that at the time you wrote it you didn't have the will to do it, but writing it conversely stimulated you, and you finally brought it into action. Is that so impossible to imagine? Surely your own rich powers of imagination . . ."

"No, now, if you have that much imagination, you should become a novelist yourself!"

"And the next issue: people are saying that there's another person who is also a model in this story—the man who gets murdered, this Codama-Cojima. There is after all the Nakajiro Cojima who was murdered the other day.—You probably realize that, too. No, I'm sure you realize it. Where you meant to write 'Codama,' you carelessly wrote 'Cojima.' Further, you phoned *The People* about it. When that staff member, Nakazawa, visited you, you were still worrying about it. These various fact show that you were at least conscious of the resemblance between the model and the actual person."

"It was after I wrote it that I got worried. But I wasn't conscious of it at the time I wrote it . . ."

"Well, that's something that can be known only in your heart, so let's leave it. Even to ask about it is useless. We can believe it or not as we wish. So it comes to this: On the one hand, there's this story, 'To the Point of Murder.' And on the other, there is totally parallel to it—at least on the face of it, it's totally parallel—time, place, person: there is the reality that 'a man was murdered.' You are the author of the story. The protagonist in the story and you in the real world are parallel. I'm repeating myself, but at least *on the face of it* you can't deny it. Particularly important is that the actual crime occurred in the same month, on the same day, at the same time as the crime in the story. You came back from your stroll on the evening of November 15, you borrowed an almanac from the office, and it was open on your desk until the evening of the sixteenth. When Nakazawa went to your room in your absence, he saw that it was opened to the November 25 page. So in order to prove that you are not—as you are on the face of it—parallel to the story, there's nothing for you to do but make clear your movements on the day in question, that is, the twenty-fifth of November. That's only as far as our investigations have gone; we don't know anything more . . ."

"They say you hadn't returned to the boardinghouse since Tuesday evening, you know," Watanabe chimed in after him.

"Ah, yes, well, there you are, that's where I'm in trouble. I expected that your questions would come down to that, but to explain why I hadn't been back since Tuesday evening, I have to present a certain woman to you. The only person who knows what I was doing on the evening in question, the twenty-fifth, is this woman. However, not only do I not know her name, I also don't know her identity or even where she lives. So if you say she doesn't exist and is only a fabrication—even if you say it sounds like a fairy tale— unfortunately I can say nothing in my defense. I did in fact, around one in the afternoon on Tuesday, go into a diner at Sakuragicho station with a woman who looked like a typist, wearing Western clothes, and I'm sure the waiter could testify that for me. The fact is, I ran into this woman on the evening of the sixteenth at the London Bar, and subsequently we entered into a certain kind of arrangement. She is a 'professional woman' who takes on mostly foreign clients, and where I was on the night of the twenty-fifth was this woman's house. But if you ask me where her house is, I couldn't point it out and say for certain that this is it. I made a contract with the woman for a month. We were supposed to meet every week on Tuesday and Friday. But ever since the Tuesday following the twenty-fifth, the woman has totally disappeared. The only small hope I have is that you people will get the Yokohama police to look into it for you, and they will grab her. That's all I can hope for. But maybe she can't be caught. Even supposing you catch her, she could deny it in order to avoid being involved in this messy business, because there's no other proof. If that happens, the only things other witnesses can say are that I went to the station cafeteria with her, that we went to a hotel in Kamakura, that we sat at a table at the London Bar, that I took care of her as she sat dead drunk on a platform bench at Yurakucho station—things like that. And all of those things happened before the twenty-fifth. After the twenty-third, until the morning of the twenty-fifth I was at a hotel. If you check with the hotel, they'll know. And yet, for the critical twenty-fifth, from 4:00 P.M. on I was alone with the woman. Even supposing you made certain of the house where we stayed in Honmoku, not a single person other than the woman saw my face. Even the limo that carried us there was one that the woman called specially, and I know nothing about either its make or license number.—To put it in a word, Fate has ensured that just at the instant the event occurred that would most make me the object of suspicion, I was made to disappear from the face of the earth. As in a fairy tale, the woman threw a cloak of invisibility over me. Or to speculate even more strongly, someone is trying to destroy me, and used the woman as his tool . . ."

"Aha, so that's the Shadow Man who appears in the sequel! I saw it in the galley proofs from *The People*, but we'll wait to see it when it comes out as a book."

"Oh, hey, wait a minute—Mr. Mizuno is pretty afraid of being hurt . . . ," Watanabe said, giving his superior a strange eye signal.

"That's right, he said he was quite a coward, and if he were threatened with pain, he'd confess right away.—How about it? Shall we try a little . . ."

"Th-that's . . . isn't that cowardly?" Mizuno immediately cried out in a tearful voice, but the boss laughed loudly as if to deny it.

"Oh no . . . It's just that you said you didn't feel the pricks of conscience, and so we'd only be helping with a few pricks from the outside, you know."

"Oooh," Mizuno groaned, collapsing face down on the desk. But immediately someone grabbed his right hand from behind.

He heard a voice saying, "It'll only hurt a little." And at the same moment, he felt something like a pencil being pushed between his fingers.

AUTHOR'S APOLOGY
ON THE CONCLUSION

From the author: *In Black and White* has gone on quite a bit longer than the initial projection of three months, so I've decided to end it here. I earnestly beg the readers' indulgence.

TRANSLATOR'S AFTERWORD

As mentioned in the translator's preface, this 1928 novel has been invisible for more than eighty years, even though it was available in Tanizaki's collected works (*zenshū*) all along. It was never published as an independent volume, and Japanese scholars have almost totally ignored it. (The late Kōno Taeko is the only critic I have found who even talks, albeit briefly, about this novel.)[1] Many Western scholars have not even known that it exists, apparently. Why the novel has been hidden lies only in the realm of speculation; nevertheless, a fresh look at the work reveals it to be an important window into the writer and his relationship with his literary and personal world, at a time when that world was seriously debating the connection between fiction and real life.

In the half century since his death, in 1965, Tanizaki Jun'ichirō has been one of the most read and studied Japanese writers of the twentieth century. Thanks to a masterful bibliography, we know that as of the year 2000 close to eighty of his works had been translated into at least seventeen Western languages (with French, Italian, and English leading the pack), many of them more than once, and at least twenty-two of his stories have been realized in film, some of them several times, and not all just for Japanese audiences.[2] New translations like this one continue to appear. The work of dozens of non-Japanese scholars has added significantly to the wide variety of Japanese Tanizaki scholarship. Exhibitions of his life and work continue to be organized in Japan, most recently at the Kanagawa Kindai Bungaku-kan in 2015 to commemorate the fiftieth anniversary of the author's death. There was even an international Tanizaki symposium in Venice in 1995. Some studies are about Tanizaki alone; others see his work in company with other writers'. Tanizaki, who at his death was considered a likely candidate for Japan's first Nobel Prize in literature, is seen as standing for himself; through him, we are to see "Japan," "modern Japanese literature," or even "modernity" itself.

Kokubyaku, translated here as *In Black and White*, was written at a time of extraordinary productivity for Tanizaki after a long relatively fallow period and is one of three novels he began in a single year, 1928. It was the only one completed within that year. The other two 1928 novels, *Manji* (*Quicksand*, 1994) and *Tade kuu mushi* (*Some Prefer Nettles*, 1955) quickly became classics among his works, their titles known in Japan even to those who haven't read the novels themselves, and worldwide to readers of translations of Japanese literature; they have been studied heavily ever since their publication.[3] But *In Black and White*, which is longer than either of them, is never even mentioned in those anthologies of modern literature so popular in Japanese publishing. This singular concatenation is worthy of attention.

In Black and White is a fictional story about a fictional story. But it can also be seen as a response to an actual argument between Tanizaki and a famous fellow writer, Akutagawa Ryūnosuke (author of the two short stories that provided the plot for the classic film *Rashomon*), the literary world (*bundan*) they inhabited in the late 1920s, and the literary establishment that approved, disapproved, critiqued, and ratified individual writers, especially in the

1920s and 1930s. The novel has what would then have been called a typical Tanizaki "ingenious plot," but in its storyline is also a pointed critique of the art of fiction as practiced in that literary world.[4] Through the fiction of a sexual adventure and murder mystery, Tanizaki meditates on the writer's craft, literary issues, and the complicit culture of the *bundan*, and he explores the literary values he both participated in and, especially, resisted. In part, *In Black and White* satirizes the conventions of Japanese autobiographical fiction in an ironic parody of the "I-novel" (*watakushi shōsetsu* or *shishōsetsu*), a genre in which the author and other actual people can be more or less clearly discerned as characters in the story, and which was being much debated at the time. This novel is thus in part a parody of *bundan* issues.[5] *In Black and White* is comic (imagine a man trying to establish an alibi by pretending he has gonorrhea)—if you find the preoccupations of *bundan* life amusing. Its failure to garner critical consideration might even suggest that the *bundan* itself was not amused at the satire. But beyond the local issues, *In Black and White* is a kind of concordance to themes and tropes Tanizaki had been working on for fifteen years, and it reveals subtle connections to issues in Tanizaki's life that underlie his work, as the author was entering a transition in his personal life. Thus we can see this novel as Tanizaki's commentary on where he had been and where he was at the time, and we can see (in retrospect) where he will go. It shows us the pivotal moment when Tanizaki leaves behind—kills off—his old career and begins the second half of his life with the mature work that established him as a master.

In Black and White is recognizably a Tanizaki work, with echoes and presages of other stories he wrote, yet it is clearly distinct from his other work. There is no secondary work on this novel and this particular moment in Tanizaki's life to place it in the company of the two other stories he was writing, *Some Prefer Nettles* and *Quicksand*. The salient tone of the story—unease even to the point of terror—seems to run counter to the received "Tanizaki success" narrative of that time in his life. Tanizaki himself seems not to have written about the novel, other than the peculiar "preface" (*maegaki*) and "apology" (*atogaki*) he attached to its newspaper serial publication (included in this translation).[6] The novel must of course speak for itself. Following are some literary and personal aspects of the story that point to some of the pleasures the novel did, however, provide to readers of the day.

LINGUISTIC GAMES

Both the title of the novel and the plot "hook" rely on word plays. The Japanese title, *Kokubyaku*, is formed of two ideograms that mean literally, *black* and *white* (hence on the simplest level the translation title, *In Black and White*). Anyone literate in Japanese knows that the ideogram for *black* is commonly pronounced *koku*, and *white* is *haku*. That would seem to indicate reading the title as *kokuhaku*. But in its initial newspaper appearance, the author indicates that the "white" should instead be pronounced *byaku*. And *kokubyaku* is actually the correct, or at least preferred, pronunciation for this compound. Is Tanizaki just conducting a language lesson? Well, no. Reading the ideograms silently will not show what is at stake, but to *hear* them immediately conjures up a common homonym: *kokuhaku*, meaning "confession." And of course, in English, too, "in black and white" hints at truth, and at matters of proof and trust. The plot of the novel does culminate in a confession; in fact, the whole novel is a confession. The fictional *In Black and White* is the confession of a fictional writer who lives in the world of writers and is caught in a fictional trap: he has made a terrible mistake and finds that he cannot undo that mistake. He believes he is a true artist but is under attack from the *bundan*. He desperately tries to shake off the entanglements of the past and present—guilt, miscalculations, and dependencies—but he is hopelessly enmeshed. In a sense, that was the situation of the real author, too, at the time, making the bizarre plot actually work like that of an "I-novel." The title itself thus slyly draws attention to a "misreading" that is not a misreading—it is a confession in black and white.

Also central to the plot of *In Black and White* is a play on words, or a word mistake, hinging on the name of one of the characters. There are three main characters in the story: Mizuno, Cojima, and the Shadow Man. It is the relationship between Mizuno and Cojima that sets the story in action; the Shadow Man's significance emerges later.

To recapitulate the situation of the novel: the writer Mizuno has written a story about a perfect murder. Mizuno's story, "To the Point of Murder" ("Hito o korosu made"), is not autobiographical, he claims, but as is the general I-novel practice, he has used real people as models for various characters in the story. Mizuno chose as the model for the victim an actual fellow writer named Cojima, whom he names "Codama" in the story.[7] As the novel opens, Mizuno awakens to realize that he has slipped up a couple of times in the manuscript he just sent off to the press and used the real writer's name, "Cojima." Suddenly he is terrified that if the actual Cojima is murdered, he will be suspected, because—in a literary milieu dominated by the I-novel—in this slip-up name error, readers who know Cojima will recognize him in the description of the character Codama and will naturally associate the murderer-protagonist with the author, especially since Mizuno, the author, actually has modeled that character on himself. The problem is spotlighted in the spelling of Cojima's name. While "Kojima" is a common name, most frequently it is written with ideograms that mean "Little Island." Cojima, however, spells his name with characters meaning "Child Island," and Mizuno used not "Little Jewel" for the Codama in the story but "Child Jewel," which, Mizuno decides, sets up a potential association of the fictional murder victim with the real writer. (Hence, in this translation, the two spellings, "Kojima" and "Cojima.")[8] Mizuno's story has gone to press, so it is too late for changes. The remaining two hundred or so pages of *In Black and White* recount Mizuno's attempts to establish an alibi in case the actual writer Cojima is murdered. Of course, Cojima *is* murdered, and Mizuno is entangled in the crime, trapped not by facts and acts but by the assumptions of his literary world. In short, *In Black and White* is a parody I-novel nightmare, propelled by name spellings.

MIZUNO'S PARANOIA AND THE I-NOVEL

Mizuno is a typical I-novel antihero authorial persona: "Look at the mess I have made of my life, but really, I'm actually a sensitive artist and highly misunderstood by the philistines around me." (Think of Naoji in Dazai Osamu's *Shayō* [*The Setting Sun*].) He is alternately grandiose and craven. He feels harassed and insulted by his publisher and hounded by his two-faced editor (whose contemptuous flattery Mizuno sees through). His insistence that his story is a *story*—despite real-life resemblances—is ignored. Several years earlier, letters of sympathy had flooded in to Mizuno's now ex-wife from readers after he wrote a series of wife-murder stories; the *bundan* had been more interested in circulating rumors—in poking at his life—than in discussing his artistic achievements. That's the problem inherent in the I-novel: readers and critics alike may take your fiction as fact. *In Black and White* raises the stakes to the ultimate level: Mizuno may have to pay *with his life* for the *bundan*'s arrogance and obtuseness.

As Mizuno resists his critics when his latest "diabolistic" story is dismissed by them—"What, this again?"—we hear Tanizaki's actual enmity toward his own critics, including Akutagawa, who had recently denounced Tanizaki's "diabolist tendency" (*akumateki keikō*).[9] The novel's intensity takes it to a level beyond a writer's mere irritation, though. At issue is the plot itself. Mizuno has written a story about the perfect murder of a writer. What is Tanizaki saying in a story about a writer killing—or not killing—another writer through his writing? And where would Mizuno (or Tanizaki) even *get* the crazy notion that just because he wrote a story, a man would be murdered? Where did this obsessive and hermetic plot come from, when at the same time Tanizaki was writing such rich and vibrant stories as *Quicksand* and *Some Prefer Nettles*? A simplistic psychological reading would suggest an answer: Mizuno *wants* to kill Cojima. Tanizaki wants to kill—whom?

Tanizaki's own internal disarray is signaled in the delusional quality of the basic plot. Mizuno's disorder and then the mysterious trigger that drives him into needing an alibi create an atmosphere not really explained in the action of the story. That suggests that there is more story than Tanizaki put on the page. Mizuno's proposition about Codama/Cojima is ludicrous, but so is Tanizaki's in writing the story. Both of them are more touched by death than they want to admit. Mizuno is only a fictional character in a story Tanizaki is writing, as Codama is in Mizuno's fictional story. Mizuno thinks, I have written a story. In it a character is murdered. If the real person who is the model for the victim in my story is murdered, I will be suspected. And if/when he is murdered, I will not have murdered him. But (we ask) why *should* the real person be murdered? If there is a reason, the story has to give you a hint. Would you imagine that some real person would be murdered just because you wrote a story about a fictional character being murdered? Mizuno's story-within-a-story, "To the Point of Murder," gives a motive to the murderer. But *In Black and White* gives no motive to the Shadow Man, a non-character who casts a stronger light than his nonexistence would warrant, other than Mizuno's conviction that someone is out to destroy him. And there is no explanation in the story for why anyone would want to do that. He's not a pleasant person, but he doesn't merit extermination. Hence the fundamental craziness: Mizuno's groundless, paranoid conviction that someone is trying to kill him.

Tanizaki did write stories with mad, paranoid murder plots. There is, for example, "Yanagi-yu no jiken" (1918; "The Incident at the Willow Bath House," 1997). A man fears repeatedly that his wife is dead and sunk to the bottom of the pool at the public bathhouse, only (he discovers repeatedly) she is not dead; then finally he does kill her in the bathhouse pool. But a coda at the end of the story tells us that the man was insane, that he was hallucinating and in fact didn't kill his wife but killed another man in the bath, and now instead of being sent to prison, he is in an insane asylum. If Mizuno is insane, then his terrors, and the story, paradoxically make sense. But there is not even a hint of this in *In Black and White*.

Mizuno's delusional fears turn out to be true. Within the novel, there are no grounds for Mizuno's fears. He is not a murderer. Only the literary ground rules of the I-novel—that there is an essential, and not *contingent*, connection between real people and fictional people in a story—make Mizuno vulnerable. Mizuno debates this issue with the detectives near the end of *In Black and White*, which is realistic enough about Tanizaki's literary world. There is no rational explanation for Mizuno's terror unless we take into account the social mores of the literary world he inhabits— and, beyond that, Tanizaki's relationship with Akutagawa. These are reflected in the character, or non-character, Mizuno refers to as the Shadow Man.

TANIZAKI AND AKUTAGAWA

Literary Matters

The last stage of the long-standing relationship between Tanizaki and Akutagawa Ryūnosuke suggests that Akutagawa is a shadow participant in *In Black and White*. In 1927 the two writers entered into what is now known famously as the "plot debate," or *shōsetsu no suji ronsō*. Neither was known as a writer of I-novels although both had written stories with obviously autobiographical referents, especially Akutagawa in his late work. Rather, both were primarily writers of intellectual, often witty, well-crafted, highly plotted shorter fiction. Tanizaki also (like Mizuno) had a special reputation as an *akumashugi-sha* or "diabolist" who brought his readings of European decadent and Symbolist writers (including the "opium eater," Thomas De Quincey, referred to in *In Black and White*) into his own creative mix.

The debate was carried out over a period of five months in 1927 largely in the pages of the journal *Kaizō* in dueling essays: Tanizaki's "Jōzetsu-roku" (Garrulous Record) and Akutagawa's "Bungetekina, amari ni bungeitekina" (Literary, All Too Literary).[10] Tanizaki is usually credited with—or blamed for—starting the argument, but in fact his first volley was not even lobbed directly at Akutagawa. Each of them just happened to publish literary opinions in the same month but in different venues. In February, Tanizaki began writing a monthly opinion column for *Kaizō*. In the first installment, he made some provocative but general comments about the current fashion for what he called self-involved, meandering, boring, "stories"—that is, what were being called *watakushi* or *shinkyō shōsetsu* ("internal state stories"). Rather, he asserted, structure was important in storytelling, and structure meant "plot." For his part, at a roundtable discussion in the journal

Shinchō, Akutagawa (in company with Tokuda Shūsei, Hirotsu Kazuo, and other well-known literary figures) the same month passingly referred to Tanizaki's and his own writing as problematic, expressing uneasiness about highly plotted fiction. Yes, it was entertaining, but was it "pure," he asked. Shiga Naoya was his model for the "pure artist" (*junsuina sakka*)—and he and Tanizaki were not.[11] The cultural critic and writer Masamune Hakuchō had jocularly warned Tanizaki not to seek controversy in his new literary column: "There will be many people who will argue with you, and you won't be able to stay silent, and you'll respond, and it'll become an issue in the *bundan,* and you know how *urusai*—noisy—that will be!"[12] But Tanizaki rose to Akutagawa's bait.

The operative terms in the debate were *hanashi no suji* (story plot), *junbungei* (pure art) and *suji no omoshirosa* (plot interest). Soon Akutagawa added a fourth even more resonant term: *hanashirashii hanashi no nai shōsetsu* (literally, "stories without story-like stories," or as it has come to be transformed into less-tortured English, "plotless stories"). The debate has been much discussed and analyzed.[13] Suffice it to say that *In Black and White* was written in the aftermath of an increasingly ad hominem discussion of literary value—that is, the core of a writer's self-definition.

Tanizaki vigorously resisted Akutagawa, but that only revealed him to be even more of a *bundan* outlier, like the "diabolistic" protagonist of *In Black and White.* The debate continued in *Kaizō,* with Tanizaki alternating monthly with Akutagawa; then it came to a crashing halt, when on July 24—Tanizaki's birthday— Akutagawa committed suicide, thereby effectively leaving him with the last word and ending the debate as victor. Tanizaki was pulled into the aftermath, with requests from publishers for commentaries and memorials; he was asked only a month later to write some words of introduction to a new Akutagawa "collected works" that was rushed into press. Within eight months of Akutagawa's death, he began the unprecedented flurry of publication that resulted in the three 1928 novels. Two of the novels began newspaper serialization at the same time: *In Black and White* and *Quicksand*. *In Black and White* was finished in only five months, published in Osaka and Tokyo newspapers over exactly the same time period the Tanizaki-Akutagawa debate had taken place the previous year. *Some Prefer Nettles* began serialization in December; *Quicksand* did not finish serialization until 1930.

Matters of Real Life

Another more intense and personal, rather than intellectual, part of the Tanizaki–Akutagawa relationship may be implicated in the terror Tanizaki visits on poor Mizuno. It has to do with the internal similarities Akutagawa's suicide forced Tanizaki to see between himself and the other writer. Within a month of Akutagawa's suicide, he wrote a short memorial piece, "Akutagawa-kun to watakushi (Akutagawa and Me).[14] It was written in a conversational style as if Tanizaki were thinking of Akutagawa as a "younger brother" (using the suffix *-kun*, a diminutive form of *-san*, in referring to Akutagawa), and it drew attention to similarities Tanizaki saw between himself and Akutagawa. He saw strong karmic connections (*in'en*) between them: both sons of *shitamachi* (the old, traditional incarnation of Tokyo); both went to the same middle school (or its successor), with the same principal and several teachers in common; both entered the *bundan* through the literary coterie magazine *Shinshichō*, Tanizaki in its first generation, Akutagawa in its third; both made their debuts with stories (Tanizaki's was a play) set in the classical Heian period, thus setting them against the current of other young writers who at the time were enamored of the West. Their families used the same temple cemetery. The congruence culminated, Tanizaki observed, when Akutagawa chose Tanizaki's birthday as his death day. Six years older than Akutagawa, Tanizaki said he felt that they could have been closer if the younger man had not always treated him awkwardly as his *sempai*, or senior. He quotes Akutagawa as commenting to him, "*Shitamachi* kids have a certain weakness in their spirits"; Tanizaki sees that as one of the bad qualities of Tokyo people—of whom he was one. (The standard narrative has Tanizaki immersing himself in Kansai culture, the Kyoto-Osaka area, at this time; Akutagawa's death seemed to remind him he was after all a Tokyo man.) He concludes by confessing that he is ashamed to have been a bad *sempai* to Akutagawa. Additionally, the ability in the Japanese written language for one ideogram to have multiple pronunciations provides Tanizaki a further mechanism to indicate subtly an intimacy that enforces visually the emotion of the essay: the word Tanizaki uses as a suffix of address for Akutagawa's name in the essay, *-kun* (Akutagawa-kun), which initially means "Mr.," can be pronounced *kimi* when used in isolation, without the addressee's name, (which is how it appears in most of the essay), in which case it can mean "you." In essence, the piece turns out to be a personal conversation Tanizaki is having with "you," Akutagawa.

There is, beyond that, an even more personal, extra-literary, element implicated in Tanizaki's complex sensitivity to Akutagawa's death. Had it not been for Akutagawa, Tanizaki might never have met Nezu Matsuko, who in 1935 would become his third and final wife. When Tanizaki first encountered her, in 1927, she was married to another man, but his bizarre and inappropriate account of their meeting in another essay about Akutagawa shows that, as he recollected it, from the start he was intensely aware of her.

On the surface, the encounter sounds innocuous enough: Akutagawa had been invited to give a lecture in Osaka. Mrs. Nezu admired his writing and had asked to be introduced to him. Tanizaki happened to be at Akutagawa's inn, where the two friends were continuing their conversations on life and art more informally and more personally then they were currently doing in print, when Mrs. Nezu paid her visit. As a good hostess, she invited them to go to a dance hall the next day—a popular entertainment at the time. But see how Tanizaki describes the encounter, in an unusual place, the short essay "Itamashiki hito" (That Poor Man) included in a memorial issue of the journal *Bungei Shunjū* only two months after Akutagawa's death: "The next day, too, he kept me from leaving, and, happily invited by Mr. Nezu's wife, he said he would go to see a dance hall. When out of respect to Mrs. Nezu I changed into a tuxedo, she purposely stood up and buttoned the buttons of my formal tuxedo shirt for me. It was a kindness utterly like that of a sweetheart."[15]

That he uses the word "sweetheart" (actually, a nicer translation of *iro-onna*) surely raised more than one reader's eyebrows on first reading it. In any case, it is a strange word to use, and a strange scene to describe, in a memorial essay for a writer who has just died a suicide, and using the socially well-placed married woman's actual name, too—a married woman he had only just met. Whether at the time Tanizaki was entirely conscious of it or not, and even though his own troubled marriage still had three years to run, he shows us here that he was far more aware of Nezu Matsuko than the circumstances warranted. And Akutagawa was a part of the story.

The Shadow Man

That leaves the problem of the Shadow Man, and how we can see him entangled with Tanizaki and Akutagawa. This strange figure is not a ghost, not a hallucination, not a mirage. He is not formally

in the list of characters. But from Mizuno's perspective, he is running the action even though he never appears physically in the
story. No one else even imagines he exists in Mizuno's life, and
Mizuno doesn't know who he is. We don't know *if* he exists, since
the story never shows him. We don't know why or if he has it in
for Mizuno. To get at how the Shadow Man works in the story at
a deep level, we have to look beyond Mizuno.

In his mounting paranoia, Mizuno starts to imagine this figure
he calls "the Shadow Man" (*kage no hito*), who is manipulating
events to destroy him. Well before the murder takes place, Mizuno
plays out the deadly possibility that he might be convicted of a
real murder he had created only in fiction, perpetrated by some
unknown person standing in the shadows. In an effort to forestall
this Shadow Man, Mizuno sketches out a sequel to his story in
which the plot of "To the Point of Murder" will be shown to have
been used by a real murderer, not the innocent author of the story,
but this innocent fictional author will be convicted and executed;
only then will the real murderer be revealed.[16] He agonizes over the
title of the sequel, finally arriving at the preposterous "To the Point
Where the Man Who Wrote 'To the Point of Murder' Is Murdered" ("Hito o korosu made o kaita hito ga korosareru made"). In
the sequel to this story-within-the-story, the Shadow Man is of
course shown to be the real murderer. The Shadow Man will win,
Mizuno decides, even though the executed writer is later—too
late—exonerated. *In Black and White* allows only Mizuno's imagination for disaster, however; it does not allow for exoneration.

Who is the Shadow Man? On the surface, we can say the
Shadow Man embodies Mizuno's internal sense of being out of
control—he is a paranoid figment of Mizuno's imagination. He
is also obviously Tanizaki-as-author, the manipulator who put
Mizuno in this situation. But then, Tanizaki is also Mizuno, the
abused writer, and not just his manipulator, so the Shadow Man

can be separable from Tanizaki-as-author who created him. Symbolically, he could be Fate, similar to the way the director Shinoda Masahiro used the *kuroko* to manipulate Koharu and Jihei in his 1969 film of Chikamatsu's *Shinjū ten no Amijima* (*Double Suicide*)—the same puppet play Tanizaki used to such strong effect in another of the 1928 novels, *Some Prefer Nettles*.

But there are two more possibilities for the Shadow Man, if we think of *In Black and White* as a representation of Tanizaki's intellectual and emotional life. The first is, clearly, Akutagawa. As a result of Akutagawa's "machinations"—his suicide while Tanizaki is debating literary value with him—a fellow writer, Tanizaki, could be made to feel somehow responsible for the death. *In Black and White* thus is a way for Tanizaki to recognize yet disavow guilt and insecurity about his writing talent. Mizuno did not kill Cojima— the Shadow Man did. Tanizaki did not kill Akutagawa—the Shadow Man did. Akutagawa killed Akutagawa.

In one of the commentaries Tanizaki wrote soon after Akutagawa's death, he expressed a surprisingly tender and pained recognition: "I had no idea at the time that he was under so much pressure. I was just happy to have found such a worthy sparring partner. Had I known, I wouldn't have been so vociferous."[17] Only in retrospect could he—or anyone—read clearly what Akutagawa was writing at the end. Akutagawa's late stories "Shinkirô" (1927; "The Mirage," 1965), "Haguruma" (1927; "The Cogwheel," 1965), and even an entertaining satire, the seemingly frivolous "Kappa" (1927; "Kappa," 1949), are far more chilling when read as the thoughts of a man within months of suicide. Akutagawa's espousal just before his death of the "plotless novel" is a repudiation of his entire writing career, a kind of *intellectual* suicide. The Shadow Man makes Tanizaki's parody a much more dire parable about the dangers of literary life. Suicide was in fact a common peril for twentieth-century Japanese writers.

There is also a fourth possibility for the Shadow Man: he may embody Tanizaki's own emotions and feelings about himself and his life, some of them antisocial and unacceptable, many of them not conscious, but all triggered by Akutagawa's death. In this story about false confessions, Tanizaki makes a real "true confession." Whatever the crimes in his mind—guilt, anger, failures, overreaching, underachieving—he recognizes them, and that means he can master them. Tanizaki genuinely recognizes that the Shadow Man is within himself, and that recognition means that he can surmount limitations that are holding his creativity hostage. The Shadow Man appears as Tanizaki is freeing himself from what his internal shackles had kept him doing: "the same old thing." He could kill off Mizuno *and* the Shadow Man. In the second half of Tanizaki's life, we see in many of his stories a selfish man-child grown strong, not the groveling masochist of his earlier stories. No more Seikichi ("The Tattooer"), seemingly a sadist but obviously at heart a masochist looking for a controller, or Mizuno; instead, the Old Man (*Some Prefer Nettles*) and the Mad Old Man (*The Diary of a Mad Old Man*), who openly and unapologetically control their worlds, and Sasuke ("Portrait of Shunkin"), whose controlling sadism lurks within his apparent masochism. We see in *Some Prefer Nettles*, *In Black and White*'s fellow story, Kaname beginning to explore a new freedom, as Tanizaki was on the brink of doing in his life. While scholars point to autobiographical elements in *Some Prefer Nettles*, *In Black and White* is more deeply, personally, about Tanizaki. Revealing the conviction that Mizuno must go, it is thus both a fiction *and* an I-novel. Tanizaki wins, having written his way out of the hole from which he worked in the first half of his creative life.

We cannot say that Tanizaki was following Akutagawa's cheeky advice during the 1927 debate to find a "healthier and more humanistic" idiom that "let in more circulation of light and air."[18] Without question, however, the three 1928 novels mark a new energy and direction for Tanizaki's work, with *In Black and White* the pivot point. Perhaps in the short run Akutagawa won the debate by closing it down (as Tanizaki himself acknowledged).[19] But in the long run his death may have worked to free Tanizaki's imagination, leading to the succession of stories that has assured his reputation as a literary giant.

NOTES

1. *Tanizaki Jun'ichirō to kōtei no yokubō* (Tokyo: Chūōkōron-sha, 1980), 64–68.

2. Adriana Boscaro, *Tanizaki in Western Languages: A Bibliography of Translations and Studies* (Ann Arbor: Center for Japanese Studies, University of Michigan, 2000).

3. My text source here is *Kokubyaku*, in *Tanizaki Jun'ichirō zenshū* [hereafter abbreviated *TJZ*] (Tokyo: Chūōkōron-sha, 1967–68), vol. 11. *Manji* appears in vol. 11 and *Tade kuu mushi* in vol. 12.

4. "Bungeitekina, amari ni bungeitekina," in *Akutagawa Ryūnosuke zenshū* [hereafter abbreviated *ARZ*] (Tokyo: Kadokawa Shoten, 1968), 9:205.

5. I thank members of the Association for Japanese Literary Studies for comments on my article "Tanizaki Fights the *Watakushi Shōsetsu*: *Kokubyaku* as *Bundan* Parody," *Proceedings of the Association for Japanese Literary Studies* 9 (2008).

6. *TJZ*, 23:109, 23:111.

7. "Cojima" and "Codama" are peculiar transliterations into English; see n8 below.

8. I am indebted to Stefania Burk for suggesting this spelling stratagem. The strangeness of "Cojima" to English readers who know how Japanese is commonly transliterated produces just the instability Tanizaki wants Japanese readers to recognize in the slip between the "little" and "child" ideograms they are reading.

9. "Taishō hachinendō no bungakukai," in *Bungeitekina, amari ni bungeitekina* (Tokyo: Kodansha, 1972), 135.

10. Akutagawa's title of course alludes to Nietzsche's "Human, All Too Human," an ominous hint that Akutagawa may have been identifying his own growing fear of insanity with Nietzsche's madness.

11. *ARZ*, 9:209.

12. "Jōzetsu-roku," in *TJZ*, 20:72.

13. For a few of the sources that discuss the debate in English, see Tomi Suzuki, *Narrating the Self: Fictions of Japanese Modernity* (Stanford, CA: Stanford University Press, 1996), 152ff; Irmela Hijiya-Kirschnereit, *Rituals of Self-Revelation: Shishōsetsu as Literary Genre and Socio-cultural Phenomenon* (Cambridge, MA: Harvard University Council on East Asian Studies, 1996), 155–56; and Karatani Kōjin, *Origins of Modern Japanese Literature* (Durham, NC: Duke University Press, 1993), 155–68.

14. *TJZ*, 22:224–26.

15. *TJZ*, 22:228.

16. A reverse real-life event astonishingly similar to what the terrified Mizuno imagines in Tanizaki's fictional story occurred in Poland in 2000, only in this case the real author-murderer was identified and is now in prison for twenty-five years—discovered by a novel he wrote a couple of years later about the "perfect murder." Krystian Bala had given the murderer in his story, Amok, "a biography similar to his own, blurring the boundary between author and narrator." Like Watanabe in *In Black and White*, a tenacious detective broke the cold case. In another similarity, the author of the article about the event even tells us, "Throughout the book, Bala plays with words in order to emphasize their slipperiness." See David Gann, "True Crime: A Postmodern Murder Mystery." *New Yorker*, February 11, 2008.

17. "Itamashiki hito," *TJZ*, 22:227.

18. *Bungeitekina, amari ni bungeitekina* (1972), 135.

19. "Akutagawa zenshū kankō ni saishite," *TJZ*, 23:100.

TRANSLATOR'S
ACKNOWLEDGMENTS

T his novel was first published in 1928 as a newspaper serial novel in the *Osaka* and *Tokyo Asahi Shimbun*. It was included in anthologies as early as 1930 but has never been published as an independent volume in Japan. It was published in 1957 and 1966 editions of *The Complete Works of Tanizaki Jun'ichirō* by Chūōkōron-sha, which oversaw the copyright until Tanizaki's works entered the public domain in Japan in 2015, on the fiftieth anniversary of his death. I thank Irie Norio, emeritus editor at Chūōkōron, who explored the Japanese copyright situation for me. Chūōkōron-sha commenced publishing a new edition of the complete works in 2015.

My thanks to Russian literature scholar and poetry translator Clare Cavanaugh, who first, in an unrelated context, listened to my intense synopsis of the novel, pondered my puzzlement that it was so unknown, and then said, "Why don't you translate it?" The idea hadn't occurred to me until then, and that was the beginning of the project.

Kirk Morrow, my student assistant from the International Studies Residential College at Northwestern University, did not know Japanese literature but became a good Tanizaki reader in the course of typing my handwritten manuscript into the computer, sharing his thoughts on that first draft.

My deep gratitude goes to friends, colleagues, and family who have patiently given moral and intellectual support to this work long in the making.

And my thanks to the copyeditor, Glenn Perkins, and to the editors of Columbia University Press, especially Jennifer Crewe and Jonathan Fiedler, who prevailed through the complexities of international copyrights to make this novel available to the rest of the world—perhaps even before Japanese readers have begun contemplating it.

WEATHERHEAD BOOKS ON ASIA

WEATHERHEAD EAST ASIAN INSTITUTE, COLUMBIA UNIVERSITY

LITERATURE

DAVID DER-WEI WANG, EDITOR

Cao Naiqian, *There's Nothing I Can Do When I Think of You Late at Night*, translated by John Balcom (2009)

Park Wan-suh, *Who Ate Up All the Shinga? An Autobiographical Novel*, translated by Yu Young-nan and Stephen J. Epstein (2009)

Yi T'aejun, *Eastern Sentiments*, translated by Janet Poole (2009)

Hwang Sunwŏn, *Lost Souls: Stories*, translated by Bruce and Ju-Chan Fulton (2009)

Kim Sŏk-pŏm, *The Curious Tale of Mandogi's Ghost*, translated by Cindi Textor (2010)

The Columbia Anthology of Modern Chinese Drama, edited by Xiaomei Chen (2011)

Qian Zhongshu, *Humans, Beasts, and Ghosts: Stories and Essays*, edited by Christopher G. Rea, translated by Dennis T. Hu, Nathan K. Mao, Yiran Mao, Christopher G. Rea, and Philip F. Williams (2011)

Dung Kai-cheung, *Atlas: The Archaeology of an Imaginary City*, translated by Dung Kai-cheung, Anders Hansson, and Bonnie S. McDougall (2012)

O Chŏnghŭi, *River of Fire and Other Stories*, translated by Bruce and Ju-Chan Fulton (2012)

Endō Shūsaku, *Kiku's Prayer: A Novel*, translated by Van Gessel (2013)

Li Rui, *Trees Without Wind: A Novel*, translated by John Balcom (2013)

Abe Kōbō, *The Frontier Within: Essays by Abe Kōbō*, edited, translated, and with an introduction by Richard F. Calichman (2013)

Zhu Wen, *The Matchmaker, the Apprentice, and the Football Fan: More Stories of China*, translated by Julia Lovell (2013)

The Columbia Anthology of Modern Chinese Drama, Abridged Edition, edited by Xiaomei Chen (2013)

Natsume Sōseki, *Light and Dark*, translated by John Nathan (2013)

Seirai Yūichi, *Ground Zero, Nagasaki: Stories*, translated by Paul Warham (2015)

Hideo Furukawa, *Horses, Horses, in the End the Light Remains Pure: A Tale That Begins with Fukushima* (2016)

Abe Kōbō, *Beasts Head for Home: A Novel*, translated by Richard F. Calichman (2017)

Yi Mun-yol, *Meeting with My Brother: A Novella*,
translated by Heinz Insu Fenkl with Yoosup Chang (2017)

Ch'ae Manshik, *Sunset: A Ch'ae Manshik Reader*,
edited and translated by Bruce and Ju-Chan Fulton (2017)

HISTORY, SOCIETY, AND CULTURE

CAROL GLUCK, EDITOR

Takeuchi Yoshimi, *What Is Modernity? Writings of Takeuchi Yoshimi*,
edited and translated, with an introduction,
by Richard F. Calichman (2005)

Contemporary Japanese Thought, edited and translated
by Richard F. Calichman (2005)

Overcoming Modernity, edited and translated
by Richard F. Calichman (2008)

Natsume Sōseki, *Theory of Literature and Other Critical Writings*,
edited and translated by Michael Bourdaghs, Atsuko Ueda,
and Joseph A. Murphy (2009)

Kojin Karatani, *History and Repetition*, edited by Seiji M. Lippit (2012)

The Birth of Chinese Feminism: Essential Texts in Transnational Theory,
edited by Lydia H. Liu, Rebecca E. Karl, and Dorothy Ko (2013)

Yoshiaki Yoshimi, *Grassroots Fascism: The War Experience of the Japanese
People*, translated by Ethan Mark (2015)